Must Be Friends

Must Be Friends

Corey Johnson

IZZARD INK PUBLISHING
www.izzardink.com

Library of Congress Cataloging-in-Publication Data

Names: Johnson, Corey (Novelist) author
Title: Must be friends / Corey Johnson.
Description: First edition. | Salt Lake City : Izzard Ink Publishing, 2026.
Identifiers: LCCN 2025054454 (print) | LCCN 2025054455 (ebook) |
ISBN 9781642281354 hardback | ISBN 9781642281347 paperback |
ISBN 9781642281330 ebook | ISBN 9781642281361 audiobook
Subjects: LCGFT: Fiction | Novels
Classification: LCC PS3610.O3247 M87 2026 (print) |
LCC PS3610.O3247 (ebook)
LC record available at https://lccn.loc.gov/2025054454
LC ebook record available at https://lccn.loc.gov/2025054455

Designed by Daniel Lagin
Cover Design by Andrea Ho
Image illustration by Sophie Johnson.

First Edition

Contact the author at info@izzardink.com

Hardback ISBN: 978-1-64228-135-4
Paperback ISBN: 978-1-64228-134-7
eBook ISBN: 978-1-64228-133-0
Audiobook ISBN: 978-1-64228-136-1

Contents

Chapter 1

Billy Rose

It was 1927, the first day of summer. Not the first day of summer as reckoned by the solstice, but rather the first day after the last day of school. The neighborhood boys were still giddy from yesterday, when they burst through the school doors and into the summer. They had assembled to inaugurate the yearly institution that defined their summer: a pickup baseball game. In 1927, baseball ruled the souls of all young boys who worshipped at the altar of Babe Ruth and Lou Gehrig. When they weren't playing baseball, they were thinking about it. They obsessed over homerun counts, batting averages, ERAs, and won/loss records. They traded Major League Baseball cards like currency. Each boy had a short list of favorite players that he followed in the sports pages. Arguments among the boys as to the proper order of greatness were frequent and vocal. What often started out as a statistical defense of one kid's champ usually ended in an attack on the other kid's champ and included terms like *bum*, *whiffer*, and *noodle arm*.

Consequently, the worth of a boy, as determined by his peers, was based on his bat, his mitt, and his arm. Their gathering place was not a groomed field with chain-link backstops and chalked baselines. There was no home run fence, no lights, no concessions, and certainly no public toilets. It was a vacant lot just off Maple Street. The field was mostly weeds and undisciplined patches of grass through which baselines had been worn by the leather shoes of countless boys running—and often sliding—for glory. The encircling trees framed a grand stadium, and it was easy to imagine the breeze through the leaves as the low roar of an adulating crowd. The bases were homemade: gunny sacks filled with rocks and tied with twine.

The backdrop was a medium-sized Midwestern city like any other in America. The early June sun made good on a promise of hot and heavy afternoon air. Nobody cared. It was baseball, and the heat was part of the game. Fourteen assorted boys from eight to twelve years old milled about in their knickers and baseball caps. Not everyone had a mitt.

Seven-year-old Scotty Jones, Jimmy's little brother, wore a cowboy hat and leather chaps and carried cap pistols in holsters on each hip as he galloped about the field on his stick horse—a six-foot-long willow. The bridle was a thin leather strap he'd looped onto the stick and held deftly in his left hand so he could "shoot" with his right. He named his cellulose horse Shiner. None of the kids knew why.

When it came to baseball, all the boys knew one another. They knew who was good and who wasn't. They knew who could hit, who could catch, and who could throw. They also knew which boys always struck out, which ones turned their faces away while fielding a jittery grounder, and who had the loudest mouth. Only two of the kids were decent pitchers. By time-honored but tacit rules of the unsanctioned game, the pitchers had become the default captains of each team. Other standard rules applied too. One: The captains took turns picking players until the last boy was chosen—and everybody knew who that would be. Two: The team in the field got to use all the mitts. Three: Since there were never enough boys for two full teams, the batting team had to supply the catcher. Four: Balls and strikes were called by consensus. A practice conceived in folly and resulted in endless bickering. And then there was chatter. Lots of chatter. And laughing and teasing and goofing around as well as some whooping and cussing, like real ballplayers. It was summer. It was baseball. The best part? There were no girls, no parents, no pianos, no Sunday school teachers, and no square dancing. Just boys and baseball.

The boys huddled up around home plate like herd animals while the two captains, Billy Rose and Stan Obermeyer, stepped out in front, facing the motley and animated gaggle. Billy Rose was one of the eldest boys at age twelve. A head taller than most of the group, athletically built with a precocious swagger, he was indisputably the best player. Billy had that intangible possessed by great ball players such that he could leverage all of his strength into the tiny focus required for baseball prowess. He was red-headed and freckle-faced with a pointy nose and reverse-buck teeth. The other boys thought he looked like a giant red rat. At least, that's what they said behind his back. But no one said it to his face. To go along with his generally nasty and locally infamous disposition, Billy had a hair-trigger temper.

Stan Obermeyer was the son of German immigrants. Stocky, light-complected, and round-faced with a prodigious Babe Ruth nose, he looked more like a butcher than a baseball player—as did Babe Ruth. But he could throw the ball hard and straight. He got on well with the other boys and was generally regarded as a cutup. His persistent joking and pranking endeared him to his sixth-grade colleagues but exasperated his teachers. Stan was also the only kid big enough and respected enough to escape the wrath of Billy.

The selection ceremony began with a traditional hand-over-hand bat contest to determine the first pick. Stan won. He started the bidding with gusto, as if he'd already won the game, shouting, "I'll take Jimmy!"

Billy responded next. "I'll take Bart."

"Kelly."

"Mike."

"Casey."

"Jack."

On it went, like two Saint Peters selecting supplicants for admission into heaven, until there was one boy left standing—facing those already anointed by the holy hands of the two captains, standing in the loneliest spot of a boy's childhood.

The last pick fell to Billy. "All right," he conceded, "I'll take Dugan." Billy was holding the only bat on the field. As Dugan stepped forward to take his place with the team, his progress was abruptly halted by the butt end of Billy's bat, which thumped sharply off his chest like a long, bony finger.

"Try to get a hit for once in your life!" Billy scolded the shoulder-slumped boy.

Billy's team took the field while Stan barked out the batting order for his team, and fourteen raucous boys wildly anticipated the first pitch of summer. The midday sun cast truncated shadows as a light breeze toward left field tempted right-handed hitters. Cottonwoods gently snowed from the stands. The ubiquitous fluff drifted over the first baseline and tumbled across the infield. With Stan serving as catcher, Billy threw a few warm-up pitches, which Stan casually snapped up and tossed back to him. Without regulation equipment, the catcher would have to stand well behind the batter to avoid taking a foul-tipped ball to the eye. Little Scotty Jones was mounted on Shiner, ready to fetch errant balls missed by the catcher or fouled out of bounds. That was his job until he was old enough to play, and he didn't complain about it.

The chatter began and the excitement escalated as the lead hitter, Jimmy, Stan's first-round pick, took some ghost swings and eyed up the pitcher—like all good hitters do. The time had come and the anticipation was nearly fatal. But just before Jimmy stepped to the plate, something unexpected happened to change the course of the game.

The boys had become so acquainted with their familiar baseball routine, with its known cast of characters and predictable banter, that when a new kid appeared, everyone went silent. The boy walked right up to home plate out of nowhere like he owned the place. He was slight of build, wearing overalls and a too-small brown cap pulled down so tightly his ears jutted straight out. There was a large bruise on his right temple and cheek. Surprisingly, he had a well-trained mitt on his left hand and was pounding the pocket with his right fist. All fourteen boys began sizing this kid up.

Where did he come from?

How did he find the game?

Why wasn't he in school with us the day before?

More importantly, *Can he hit? Can he field? Can he throw?*

No one spoke. It felt like the game was on rain delay. Everyone stared at him as if they'd never seen a new kid before, the way every new kid gets stared at.

Finally, the new kid asked that immortal question. The question that starts out as a simple and hopeful childhood query of inclusion but ultimately marks the onset of every stage of human endeavor: "Hey, can I play?"

"Beat it, kid!" Billy yelled from the mound. "We got even teams."

The new kid calmly turned toward the mound to face the hostile voice, calculating the distribution of the boys. "I see you have no third baseman."

It was true. With only seven players in the field, the shortstop, Bart—Billy's first-round pick—had to cover short and third and was already positioned accordingly.

"What's it to you?" Billy snorted.

"I can play third," he responded flatly.

Everybody knew third base was the most difficult position on the field because right-handed batters—which was most of them—tended to hit line drives and hot grounders down the third baseline. They knew that most players couldn't handle them, especially scrawny little kids like this one. Even if the third baseman managed to stop the ball through skill, luck, or divine providence, throwing it to first base before the runner got there was a challenge at any level, particularly in the bush leagues.

Billy snarled, which only enhanced his rat-like features. "Listen, kid, there's no way anyone with little weenie arms like yours could make that throw to first!"

"Well, why don't I just show you," the boy suggested matter-of-factly. Without waiting for an answer, he turned and jogged briskly toward third base. He had no way of knowing that challenging Billy could be dangerous. The other boys approached this face-off with caution. They loved to watch Billy self-incinerate, so long as they didn't get singed in the process.

Billy's temperature went up a couple of degrees at this intrusion, and when the new kid reached the tied-up bag of rocks that posed as third base, Billy threw a fastball at him and screamed, "One throw!"

The new kid clearly wasn't ready for the fastball hurling toward his midsection, but he managed to stab it with his mitt, an act of self-defense to be sure, just in time to avoid a gut punch. Brushing off the near miss, he pulled the ball from his mitt and prepared to throw it to first. One thing was certain: None of the boys were prepared for this throw. After a couple of jerky, abbreviated side hops, he pivoted hard to the left toward first base. His right arm came back behind his head but didn't stop near the ear as in conventional throwing form. Rather, his arm cocked way back and stayed there like some kind of spring-loaded device. Then he planted his right heel and stretched his left leg out so far in front that he was practically doing the splits in the dirt. As his torso spasmed in retching fashion, his arm came forward like something halfway between the wing of a wounded stork and a trebuchet. The whole disturbing process happened in a split second, but the painful image lingered like a welding flash. The ball came out of his hand in a tight spin and flew past Billy's head toward first base, making the distinctive whirring sound of a high-speed baseball with a couple of flagged stitches. It hit the first baseman's frozen mitt on a trajectory with practically no visible arc and popped like a handgun.

The first baseman, ten-year-old Mike Saunders, instantly dumped his mitt on the ground and frantically shook his left hand. "Geez kid! Take it easy."

Although the throw was perfectly placed and had enough speed to beat the fastest runner, Billy instantly shouted his contempt. "That's the single ugliest thing I've ever seen in my whole life!" As he raised his right arm in full extension and pointed in a direction where the third baseline dugout should have been, he screamed, "Get the hell off my field!"

Stan busted into laughter at Billy's fuming outburst. The new kid stared blankly at Billy, then looked at the other kids for understanding. But no one spoke up to explain the breach of baseball protocol that had set Billy off. Instead, they snickered at Billy's antics and mimicked the ungainly throw, each spinning his own exaggerated interpretation. What was supposed to be the beginning of a consequential "Opening Day" game had descended into giggling tomfoolery. Bart jumped to the ground and attempted to do the splits as Jack pretended to throw a ball to first by rotating his straightened arm over his head in a stilted motion, like the hand of a clock. Some pretended to vomit, while others covered their eyes in feigned agony as they laughed and carried on.

As the revelry and chaos lingered, an unfamiliar voice from behind second base pierced the scene. "I didn't think it was so ugly."

The laughing stopped as the boys wheeled toward second base to discover the source of this unsolicited opinion.

Lightning had struck twice in the same place. There was a second new kid. He had ambled in from somewhere in center field, and nobody had noticed because of the exchange taking place between Billy and the first new kid. He looked to be about eleven years old, of average height and weight. He was wearing dark pants, tattered and a little baggy in the seat, with a dirty white shirt, and the sole was coming off his left shoe. His worn black newsboy cap had no chance of containing the shafts of unruly blond hair that stuck out like arrows of straw. His face was dirty too. With a bat perched on his right shoulder, he began walking toward the mound with purpose and candor, his shabby appearance notwithstanding.

"And who the hell are you?" Billy demanded.

"I'm Sam," he said flatly.

Billy glared at him, then gave a nod toward the bat on his shoulder. "What do you think you're gonna do with that?"

"I think I'm gonna hit baseballs with it."

"Did you now?" Billy said snottily. "If you ask me, a kid who brings his own bat can't bring much else to the game. He's gonna be all bat and no hit."

Sam gave Billy the once-over before responding, as if taking time to make a calculation. "I know kids like that," he answered, seeming to agree. "Kids with shiny new bats. But here's the difference, Red. A kid with a shiny new bat may or may not know how to use it. With a new bat you just can't tell." Sam spoke with an air of philosophy as he dislodged the bat from his right shoulder and shoved it inches from Billy's face. "But you take a hard look at this one." Everyone could see that the bat was scratched and dented, the surface weathered and smudged with ball marks and a couple of blood stains. The number thirty-one had been crudely etched by hand over the Louisville Slugger logo—probably by a pocket knife—which was worn and barely visible. The handle was soiled with the grips of a thousand hands, and a third of the lip was missing. Billy studied the well-traveled bat, then peered at the strange and disheveled owner but said nothing.

"Well, do you think I'm one of those kids?" Sam asked.

"I think if you call me *Red* again, you're dead!" Billy threatened.

That's when Stan leveled a little ball field diplomacy at the situation. "All right, all right! Sam, you're on my team, and the first new kid stays in the field on Billy's team. Now let's get to it!"

Sam ran to join the team at bat, and the other new kid staked an official claim to third base. Jimmy stepped to the plate, and Billy slashed the first pitch through the heart of the strike zone.

"Strike one!" Stan admitted reluctantly.

And the first game of summer was underway.

By the top of the seventh inning, the score was tied five to five. As expected, Billy had pitched a good game from the mound and hit two doubles and a triple. Young pitchers tended to be good hitters. When they got to the majors, most of them became bat-stupid. Stan's performance did not disappoint. He threw a decent game and hit well. The first new kid acquitted himself with notable distinction from third base, skillfully handling a series of zippy, unaccountable grounders that contoured every defect in the bumpy field in search of the perfect place to ambush his face. Each time thereafter he reproduced that hideous disconnected throw, and each time with the same result: a liner to the first baseman with heat from the center of the earth, arriving counts before the runner. And Sam, the kid with the trained bat, had blasted two of Billy's fastballs for home runs.

As Billy's team took the field, he pulled Stan aside. "I'm starting to get sore at that Sam kid. He got a couple of lucky hits, but I'm gonna throw him the curve ball this time. I'd like to see him hit that!" He turned and paced to the mound, kicking up dirt angrily.

Sam stepped to the plate for his third at bat, venerable number thirty-one clutched tightly in his hands, and took his stance: feet widely spaced, weight shifted slightly to his right foot, knees bent, leaning forward into the pitch, butt pointed to the sky, and eyes drilled into the pitcher.

Billy gave Stan the look of an inside trader. He took his windup and fired a brushback pitch high and inside. The searing fastball looked like it might clip Sam in the chin. All the boys froze, expecting him to jump out of the way. But he effortlessly flicked his elbows slightly up and let it pass an inch from his Adam's apple—unflapped. Billy's face showed satisfaction with his set-up pitch. This time, he threw Sam the curve. Most twelve-year-olds couldn't even throw a curve, but Billy could. On first sight, the ball appeared to be coming in high and inside like the last one, but then it broke, sidled over the center of the plate, and dropped into the strike zone. Sam studied it all the way to the bat. Level and calibrated, he torqued his swing with full measure and no waste. A sharp report signaled a massive transfer of energy. The ball accelerated away from the bat at zero angle, a line-drive shot straight at the pitcher.

With his head and arms down in a helpless follow-through position, balancing on one foot with his torso parallel to the ground, Billy was in grave peril as the ball rocketed toward his face. A split second of panic bore down on the players as they watched in horror. At the last possible instant, he tiptoed and squirmed his pelvis upward while extending both arms and legs downward, looking like a gangly sawhorse suspended an inch above the ground. The ball skinned his nose and painted a streak down the length of his sternum and across his belly, fortunately without incident. But when it reached his groin, being the lowest hanging fruit, you can bet there was an incident. An epic one. The ball made contact with a sickening thud, and he dropped to the ground like a bag of sand.

Billy let out a "humph" that soon evolved into a long, mournful groan as he curled into the fetal position. A collective gasp sounded as each boy reflexively assumed a male sympathy posture: knees together, bent at the waist, both hands over their groin, chin down, and teeth clenched tightly.

Except for Sam, who dropped his bat and ran for first base, and the first new kid, who seemed strangely unsympathetic to Billy's plight. Billy didn't get up. He wormed around on the ground, still groaning pathetically while holding his groin. All the kids gathered around, looking down on him with fear and trembling, wondering how painful a hit like that would be. But therein lay the paradox. All the boys had known the pain of groin trauma at some time or another, to some degree or another. Yet nothing was funnier than the torture of male trauma when it happened to someone else. At the very moment that a boy assumed a male sympathy posture, he had to choke back the laugh that invariably must emerge. The gangly and hilarious sawhorse image seen by them all made it even worse. But nobody dared to laugh at Billy, even though they all wanted to. Several held their hands over their mouths to hide an irrepressible smile; others had to turn away and bite their lips.

But all of their attempts at proper demeanor and requisite regard for the injured were to no avail when little Scotty Jones, still astride his stick horse and hovering over the groaning Billy, blurted out the obvious in the way only a young child can. "Wow, right in the *nuts*! I'll bet that *really* hurt!"

The squelched laughter exploded into uncontrolled giggles and outright belly laughs.

But little Scotty wasn't finished. "Did you see that, Jimmy?" He turned to look at his older brother. "I never saw anybody get hit like that before! I bet that ball was going a hundred miles an hour. And then *pow*! Right in the *nuts*! Jeepers, I'm glad that wasn't me. I never want to get hit like that!"

The more Scotty carried on, the more the boys laughed.

Sam finally left the safety of first base and approached the mound to see the spectacle up close.

Stan, harboring a poorly concealed snigger, leaned over Billy and whispered in his ear. "Hey, Billy, it looks to me like Sam can hit your curveball—and all your other balls!"

And then, when it seemed it couldn't get any worse for Billy—rolling in the dirt, in visceral pain, humiliated and defeated—he turned his head and threw up.

When Billy finished spitting the barf from his mouth and sleeving it from his lips, he climbed gingerly to his feet, pausing several seconds with his hands on his knees before attempting to stand up straight. The laughing quickly petered out, and everyone stared at him. Sam just stood there without much expression. He seemed oddly unconcerned and almost impatient to resume the game.

That's when Billy's hair trigger went off. Without warning or context, Billy slugged Sam in his left eye, sweeping him cleanly from his feet and knocking him to the dirt where he landed on both shoulder blades. "Nobody hits me in the nuts, you little butterknife haircut freakshow!" he charged.

Everyone knew something like this was likely to happen, even though it was obvious that Sam had not hit him on purpose. Swinging a bat at a fast-moving baseball and hitting it anywhere inside the ninety degrees of a baseball field was an accomplishment on all accounts, let alone intentionally directing it at some kid's nuts. Everybody knew that. But Billy made it clear that he had no tolerance for such "mistakes."

With Sam flat on his back and Billy lurking over him, threatening more violence, the crowd slowly radiated away like concentric ripples on a pond, creating a clearing in the middle. None of them knew this Sam kid, so they had no idea what to expect next.

Sam came to his senses and, with the quickness of a cat, rolled off his back and sprang to his feet. In a single fluid motion, he grabbed the stick horse from between Scotty's legs by its tail and swung the thick end at Billy's face. With a full six feet of leverage and a broad, well-aimed arc, the willow smacked Billy's left cheek with a crack and jerked his head sharply to the right. Billy wobbled and dropped to one knee, eyes wide open but clearly not seeing anything. Shock reverberated through the crowd of dumbfounded boys as the circle widened even more. Surely this ignorant kid had just signed his own death sentence. Finishing the follow-through of his right-handed swing, Sam quickly switched to a left-handed grip and swung again, placing a matching crack on Billy's right cheek and snapping his head to the left. Billy dropped to both knees and stared blankly ahead, arms raised in front of him in a searching manner, as if he were looking for a light switch in a dark room. With the willow once again in the right-hand position, Sam lowered his aim and took a homerun swing at Billy's solar plexus, laying the final blow just below his ribs. Billy folded and crumpled into the fetal position for the second time.

Having witnessed the unthinkable, the crowd of boys was utterly petrified. And Billy, after absorbing that paralyzing hammer to the diaphragm, could not breathe. He opened his mouth and thrust his abdomen forward and backward, but nothing happened. No air went in, no air went out, and no sound was made. He was like a fish out of water, flexing its gills in vain.

The circle tightened around Billy as expressions of alarm and concern rapidly turned to terror and panic as they realized he could not breathe.

"He's not breathing!" Mike cried.

"Sam killed him!" Bart screamed.

Sam coolly watched the drama play out but showed only mild annoyance toward the hysterical mob. Billy received no sympathy as he grappled helplessly for air.

"He's not going to die, you sapheads!" He just thinks he's going to die," Sam said. "He got the wind knocked out of him is all."

Billy's face was now bright red, and the veins in his neck were bulging as he gave Sam a look of desperation.

"It's a funny thing . . ." Sam said nonchalantly as he sat next to Billy in the dirt and gently probed the tenderness of his briskly swelling left eye with his index finger. "When you get your wind knocked out, it's the first time in your life that you feel like you are going to die. It's not that you're afraid you might die; you're sure of it! And suddenly you can't feel anything else. You're not hungry or thirsty or tired. You're not hot or cold or in pain. You don't care about your bike, your dog, or your friends. You don't care about baseball or going to the circus. You get your wind knocked out, and you only care about one thing: breath. And you feel alone and small 'cause nobody can help you. You can't even help yourself. I heard one guy put it like this: 'You show me a guy with his wind knocked out, and I'll show you a guy with a brand-new priority!' Then, just before you pass out and die . . . you don't. Instead, your wind comes back, and you feel a relief like you've never felt before."

On cue, as Billy's diaphragm began to respond in fits and starts to the demands of hypoxia, he made some tiny stuttering grunts, followed by a gasping series of prolonged low vowel sounds. "Aaaaaaa . . ." *Gasp!* "Eeeeeee . . ." *Gasp!* "Ooooooo . . ." *Gasp!*

Sam rose to his feet and retrieved his bat from home plate. As he returned to the mound, the less-distraught assembly of boys began to murmur sentiments of reassurance upon realizing their feared captain was not dead.

Billy was taking deep breaths and appeared to be savoring every single one. He didn't seem to notice the rigid welts erupting across each cheek or the hematomas that were beginning to form. He stood, brushed off the dirt, and glared at Sam.

Once again, the circle of boys began to slowly expand as the tension escalated. Billy had survived. That he was now going to kill Sam was a foregone conclusion. But that's not what happened. Sam held his ground and glowered at Billy with his bat affixed to his right shoulder and his eye nearly swollen shut. A tense and awkward moment ensued.

It was Sam who spoke first. For a second time, he shoved his hickory bat in Billy's face where he could get another good look at it. "If I ever see you again, I won't be swinging a willow!"

But all the bluster had been beaten out of Billy, and he offered no rebuttal.

Just then, a 1925 Chevrolet sedan pulled up to the field driven by an attractive thirty-two-year-old woman smartly appointed in the style of the day. She opened the door, stepped out halfway, and called to her two sons. "Jimmy! Scotty! It's time to come home."

Little Scotty quickly mounted his stick horse and trotted toward his mother. And boy did he have a story to tell her. The arrival of somebody's mother usually signaled the end of the game. Certainly this game was over, and all the boys went home.

Sam watched everyone leave. Once again, he was alone as he had been when he first appeared in center field. Or at least, so he thought. From behind, he heard a voice say, "Well, Sam with the butterknife haircut . . ."

Sam turned to discover the identity of the lone voice. Standing in front of him was the first new kid but without the tight hat, revealing a pile of long, tangled dark-brown hair. They stared at each other as Sam let the revelation sink in. Let the frame change. Then Sam's cap came off, validating the extent of the botched haircut. At once, each of them formed the faintest smile.

"So, when did you figure out I was a girl?" the first new kid asked.

"The instant you threw that first ball," Sam replied. "Let's face it. No boy could throw like that. Then I was sure by the way you flinched when that kid chucked that mitt at your chest. How long did it take you to figure out I was a girl?"

"About one second," the first new kid said. "And I was certain when that line drive hit that Billy kid and you didn't instantly hold your groin and lose your mind like all the others."

"So, what's your name?" Sam asked.

"I'm JoAnn, but everyone calls me Jo. Are you really Sam, or is that just the baseball name you use so the boys will let you play?"

"Samantha," she affirmed, "but I've been Sam for so long now that I just go with Sam."

"Do you think any of those dopes knew we were girls?" Jo asked.

"Not a chance," Sam said patently. She stared at Jo until she was certain of mutual understanding.

Twin smirks evolved, and both girls declared simultaneously, "Because boys are dumb!"

"Where did you learn to play the infield like that?" Sam inquired.

"My cousin. He's fifteen. He taught me. Where did you learn to hit like that?"

"Oh, I don't know . . . Picked it up along the way," Sam said dismissively.

"I never saw anybody swing a bat like that," Jo said. "Or a stick!"

"Well, I never saw anybody throw like you!" Sam said. "So, do you live around here?"

"Just a couple blocks away," Jo said. "What about you?"

"Same," Sam said curtly. "Did you just move here?"

"About three months ago. You?"

"Same," Sam repeated. She wasn't sure Jo believed her, yet she didn't want to tell her the truth. "I suppose you live with your mom and dad and your little brother and your big hairy dog?" Sam asked.

"No," Jo said flatly. "I live with my stepdad. Does your eye hurt?"

"Of course, but it's not my first black eye, and it won't be my last. Where did you get that bruise on your cheek?"

Now it was Jo's turn to be dismissive. "I don't know. Maybe a baseball hit me."

"You mean one of those jumpy grounders popped up and hit you in the face?"

"Yeah, probably. I don't really remember."

Sam was not buying it. "Let me tell you why that's not a baseball bruise. I watched you field those ground balls. As soon as the ball was hit in your direction, you charged in. You didn't wait to see how it would bounce; you didn't get caught on your heels. You attacked it every time without hesitation. Then you put your mitt all the way to the dirt and stuck your face right in the middle. You didn't turn your head like most kids. You kept it down and held the line so you could see the ball all the way in. Takes courage to do that, which is why you don't miss grounders. It's also why that bruise clear over on the side of your cheek wasn't made by a baseball. If you were going to get hit by one, the bruise would be right in the middle of your face."

Jo looked a little sheepish as she gently stroked the healing bruise on her cheek. Then she changed the subject. "Did you say you moved here three months ago, and your house is only a couple blocks away, like mine?"

"Yeah," Sam said.

"That's funny. I've never seen you around." Jo stared into her eyes.

This time Sam was sure she didn't believe her. But there was no sharpness to the exchange. Sam didn't feel like Jo was accusing her of a crime she herself was not willing to commit. The two seemed to be dual frauds; therefore, neither showed signs of offense. Sam was increasingly intrigued with the possibility of common ground. The intensity of the afternoon sun chased them from the field. They replaced their hats and migrated toward the shade of a leafy maple tree where Jo had left a twenty-pound cotton flour sack.

Sam was the first to confess, without any remorse or embarrassment. "I don't have a home. I ride the rails and live on the streets. That's why I dress like a boy. It's safer this way, and the men leave me alone." She looked at Jo, waiting for some kind of matching revelation.

"My stepdad hit me with the back of his hand," Jo admitted, her head bent down, clearly ashamed and embarrassed to speak the truth. "That's where I got the bruise. And I only dressed like a boy today because I didn't think they would let a girl in the game."

"Where's your mother?" Sam questioned.

Jo started to speak, then abruptly cut herself off. She stared at Sam with struggling eyes. She tried again, but failed a second time.

Perceiving her difficulty, Sam asked the obvious. "Is she dead?"

"No!" Jo declared sharply. "It's just that everyone in my life already knows where my mother is, so I've never had to answer that question. Look, I'm going to say some words I've never said before, and I'm going to hear myself speak the truth out loud for the first time." Jo took in a deep breath and then let it out. "My mother is in prison, and my stepdad beats me when he's drunk. That's my life. That's who I am." She picked up the sack and walked away.

Sam, undeterred, ran to catch up with her. "No, Jo, you're wrong. That's not who you are. That's just what happened to you. And besides, look at me. I have no home and no people. I beg for food. I've been called a tramp, a hobo, and even a thief. I never knew my mother. Don't know if she's alive or dead. If she walked right up to me now, I guarantee she wouldn't even recognize me. And I wouldn't recognize her. That's what happened to me."

They walked in silence for a few minutes, Sam occasionally glancing over at Jo.

Sam broke the silence. "What's in the sack?"

This time there was no hesitation in Jo's response. "Four quarts of moonshine."

"Where did you get that?" Sam asked, shocked.

"I buy it from my stepdad's moonshiner and take it home to him. He's going to be mad that I'm late. Maybe I'll get a bruise on the other side of my face. But if you're not afraid to come with me, I'll get some ice for your eye."

Chapter 2

Steven Toone

Jo's house was the last one on a dead-end street. A small, boxy row house in need of paint with a modest front porch and a single outbuilding. A dandy little house in its day, it was now the victim of neglect, yet still solid enough to call home.

Jo gingerly squeezed through the front door carrying her sack with Sam in tow. Her stepdad, thirty-five-year-old Steven Toone, was waiting for her, as expected. Rail thin with a yellowish hue to his skin and a grossly distended belly, he did not appear well. His worn and filthy overalls were only buckled on one side. He was shirtless and barefoot. His dark, greasy hair was uncombed and flattened to his head on one side, and he stank of body odor, urine, and alcohol.

Steven teetered and lurched as he approached Jo, bellowing in slurred speech. "Where the hell have you been? Where's my whiskey, girl?"

"It's right here," Jo assured, handing him the sack.

Snatching it away from her, he snapped it open and peered inside.

Hoping he would be satisfied with the four quarts of moonshine, enough to keep him inebriated for days, she proceeded toward the kitchen to get ice for Sam's eye.

Steven grabbed Jo's arm and spun her violently until she was facing him again. "You're late!" he shouted. "I told you if you were late again there would be hell to pay!" He jerked her arm and she stumbled toward him. Before she could get her footing, he slapped her face with the back of his hand while holding the heavy sack of hooch in the other.

Jo's neck flipped sharply to the side, her eyes rolled back in her head, and she lost her balance, landing on her hands and knees. As the pain of the blow registered, she looked up at him and screamed, "I got your moonshine! What do you want from me?"

"Don't you sass me, girl!" Steven yelled as he grabbed her by the throat and lifted her to her feet, shaking her like a dog with a rat. Her hat fell to the floor, and her long dark hair rolled down her shoulders and covered her face as she thrashed about wildly.

Unable to breathe or make a sound, her larynx crushed and her airway closed. She clawed frantically at his tightening grip as tears of fear and agony erupted and poured down her cheeks and across his trembling hand. Through her swinging hair, she caught glimpses of the unhinged rage on his face and, for the first time, feared for her life. She began to feel faint and was near passing out. After a minute, the darkness closed in and she lost clear sight. It was as if she were in one world and Steven was in another, and the two worlds were joined only by the length of his arm. In what she thought were her final moments, she heard Sam's voice.

"Let her go! Let her go!"

Steven Toone ignored Sam's intervening pleas and had yet to acknowledge her presence in the room. He ignored the terrified expression on Jo's face. He also ignored his own cruelty. Why? Because Steven Toone was gone. His brain cells poisoned, his higher function out of reach, an alcohol savage was all that remained of the human being born by that name. Without access to his own humanity, he persisted in his brutal assault on the innocent young girl.

Had Jo been alone with him that day, perhaps he would have killed her. Perhaps he would have killed her and fallen into a drunken stupor and only discovered his despicable crime when he awakened the next day in a window of sobriety.

But Jo wasn't alone that day. Sam was there, still holding her bat. With Steven's back turned to her, one hand choking Jo and the other holding the sack of bottles, Sam swept her bat from her shoulder and lunged at him with a full swing. The bat hit his rib cage with a crunch, fracturing two ribs. Steven let out a tortured groan as he released his hand from Jo's throat and dropped the sack of moonshine on the floor, breaking all four bottles.

Jo inhaled with a gasp as she escaped his suffocating grip, then coughed until she gagged.

Steven wheeled on Sam. "You're gonna die for that!" He swayed toward her menacingly, but she brushed him back with an air swing near his face. She gave him another one to keep him at bay, then another. Finally, he capitulated and stumbled into the kitchen, cursing and holding his ribs.

"Are you okay?" Sam asked Jo.

Jo took some deep breaths and managed a weak reply. "Yes, I'm okay." She was accustomed to Steven's violent outbursts. Mercifully, they were always brief—not due to a tempered resumption of control, but rather that the event seemed to rapidly encompass his primordial attention span. When he wandered vacantly into the kitchen, she assumed his furor was over.

But this time she was wrong.

Steven staggered toward the girls, wielding a ten-inch butcher knife, his eyes wild and searching like a predator.

"Quick, Sam!" Jo said. "Upstairs, to my bedroom!" The two agile girls bounded up the staircase and down the hall into Jo's bedroom and slammed the door, locking it behind them.

Steven tottered his way in pursuit, stumbling and missing steps, tethered to the handrail with one hand, clutching the butcher knife with the other. Cresting the stairs, he made his way toward Jo's room, brushing the walls with his body, shouting at her to open the door.

Inside the bedroom, Sam and Jo listened as he approached. Jo knew they were safe behind the door, but she was still frightened. Three sets of double clicks echoed in rapid succession from the doorknob as he tried in vain to turn it. Waves of heavy pounding followed.

"Open this door or I'll break it down!" he threatened, the dull pounding of his bare left fist alternating against the sharp staccato of the knife in his right. For several harrowing minutes, the ranting, cursing, and threats continued until he had exhausted himself. Finally, Jo heard no more sounds coming through the door. She hoped the tirade was over. But just as she was about to relax, she caught the distinctive sound of a knife tip stabbing into the surface of the door, followed by his struggle to remove it. Methodical and slow, he repeated the assault on the door over and over.

Jo knew Steven couldn't possibly punch the knife through the solid door. Why would he even try that? His mindless and futile attempts were more unnerving than the pounding and raving.

After ten minutes he stopped, and it became quiet. Letting out a sigh, she turned away from the door.

Sam followed Jo's lead that the crisis was over and set the bat on the bed. Jo watched Sam's eyes tour the room. The walls were barren; the paint faded, cracked, and peeling. The bed frame cradled a single mattress. It was heavily stained, smelled of urine, and had no sheets or bedding. There were no curtains on the window. No paintings, pictures, or knickknacks. No child art or cutouts from magazines. No dolls or toys. The closet was empty save for one ratty dress and a winter coat that looked two sizes too small for Jo. There was one tiny desk stacked with a lonely pile of books and a plain wooden chair.

"Like I said, I don't live here with my mom and dad and my little brother and my big hairy dog."

"I can see that. But it's still better than where I live," Sam said.

"You mean this room is better than your room because you have no room?" Jo asked.

"Yeah, I guess so," Sam said.

"But this room comes with a monster; is that really better than what you have?"

Sam made no attempt to answer. How could she compete with Jo's live-in threat? Had she been a professor of sociology, a seasoned legislator, a family advocate, a charity worker, or a law enforcement official, she still wouldn't have had an answer. How could a child, entwined in such a predicament, possibly have an answer to such a question. The two girls stared at each other blankly, their adrenaline subsiding.

"Why did you save me?" Jo said, locking onto Sam's eyes. "When Steven grabbed me, the front door was still open. You could have just run away. You don't know me. You don't owe me anything. We're not friends. You could have slipped out and hopped a freight train to the next town and never known what happened to me. I would have just been that girl you met once who played third base disguised as a boy. He could have easily gotten his hands on your throat and wouldn't have thought twice about choking you too! Why did you stay?"

Sam stared at the floor but remained silent. It was a simple enough question, so Jo wondered why she wouldn't answer. When Sam lifted her gaze, there was a wall across her face. Jo didn't know what it meant, and she certainly could not have known its history. But it was definitely a wall. Jo wanted to retract the question, but it was too late. It was already out there, separating the two of them. Perhaps it had been a long time since anyone had broken through that wall.

"It was the ice." The answer came out like a confession.

Jo looked at her quizzically. "The ice?"

"Yeah, the ice," Sam confirmed. "You offered to get ice for my eye."

Jo shook her head, confused.

"Well, you don't know me either. You don't owe me anything. You weren't the one who gave me a black eye. We're not friends. You didn't have to help me."

"I just offered you some ice. You hit a crazy, drunk man with a baseball bat! What I did took common courtesy. What you did took real courage. Not the courage it takes to field a grounder, but the kind that risks your life."

"No, it didn't," Sam refuted calmly. "You can only have courage if you care. If you risk your life but you don't care about your life, then it's not real courage. There was no risk for me. I don't have courage because I don't care."

Jo didn't know how to process what Sam said. She didn't believe it anyway. But she would let it go for now. "I could never do what you did. I could never attack somebody like that."

"He was choking you! Are you saying you wouldn't have hit him to save your own life if you could have?"

"No, I would rather just die."

Sam looked perplexed, like she was searching for words that refused to come out. "Why?"

"It's a long story," Jo said, "but I just couldn't."

Sam looked away and shook her head ever so slightly as she mumbled something Jo couldn't quite hear. Gradually, she perused the four corners of the room before stopping at the door. "How are we going to get out of here?"

"We're not," Jo replied. "Eventually, he'll fall asleep on the couch, and then you can escape. In the morning when he wakes up, he won't be mean."

Steven Toone, despite his relatively young age, was in the latter stages of alcoholism. He consumed vast amounts of corn whiskey every day, achieving blood alcohol levels that would be fatal to a nondrinker. Were he to go long enough without a drink, he would descend into delirium tremens. His craving for alcohol had become the driving force in his life, at the total exclusion of all else. In the mornings when he resurfaced from his alcohol immersion, he reached not for food but for whiskey. He was still in no way fit to care for a child, but at least for a few hours he was not violent. He became increasingly intoxicated and volatile throughout the day, until evening when he would reach a harmless stage before he became completely incapacitated. At that point, he'd slump into a chemical coma.

Jo knew his patterns, and she had carefully cultivated a survival strategy to avoid him during the most dangerous phase of his drunken cycle. Being late afternoon, she was confident he would drink himself into oblivion within a few hours and the episode would be over. She was counting on that.

But she had forgotten a critical detail. Steven's new supply of whiskey was slowly soaking into the living room floor beneath a pile of broken glass.

"So we're going to be in here for a while?" Sam said.

"Afraid so," Jo confirmed.

Sam wandered over to the bed and plopped down on the edge of the pee-stained mattress. Jo hoped she couldn't smell it.

"If we're gonna be in here a while, why don't you tell me how you got here," Sam said.

"You mean how did I come to live in this house with Steven?"

"Yes, how did you come to live in this house with that awful man?"

Jo pulled up the wooden chair and sat down. "Well, this is the long story. I never knew my dad. My grandmother says my mother doesn't even know who he is. When I was five, my mother married Steven. Both of them were in and out of prison, so I lived with my grandmother a lot. But she didn't want me, and I never liked her much anyway. She was always mad at my mother and constantly told me how much trouble she was. I figured I must be trouble too. When I was eight, my mother and Steven got divorced, and I lived alone with her for a while.

But we didn't have any money and got kicked out of our house. Then she got arrested again.

"I remember we were sitting in the train station. I don't know where she thought she was going to get money for train tickets, but that's where we were when the policemen came. Before they took her away, she said, 'Jo, I have to go with these policemen, and you can't come with me. I'll be gone for a long time, and I can't take care of you anymore. I'm no good for you, and I don't even want you.'

"I was crying because I didn't want her to go, so I wrapped my arms around her neck and tried to hold on. I told her I would wait for her. That we could be together again when she got out of prison. I promised her I would wait for her. I promised her and promised her, and I was sure that my promise would be good enough. I held on to her sweater and wouldn't let go. But she grabbed my arms and pushed me away until we were face-to-face. She looked straight into my eyes, and said, 'I don't want you.'"

Sam shuffled on the mattress and looked out the window but said nothing.

"I had nowhere to go," Jo continued. "My grandmother wouldn't take me, which was okay because I didn't want to go with her. So I went to live with my mother's sister and her husband. They didn't want me either, but my grandmother paid them to take me. They weren't mean to me, but they never treated me like they did their two boys, Rafe and Newel. Rafe was four years older, and he was the only one who treated me like I was part of the family. Like a little sister."

"Is he the one who taught you to play baseball?" Sam asked.

"Yes, he loved baseball and taught me everything he knew. He's the one who showed me how to stick my face into a grounder, then he hit balls at me until I could do it. I bet he hit a thousand balls at me. And I loved him for it." Jo choked out the last couple of words as a tear popped over her cheek. "I miss him every day." Then she paused her story to collect herself. She wiped the tear with her sleeve and palpated the reddened skin on the front of her neck, assessing the tenderness and swelling.

"Newel was two years younger than me, and he was a mean little shit! He teased and tortured me every chance he got. I tried to ignore him, and Rafe would pound him when he went too far, which was pretty often. But he never quit; he never gave me a minute of peace. Then one day we were getting ready to attend a church social, and I had on my only good dress. I was out in the barn being very careful not to get my dress dirty. But Newel was waiting for me, hiding behind some hay bales. When I passed by, he stuck his foot out and tripped me, and I fell face-first into the manure. My dress was ruined. My aunt and uncle wouldn't wait for me to get cleaned up, so I missed the social."

"That kid's lucky he didn't trip me into the manure!" Sam interjected.

"Well, I wanted my revenge. I was so sick of that irritating little brat, and I was going to get him good. So the next day I hid in the barn and waited for him. When he came by, I stuck my foot out and tripped him just like he did to me.

"And did he go face down into the manure like you did?" Sam asked eagerly.

"Well, yes, but on his way down he hit his face on the stall. Unfortunately, there was an old nail sticking out that cut a huge gash in his cheek. He went face-first into the manure. Newel ran away, bleeding and screaming back to the house. The wound got infected, and his face swelled up like a grapefruit. He had to have an operation to drain it, and then he got blood poisoning. The doctor told us he could die and to prepare for the worst! During that time when we didn't know if he would live or die, my aunt and uncle were suffering. Of course, it was all my fault. I had to watch them suffer. And I had to watch Rafe suffer. The guilt was more than I could stand. And I learned a new kind of suffering. I don't think there's any pain worse than guilt pain. I also learned there's no such thing as revenge. When I tripped him, I thought

I was getting even. But he tortured me much more after I got even with him than he ever did before. If revenge means getting even, then there is no such thing because it never comes out even. I prayed that he wouldn't die. And then I prayed if he did die, that I would die too."

"So, what happened?"

"He didn't die, but the wound on his face left him with a giant scar. Every time I looked at him, that hideous scar looked back at me, and I knew I had put it there. It was *my* scar on his face. And I knew it would always be there. It would show up in every photograph. Whenever he would meet a new person for the rest of his life, it would be the first thing they'd see. People would surely ask him how he got that scar. If he told them the truth, he would say, 'My cousin did this.' No matter what he did to me, he didn't deserve all of that. That's why I could never hurt anybody. The risk of going through that guilt again is not worth it to me. I'd rather just die."

"That kid got what was coming to him," Sam said. "You would never have tripped him if he had not tripped you first. He started it. It's not your fault that something much worse than what you intended happened to him."

"Isn't it? Whose fault is it then?" Jo refused to be given any grace from Sam. "My aunt and uncle never forgave me, and before long they told my grandmother I couldn't live with them anymore. That's when she made a deal with Steven. She owns this house and said he could live here if he would take me in. And that's how I got here, because I had to get my revenge. My mother committed a crime, and she went to the state prison. I committed revenge and came to this prison. I guess we're the same. We both got what we deserved." Having put a period on it, she looked at Sam for her reaction. But there wasn't much to see. Sam just stared out the window once again. After a long silence, Jo asked, "How did you get here?"

"I grew up in an orphanage in New York City. When I was nine, they put me on a train with a bunch of other orphan kids and took us to a place called Omaha. Then me and two boys went to a farm to live. The farmer was old and skinny, and he always had tobacco spit on his chin. He made us work really hard doing chores and thinning beets, but he didn't feed us enough. I was hungry all the time. My clothes got loose, and my belt wouldn't tighten enough to hold my pants up. So one night I snuck into the kitchen and stole a loaf of bread, and me and those two boys ate the whole thing. The next morning the farmer said a loaf of bread was missing, and he wanted to know who stole it. Those two boys tattled on me. So the farmer said he was going to whip me with a stick. He gave me his pocket knife and said, 'You go out there by the creek and cut yourself a willow about as long as your leg, then bring it back to me.' I went out to the creek, all right, but I didn't cut any willow. I just kept right on going and never went back. I still have that skinny bastard's knife." She pulled it from her pocket for Jo to see. "I ran away back to Omaha, but the police picked me up and said they were going to take me back to the farmer. I told them he was cruel and had starved me, and if they took me back, I would just run away again.

"So they found me another family, the Burrows. I lived with them for a while. They were kind of odd, but at least they fed me. Mr. Burrows was much smaller than Mrs. Burrows. She was the biggest woman I'd ever seen, tall and thick. One night she left for her book club meeting like she did every Wednesday. After she left, Mr. Burrows told me it was time for my bath. I didn't like the way he was looking at me. I said I didn't need a bath and went to my room. After a while he came in and said I had to take that bath or he'd give me a whipping. Then he grabbed me by the ear and hauled me into the bathroom. He started filling up the tub and told me to get in. Then he left. I undressed and got in the tub. But then he came back in the bathroom and shut the door. He said he was going to help me with my bath. That I didn't do a good enough job of it, and he was going to make sure I was clean. I told him I didn't need any help, but he insisted. I said, 'I've been taking my own bath since I was five years old, and I don't need any help from you.' He said, 'I'm gonna help you, and you're gonna sit still or I'll whip your bottom!'

"Then he took off his belt. I could tell he meant to do something awful, so I stood and reached for a towel, but he grabbed me and pushed me back down. I started screaming and hitting and kicking at him; water was flying everywhere. I was really scared and didn't know what to do. Just then, the bathroom door slammed open, and Mrs. Burrows ran in. She didn't say a word; she just grabbed that belt from his hand and doubled it up into a loop. Then she took a big old windup and swung it hard at Mr. Burrows. That belt hit him right across his lips and made a pop like nothing I'd ever heard before. His head snapped back, and his feet slipped out from underneath him. On his way down, his head hit the tub and knocked him out cold.

"I was so grateful to Mrs. Burrows because I thought she had come to save me. Naturally, I thought her instinct was to look after me like a mother would do. She handed me a towel as I cried. I thought she was going to comfort me or hug me or dry me off or something. But that's not what she did. She looked at me hard and said, 'You get your clothes on and you get out of this house. And don't you ever come back!'

"So I got my clothes and went out into the dark night and wandered off. I knew if the police caught me again, they'd put me in another home, maybe a worse one. I hid in an old shed, and the next day I went down to the train tracks and hopped a train for the next town. I've been on my own ever since."

The two young girls bonded over how they'd been betrayed by every adult figure in their short, wretched lives. Neither of them had ever encountered a single person of substance. Emotionally stunted and devoid of trust, they had lived their whole lives on the fringes of society with no concept of a loving family.

The evening sun was waning, and the girls had been trapped in the bedroom for hours. No noise had come through the door, so Jo assumed

Steven must be asleep or near incapacitation. She was thinking of taking a peek through the door. But Steven had run out of whisky, so instead of drinking himself into further disability, he had sobered up just enough to regain some of his physical faculties, but not enough to restore sanity. He had left the house for the first time in weeks and gone to the shed to fetch a sledgehammer. Still armed with the butcher knife, he carried the hammer up the stairs and silently approached the door.

Jo put one hand on the lock and the other on the doorknob, then leaned her ear against the door to listen. It was quiet, so she decided to take a look. She turned the lock until it clicked and positioned her eye in the crack of the door as she slowly turned the knob. There was still no sound on the other side.

Bam. Steven's hammer hit the door and rattled the hinges. Jo screamed and jumped back! Sam picked up her bat.

Bam. Bam! Bam! Bam!

"Steven, stop it! Stop hitting the door!" Jo screamed.

But as before, there was no reasoning with an enraged alcoholic. His only reply was more hammering on the door.

The upper hinge began to loosen, then the middle hinge. The top of the door leaned in with each successive pound. Sam dropped her bat, and the girls put both hands on the door and leaned into it with all their weight. Steven kept pounding, and each time the top of the door leaned in, the girls pushed it back. Over and over, they fought against the relentless sledgehammer.

Jo could hear him grunting and breathing heavily. As the door opened partially with each swing of the hammer, she could smell his body odor and alcohol breath. But they just kept pushing back on the door and were able to close it with each hit. Finally, a stalemate reached, Steven dropped the hammer and walked away.

The girls held their positions—waiting, hoping he had exhausted his diseased body or that the fit had run its course. They waited. Nothing happened. They waited some more, still holding up the door. Nothing. Maybe he was finished and had gone downstairs. Maybe they could let go of the door. Maybe they would be okay.

Then she heard something. It started out with the sound of faint footsteps in the distant hallway. But the steps became louder, closer, and faster. Steven was charging the door. The girls braced for the impact as best they could as Steven bulldozed into the door, knocking it free of the hinges. The door collapsed onto Sam and banged her forehead. She fell on her back, unconscious, her legs and torso trapped underneath the door. Steven landed on top of the door on his hands and knees, sweating profusely, slobbering and gasping for air, his chest heaving against his swollen abdomen. His head hung and swayed back and forth like he was too weak to lift it.

Jo had been blown back from the door and landed up against her bed where Sam had left her bat, but she was unhurt. Sam lay unconscious beneath the door with Steven on top of her, the butcher knife still clutched in his right hand. An avowed pacifist, Jo had already proclaimed she would not defend herself against violence, even to save her own life.

But would she defend someone else? Someone helpless? Would she defend the very person who had risked her own life for hers? In her conflict and anguish, she faced a sentinel moment.

Steven soon forced the decision. Recovering his marginal senses, he slowly raised his head enough to assess his position and assimilate the situation. Still trying to balance himself on his knees, he raised the butcher knife over Sam's chest. Sam remained unconscious. Jo stole a quick glance at her black eye, the goose egg rising on her forehead. Vulnerable, defenseless, and innocent Sam.

Then a rage Jo had never known engulfed her. This fury was not only directed at Steven but at her life situation, at God, at the universe. She raged at her past choices. Ultimately, she raged against the agony of dilemma and the terrible choice she was compelled to make. When she could contain it no longer, her rage erupted into a shrill and penetrating scream that she held as a single protracted note as she picked up Sam's bat and swung it as hard as she could. All of her pain, misery, frustration, loneliness, rejection, and anger went into that swing. Positioned at strike-zone height, Steven's sweating forehead absorbed the full force of the impact, and his head telescoped into his neck as a two-inch laceration opened up on his scalp. He collapsed face down onto the door in a puddle of his own blood. Jo, still holding her steady scream, lowered her face to Steven's level, swaying her head back and forth, and increased the volume and the pitch until it reached a piercing crescendo. With clenched fists and bulging temple veins, she fell to her knees, dizzy, red-faced, and out of breath. "Where is my mother?" she screamed as she burst into tears. "Where is my grandmother? Where are they?"

But no one heard her screams. The house was silent. No one was coming to help her.

Trembling, choking, and gasping for air, she jumped to her feet and leaned back against the bed, frantically analyzing what to do next. Despite her tender years, and in the aftermath of trauma that would have paralyzed a lesser person, Jo was a clear thinker. Steven and Sam both lay unconscious—one on top of the door, one halfway beneath it. The blood was still pooling from Steven's head wound. Jo took the knife from his limp hand and threw it at the window. It shattered the glass and fell one story to the ground below. Despite being unconscious with his face flat on the door, Steven was still propped up on both knees, giving the impression he was about to get up. She shook him cautiously, but he didn't move. Then Jo pushed him off the door and carefully pulled Sam out from underneath.

Minutes went by. Neither of them stirred. Jo wondered if she should go for help but didn't dare leave Sam in case Steven woke up and tried to finish the job. Jo noticed that the wound on Steven's head had stopped bleeding. His face was pale and gray. As she leaned in to take a closer look, she could no longer detect the familiar smell of alcohol breath. His body lay still in a way she had never seen.

"What happened?" Sam said groggily as she sat up and touched the knot on her forehead.

"Steven charged the door and it hit you on the head and knocked you out," Jo explained.

Sam blinked a few times, then looked at Steven lying face down on the floor, his blood everywhere. She looked at Sam expectantly but didn't ask the question.

"I hit him with your bat," Jo confessed.

"How many times?" Sam inquired.

"Just once," Jo said.

"Well, hit him again before he wakes up and kills us both!" Sam said urgently.

"I think he's dead," Jo said, still in shock.

"Are you sure?"

"I'm sure. Steven is dead." She helped Sam up and onto the bed.

The room was quiet. The fight was over. Both girls were bruised and battered, but they were alive. They sat side by side on the bed and breathed in unison.

Finally, Sam spoke. "You said you couldn't ever hit anyone, even to save your own life. What happened to that?"

"I didn't hit him to save *my* life, Sam! I hit him to save *your* life. When the door came off the hinges and fell, it trapped you from the waist down, then Steven landed on top of it. You were out cold on your back. Steven was on top of the door on his hands and knees. And when he saw you laying there, helpless, he raised the butcher knife over your chest. I swear he was gonna to stab you with it. So I reached for your bat and hit him." Jo spoke coldly, disconnected from the horror. She didn't feel like explaining her reasoning any further. Didn't want to elaborate on her moral dilemma. She didn't apologize or anticipate gratitude. She looked at Sam and repeated the only significant detail: "I just hit him."

Sam picked up her bat and confidently tapped it against her palm. "It had to be done, but now it's time to go."

"What do you mean?" Jo said. "We have to get the police."

"No police for me," Sam replied. "If the police come, they'll put me back in foster care. I'm getting out of here, and so should you. Hate to say it, but you're all out of family. Where are you going to go? Your grandmother won't take you. There's nobody else. They'll put you in foster care too." Sam paused briefly before declaring, "I think you should come with me."

Jo knew Sam was right. She was out of options and had no place to go. She threw her meager possessions, including her baseball glove, into a sack, and the two homeless girls stepped over Steven's stinking, dead body, descended the stairs, and went out into the night, closing the front door behind them. Jo was roiling with conflict as she left. Escaping her demoralizing life with Steven was exhilarating, but she was afraid of what was to come.

"Where are we going?" Jo asked.

"I know a place where we can stay the night, then tomorrow we'll hop a train out of here."

Satisfied with Sam's solution for the moment, Jo didn't ask any more questions. As they walked silently in the darkness, Jo could not settle on any one emotion. She had just killed a man and lost her home, though was it ever her real home? She had saved her new confidante from certain death, but now they were on the run. What was she supposed to feel? Was killing Steven right or wrong? Did it make any difference? Was she still a helpless child, or could she control her own destiny? Did she even have any choice in the matter? The only thing she felt with certainty was confusion.

In a flash of anxiety, questions of street survival flooded her thoughts, and she tried to imagine how her life would be from now on. It was in the midst of this turmoil and consternation, this imagining and solving, that Jo had her epiphany. She stuck out her forearm and stopped Sam midstride.

"Wait!" Jo said. "I have a better idea."

Sam stopped abruptly and looked at Jo with surprise.

"We don't need him!" Jo blurted out.

"We don't need who?" Sam asked.

"Him."

"Him *who*? What are you talking about?"

"Steven. We don't need Steven."

Sam looked even more confused. "What does Steven have to do with anything?"

Perhaps it was divine providence or merely a metaphoric coincidence that they had just arrived at an intersection requiring a directional decision when Jo received her inspiration. Emerging from the streetlight shade beneath the canopy of trees lining the sidewalk, they approached the vacant corner. There were no cars or pedestrians. No traffic lights. No crosswalk indicators. No police officers to ask for help. At a time of night when other kids were inside their homes, tucked into bed, Sam and Jo were roaming the deserted streets. Should they find another neighborhood? Should they walk left into the heart of the city? Or should they go straight, toward the train tracks? But Jo had a fourth alternative.

"Hear me out. I moved here with Steven three months ago. Since then, he has never left the house. He doesn't work, and he never goes anywhere. He just stays home and drinks. My grandmother put some money in the bank over on Cherry Street. It's called an annuity; it's like an allowance. On the first day of every month, I go to the bank and they give me money. Steven was supposed to use it to take care of me. But he never took care of me. I took care of him. Do you hear me? *I'm* the one who goes to the bank. I buy his moonshine and also a little food. He stays in the house and drinks, and nobody ever sees him."

Sam listened intently but showed no signs of understanding.

"As long as there is money in that bank account, you and I can buy food. We can live in the house. We don't need him. No one will know. We can live there by ourselves, and no one will tell us what to do. No one will beat us. No one will try to give us baths. No one will starve us. We won't have to beg for food. And we won't have to live with someone who doesn't want us." She paused to bask in the beauty of her plan. "We just don't need anybody!"

"You think it will work?" Sam asked with a hint of doubt.

"I think we can make it work. Besides, if we ever get caught, we won't be any worse off than we are right now."

Sam didn't immediately say anything, but Jo could see the wheels turning in her head. Of course, there was one problem with staying at Jo's house. A major problem. And Sam immediately addressed it with a questioning look. "But what about . . . ?"

"Simple. We have to get rid of him. We're going to throw him in the river."

Returning to Jo's dark house, the girls slipped through the front door and quickly flipped on the light. Knowing there was death in the house made the silence eerie and immediately challenged Jo's resolve. Sam appeared equally hesitant as they looked at each other for strength. They gingerly climbed the stairs, focusing on the top step. Although it had only been a short while since they had left Steven's lifeless body prostrate on her bedroom floor, there was something spooky about returning. When their eyes were level with the hall floor, they paused and peered toward Jo's bedroom. But the darkness concealed the answer.

Climbing the remaining stairs, Jo hesitantly reached for the hallway light switch, knowing that once it illuminated the area, Steven's body would be revealed. But what if he wasn't dead? Worse yet, what if he wasn't there? What if he knew she tried to kill him and had summoned the police? No, that was impossible. She knew he was dead and that no police were coming.

"Just do it," Sam said impatiently.

Jo flipped the switch. At the far end of the hall, Steven's bare feet were visible in the doorway of the bedroom, toes down. They crept closer and closer. Steven was face down in the clotted and drying pool of blood just the way they had left him. Dead.

Sam posed the obvious. "How are we going to move him?"

"Come with me," Jo said. She took Sam to the kitchen and pulled a candle and matchbook from the top drawer. Then they went outside to the shed. Jo lit the candle to reveal assorted yard tools and some old junk. Among the items were a wheelbarrow and a rusty logging chain. Jo tried to pick up the chain, but it was too heavy. She heaved it in the wheelbarrow in sections, starting with one of the hook ends. Pushing the wheelbarrow into the house, she positioned it at the bottom of the stairs.

"What's the chain for?" Sam asked.

"You know all those books in my bedroom?"

"Yeah."

"Well, I've read them all. Some are murder mysteries. Whenever the killer throws a body into the river, he always puts weights on it so it won't float to the surface. We're gonna need something heavy to sink Steven's body and keep it down."

Sam assessed the dead mass on the floor and gave Jo a nod of agreement. "We need to flip him onto his back. He'll be easier to drag out."

They rolled him over and each took one of Steven's grimy hands and pulled him through the doorway, then dragged him headfirst down the hall. As they started down the stairs, they lifted his body as best they could, but his head bounced off of each step like a bowling ball. At the bottom, they managed to slump his upper body into the wheelbarrow, then swing his legs over the front. With some extra effort, they leaned him forward just enough to wrap the heavy chain around his chest and lock the hook onto one of the links, securing it in position. Jo fetched the blanket from Steven's bed. They tucked his legs inside the wheelbarrow and wrapped the blanket around him, then carefully wheeled him through the door and into the night, with Jo on the handles and Sam balancing the front.

Their muscles strained to keep it level. If it tipped over, they would be unable to set it right, so they were slow and methodical. The stars of the night sky were overpowered by the half-moon. The light made it easy to see the road ahead, but also made it more likely that someone would see them. Jo began to tire and had to stop and rest a couple of times. Sam took over the handles and Jo balanced the front, walking awkwardly backward.

The night was warm and muggy, and the girls were soon drenched with sweat from their sustained labors. It was nearly midnight as they made their way out of the neighborhood, past a few isolated houses, and into the woods, an occasional barking dog the only threat to the quiet. Fireflies, typically an enchantment for children of all ages, darted and flashed without notice by the distracted girls. Luckily, no one saw their conspicuous procession, and they trudged onto the bridge until they reached the middle of the river.

The enormity of this final task set in. Jo wavered and lost her nerve. After all their effort, she wasn't sure she could finish. Despite her position of safety on the bridge, the thought of the cold, deep, and murky water below was suddenly terrifying. She imagined losing her footing and falling into the black void with Steven. Then she worried about getting caught.

"What if someone sees us?" Jo said, angst-ridden. "Maybe this is a terrible plan."

"Jo, we didn't ask for any of this. We didn't ask to be sent away. We didn't ask to be orphans. We didn't beat anybody or choke anybody. We didn't run away from some safe, loving home. We didn't cause trouble to nobody. And we never set out to kill Steven. We didn't ask for any of this. But here we are. So why not do what's best for us? This looks like our best chance."

In the face of such practical truth, Jo's resolution recovered, and she pulled the blanket from Steven's body. The smell confined by the blanket was released in a puff of putrid air that gagged the girls and further tested their metal. But they persevered.

Parking the wheelbarrow parallel with the side rail, they tilted Steven upright to get as much height as possible, then tipped him forward. He angled there precariously. The heavy chain wrapped around his chest clanked and rattled against the rusty steel as they heaved his lower body over the rail and watched him flop thirty feet to the river below, slapping the surface and then sinking into the void and out of their lives.

Returning to the house, Jo opened the front door and was overwhelmed with a flood of raw emotion. It was an unbridled excitement. Thrilling. Energizing. She felt a freedom she'd never known. But they still had a job to finish. Even though it was the middle of the night, they had to clean up the blood. Starting with the bedroom door, they put the bloody end in the bathtub and scrubbed it with water until it was clean, watching the last remnants of Steven Toone flow down the drain. Then they scrubbed the wood floor from the bedroom to the bottom of the stairs and even washed out the wheelbarrow. Although the bedroom door was now free of blood, it had been destroyed by all the hammering, so they put it in the shed.

Once the grisly scene was cleaned up, they were ready to rest. That's when Jo realized she was thirsty and hungry and had to pee. Surely, after such a long and grueling ordeal, Sam felt the same.

Jo didn't know how to cook, but she could manage scrambled eggs. After they took turns in the bathroom, they feasted on eggs, bread, and cheese. Sam guzzled water, but Jo took only a couple of sips.

"You can sleep on the couch for tonight," Jo said, directing Sam to the small living room.

Slipping out the back door of the kitchen, Jo went outside and retrieved her bedsheets from the clothesline. She paused to consider how normal her day had started. Washing her sheets, hanging them on the line, crashing the boys' baseball game. She'd go to bed tonight a murderer. Her brain couldn't process her new reality. She was exhausted and couldn't wait to lie down. But there was still one more thing to do. She took a hot water bottle left by her grandmother and filled it with ice from the icebox. On her way through the living room, she paused and handed it to Sam.

"Here's the ice I promised you."

Despite her exhaustion, Jo struggled to find the deep, peaceful sleep of childhood. All night long, the demons of her life slithered through her dreams and darted at her face, hideous and destructive, jerking her through the tenuous haze just before waking. It was during one of these fitful moments Jo realized she was fully awake and could hear screaming that was not in her head. It was coming from downstairs. A shrill, oscillating scream like nothing she had ever heard before.

Then she heard a pounding, like the heels of bare feet on a wooden floor, as if there was a scuffle taking place. *Sam!* she thought. *What's happening to Sam? Someone's in the house!* Her thoughts grew darker. *It's Steven! He's not dead. When he hit the water, he woke up, swam to the bank, and crawled out, dragging the chain with him. Now he's here! Downstairs! Attacking Sam!*

She jumped from her bed and ran down the dark hallway, afraid to look and afraid not to look. She flipped on the hall light and stopped at the top of the stairs, shooting glances over the handrail at the dimly lit living room. She could still hear the scream, but no one was there. Not Sam, not anyone. Confused and terrified, she cautiously followed the unnerving sound into a shaded corner behind the stairs. Oscillating louder and softer and higher and lower in pitch, it seemed to have no source but the darkness.

Jo saw faint, flashing shards of light but still couldn't make out what it was. She stared at it until a shadowy image slowly took shape. It was

Sam. She had backed herself into the corner and was swinging her bat wildly, her eyes crazed like a caged animal, screaming.

"Sam!" Jo yelled. She held her hands up as she approached, signaling she wasn't a threat. "It's me, Jo! You're safe!"

But Sam screamed louder and higher and took a lunging swing at Jo.

Jo jumped back and tried again. "Sam! You're okay. It's me!"

But the dread on Sam's face didn't change.

Jo ran to check the kitchen, but no one was there. The back door was locked. She checked the front door; it was locked too. Finally, making sure no one could possibly be in the house, she ran back upstairs to Steven's bedroom. Empty. No one had entered the house. As Jo descended the stairs, Sam's scream was becoming softer and lower in pitch. The bat hung limply by her side in one hand, and she was staring vacantly. The scream continued to deflate until it died out as she walked with a mechanical gait to the couch and laid down on her side, hugging her bat like a body pillow.

Bewildered and wary, Jo crept toward Sam. She was motionless except for her deep, slow breathing. Her eyes were fixed open in a blank stare, slightly rolled back.

Jo didn't dare wake her and wasn't sure it was even possible. She had never seen anybody who couldn't wake up from a nightmare before, if that's what this was. But she decided it was best to let her sleep, so she went back to bed.

The next day was the beginning of a new life for both of them. Jo was free of her drunken master, and Sam had a safe place to drop anchor for the first time in two years. Still strangers to one another, neither knew how well it would go. Perhaps saving each other's life was the ultimate common ground.

Jo was up first, fussing around in the kitchen. When she heard Sam stir, she went into the living room to find her sitting up on the far end of the couch. Jo sat on the other end.

"Are you okay?" Jo asked.

"Sure, why wouldn't I be?"

"I mean, after last night."

"What about last night?"

"Well, do you remember what happened?"

"Do I remember it? What do you mean? Do I remember dumping a dead body in the river?"

"No, do you remember screaming and taking a swing at me with your bat?"

"I didn't do that," Sam said.

"Yes, you did. You were making this creepy, crying sound and your eyes were opened really wide and your face was scary. You were swinging your bat at the air like you were trying to hit someone. I tried to talk to you, and that's when you swung at me. Don't you remember any of this?"

"No, none of it," Sam said blankly.

"I think you were asleep," Jo explained. "Has this ever happened before?"

"I don't know. One time I was sleeping in a box car with a couple other kids, and the next morning they told me I had started yelling during the night, and they couldn't wake me up. But I don't remember it. I guess I have nightmares. Sorry, I hope I didn't scare you too much."

"You don't have to say sorry to me. You can't help it. You don't even know you are doing it. And besides, I have my own sleeping problems."

"Oh, what's that?"

"I was trying to hide it from you because I'm embarrassed about it. But if you're gonna live here, you'll figure it out soon enough, so I might just as well tell you." She looked away so she couldn't see Sam's expression when she told her. "I wet the bed," she admitted shamefully.

"You still wet the bed?" Sam asked.

"I don't *still* wet the bed," she corrected. "I wet the bed *again*! It started after I moved here. I don't know why, and I don't know what to do about it. Every morning I have to wash my sheets and underwear in the sink and hang them on the clothesline. And I know you noticed that my mattress stinks like pee."

Sam didn't say anything in response.

The two girls, one a bedwetter and the other a victim of night terrors, sat on the couch for a few minutes in silence and watched the morning sun shine through the window. Jo didn't feel well-rested, and Sam appeared lethargic and spent. But the bright sun was subtly rejuvenating. The sweetness of the filtered light contrasted sharply against the bitter darkness of the night they had endured. They sat there, bathing in the light. Resting. Restoring. Hoping.

Gradually, Jo saw the new day as a blank canvas and contemplated the obvious question, *Now what?* Without labeling it, she arrived at a rudimentary understanding that with freedom comes self-determination, with all its thrilling prospects and thorny indecision. But Jo was not without resources in self-governance. A natural organizer, she began to establish an agenda.

"The first thing I'm going to do is clean out Steven's room for you," Jo said, shattering the silence. "I'll wash his bedding and either throw away or burn all his stuff. If anybody comes looking for him, we'll say that he just disappeared one night and never came back. Then I'm going to go buy some milk. What are you going to do first?"

Sam usually spent her days scrounging for food and shelter. Waking up with both hadn't happened since she'd been on her own. She seemed oddly lost. "I have a few things stashed in this place where I've been staying. I guess I'll go get them first."

"Do you want me to come with you?" Jo offered.

"No, I can do it myself," Sam said. "Besides, I don't really want you to see it."

"You don't want me to see what?" Jo questioned.

"I don't want you to see where I've been living. It's embarrassing."

"*You're* embarrassed?" Jo persisted. "I just told you I wet the bed!"

"Well, I still don't want you to see it. It's just something I want to keep to myself. I promise not to be long. It's only a few blocks away."

"Okay," Jo relented. "Take some of this bread and cheese."

When Sam left, Jo wondered if she would ever see her again.

Chapter 3

Ed Coltrane

Sam donned her newsboy cap and tucked her unruly hair inside as she had done for two years, once again taking on the persona of a boy. She walked through the morning sunshine like a newly paroled convict. The day was bright and cloudless with just enough breeze to animate the trees and flowers and take a deep breath. She just had one nasty job to do, then she could return to Jo's house.

After four blocks, she approached a run-down, five-story building in a junky part of town surrounded by dilapidated structures, each separated by unkempt industrial yards. Two sets of railroad tracks bisected the area. The bottom two stories were constructed of rust-colored brick, heavily stained with coal smoke. Extensive cracking was evident throughout, as if the building had survived an earthquake that should have toppled it but was somehow still standing. All the first-floor windows were boarded up. The upper floors were in worse condition. The wooden panels were rotting, the paint had mostly peeled off, and many of the windows were broken. The towering smokestack projected toward the sky like the cane of a bitter old man cursing heaven. The proximity of the derelict building to the train tracks made it a natural attraction for derelict men—and homeless children. All the hobos on the rails used it. That the boards on the northwest window were loose, granting easy access, was a poorly kept secret.

Inside, garbage and various debris littered the floor. Outdated manufacturing equipment, cardboard boxes, and assorted cans—their remaining contents easily deduced by the spillage on the outside—lay abandoned and dusty. Steel barrels retained the ashes of illicit warming fires. It was dark except for a few spears of light that pierced through the window slats. It smelled of musty old building and musty old men, of stale urine and campfire smoke. The stairwell was closed off with steel bars, confining unauthorized guests to the first floor. But Sam had found a shaft of sorts, possibly to accommodate an industrial dumbwaiter. It was covered by a grate, which she removed and carefully replaced each time she used it. Crawling up the shaft, she arrived at the second floor, bypassing the steel bars, then took the stairs to the fifth floor where she had taken up residence to avoid the other bums.

Arriving at her *bedroom*, Sam beheld her squalor. The floor was covered in rodent feces, and there was a new dead rat in the corner. Her bed was a stack of cardboard, her bedding wads and layers of soiled rags. In the corner opposite the rat, the contents of several filing cabinets had been dumped, creating a sloping mountain of folders and loose paper. A broken light fixture hung from the ceiling by a bare copper wire. The sum total of Sam's worldly possessions wrapped compactly in a small bundle served as her pillow. Despite the trappings of her wretched poverty, Sam recognized the qualities of her little penthouse suite for what they were; the roof didn't leak, nobody bothered her, and it had a single unbroken window. She lay down on the makeshift bed and rested her head on the pillow substitute. The morning sun radiating through the glass panes of the window warmed her like rising bread dough. Still exhausted from the night before, she soon fell fast asleep.

Back at the house, Jo was busy cleaning out Steven's room. Essentially the same as Jo's small room, it had one closet and a single bed. The wallpaper had been mostly pulled off, revealing the bare, unpainted lathe and plaster. No curtains covered the window, and no framed pictures or heirlooms warmed the space. Just bare walls and gloom. Alcohol had not only decimated Steven's body and mind, but his finances as well. Entirely destitute before making the deal with Jo's grandmother, he had virtually nothing to show for his thirty-five years. A dresser contained two shirts, one pair of overalls, some underwear and socks, and one pair of worn-out leather shoes. A secondhand suitcase sat alone in the closet. She decided to keep the suitcase and stuffed everything else into a pillowcase.

Next to the twin bed was a small night table. As she pulled the drawer open, a Gideon Bible slid to the front. Behind it clunked a Smith & Wesson Model 10 .38 Special. Jo did not know it was there and was a little afraid to touch it. But after some thought, she decided to keep it as well, closing the drawer carefully. She stripped the foul-smelling sheets from the bed, turned the mattress upside down, then opened the window to freshen the air. The pillow was particularly disgusting, stained by the sweat and drool that soaked through the pillowcase and stinking of alcohol breath. She determined the pillow could not be saved and tossed it into the hallway. Then she took a careful look around the otherwise empty room to ensure all traces of Steven were gone.

She finished washing her sheets and hanging them on the line in the backyard, then started on Steven's bedding—now Sam's. But before she could get far, she noticed a tall column of smoke through the kitchen window. Running out into the street, the smoke appeared to be coming from a few blocks away. It looked like a big fire, and she could soon hear the clanging bells and hand-cranked sirens of the fire engines. Eager to see the spectacle, she jogged toward the smoke.

The residual fatigue from Sam's taxing night had rendered her practically comatose. But as she slept, the fifth floor insidiously filled with suffocating smoke, first obscuring the ceiling and slowly working its way toward Sam's makeshift bed on the floor. Gradually, the smoke bore down on her like a python. But Sam slept on, oblivious to her impending peril. It had started on the first floor and burned its way through the four stories between her and the safety of ground level. Had she been awake, she would have heard the cacophony and seen the flames well before the smoke arrived. But now, the building was wholly engulfed. The conflagration reached long arms of flames through the blown windows of the lower stories as if to squeeze and crush the life out of the crippled building. A crowd had gathered outside to watch the fiery display. All the while, Sam innocently slept.

Finally, the acrid smoke reached Sam's nose and triggered a sharp gasp, filling her lungs with vicious irritant. Coughing and choking, she woke to a living nightmare. Confused, she jumped to her feet only to discover the ascending thickness of the smoke as she gagged and struggled against it. Coming to her senses, she flattened herself on the floor and crawled to a window. She tried to open it, but it was painted shut. With no tools in sight, she kicked a hole in the glass, stuck her head out, and took in a few undefiled breaths. Once recovered, she held her breath and ran for the stairs, her only path of escape. But the stairwell was like looking down into hell. Flames lashed out at her, and the curling heat blocked off her escape. Returning to the window, she kicked out the remaining glass and climbed out onto the thin ledge. Looking down at the crowd some fifty feet below, she could see the horror on their faces when they noticed a young girl perched tenuously on the ledge.

She could see them mouthing the words, "There's somebody up there!"

Sam's initial actions had been pure reflex. But now that she could breathe and was momentarily safe, she could think more clearly. And she thought of Jo, the girl with the bizarre throw. The girl she had not yet known for twenty-four hours but with whom she had traded life-saving actions. The girl who had given her a place to live and food to eat. The girl who gave her the ice. Sam saw the irony in that now as she stood next to the massive fire. In that moment, she knew she would never see Jo again. Her expectations of life in general were low, and she knew there was no way down from that ledge. So she sat there, waiting for the end, agonizing over the decision she would surely be forced to make: burn up in the fire or jump. She hoped the building would intervene by falling down first. Then she wouldn't have to make the choice.

That's when she saw Jo's face in the growing crowd. At first, Jo was looking up at her like all the other people. Gradually, her expression evolved into one of query and suspicion. She saw Jo crane her neck and squint through the smoke and flames and the dusty wind. Jo seemed agitated as she elbowed and shuffled closer to the inflamed building, all the while locking eyes with her. As she stepped from the crowd and stood alone in the expanding circle of heat, Sam saw the horror on Jo's face at the moment of recognition. Sam raised her right hand slowly and gave Jo a furtive and forlorn wave of confirmation. From her perch on the fifth-story ledge, she could hear nothing but the angry gusts and the crackling fire.

Sam saw Jo mouthing her name as she screamed up at her, then began pacing back and forth, wringing her hands. She ran to the tanker truck where two firemen were hooking up hoses and turning valves. Jo yelled something to them that Sam could not hear. They stopped what they were doing and followed Jo's pointing finger. As they peered up at her, Sam was disheartened to see the fear on their faces. She didn't want to see fear from the only people who could possibly help her; she wanted to see confidence. She slumped her back against the warm wall next to the smoking window and watched as the firemen waved over the ladder truck. Jo's animated shouts at the firemen played like a silent movie. Sam could see the angst in Jo's face and the tears falling from her cheeks. Events of the past twenty-four hours flashed through her mind.

She wondered if Jo would stick to their plan and go back to the house, even though she'd be alone. Maybe she'd find someone else to live with her. Perhaps another rail kid.

Two firemen positioned the ladder beneath Sam and recruited a third fireman, thirty-six-year-old veteran Ed Coltrane, to climb the ladder and retrieve the child. But after the final extension was employed, it came up about eight feet short. Ed started up the ladder anyway. The crowd below—consisting of everyday people, passersby, housewives, taxi drivers, mothers, fathers, and kids—watched in anticipation as he climbed until the ladder ended in midair. Newspaper reporters flashed photos as the drama rolled out. Pieces of the building crumbled and fell to the ground; occasionally, a window exploded like a rifle shot. The smoke streamed hundreds of feet into the air, and Sam could feel the heat increasing within the wall.

When Ed reached the top of the ladder lugging his bulky protective gear, he was breathing hard, and his face was beaded with large drops of sweat. As Sam looked down at him, the eight-foot chasm between them was ominous, and she shook her head. The ladder swaying back and forth four or five feet in either direction made it seem even farther, and she became acutely aware of the height. Paradoxically, the fifty feet to the ground didn't bother her, but the eight feet to the ladder was terrifying. The ladder swung, disorienting her, making her feel like she was the one moving. She tried to curl her fingernails into the surface of the building, yet remained determined not to show fear. As he stopped climbing and stood still, the ladder eventually stabilized.

"What are you doing up here, son?" the fireman asked.

"I'm not your son," Sam replied defensively. "And even if I were a boy, I still wouldn't be *your* son or anybody's son."

"Okay," Ed said apologetically. "So you're not a son; you're a girl. My fault. Tell me your name."

"My name is Samantha. I go by Sam."

"So tell me, Sam, how is it you came to be stuck on this ledge?"

"I fell asleep, and when I woke up the stairs were on fire, and I couldn't get out."

"What were you doing in this old building?"

"Just sleeping," Sam replied flippantly.

"Are you scared, Sam?" he asked.

"I just want this to all be over," Sam said, evading the question.

"Well, I want it to be over too," Ed said with some softness in his voice. Ed Coltrane was six-two and two hundred forty pounds. He was a heavyweight state wrestling champion in high school who grew up on a turn-of-the-century farm with his six siblings where he had earned every muscle in his body. He married his high school sweetheart and became a fireman. He was a decorated veteran of the Hundred Days Offensive in Amiens, France, that ended The Great War. He was a fighter, and he knew how to win. Straight as an arrow, Ed had an old-fashioned understanding of *duty first.*

"Listen, Sam," he continued calmly, "we're in a bad way, and we don't have much time. We've got to get out of here."

He waited for her, but she just stared down at him, unmoving. "You know what I'm going to say next, don't you, Sam?"

Sam's fingertips began to burn, and she had to let go of the building. She poked her head inside the window, but the advancing flames punched wildly at her face. "Yeah, I know what you're going to say next. You want me to jump down there," she said skeptically.

"That's right, Sam. You're going to jump, and I'm going to catch you."

But Sam was having none of it. The lid blew off her calm demeanor, and she attacked him. "Listen, mister, I've jumped a lot of times in my life, and no one has *ever* caught me!"

"Kid, I don't know anything about your life or your people. Right now, I only know one thing with certainty. I *know* I can catch you."

"How do I know that?" Sam retorted. "I don't know you."

"My name is Edison Coltrane the Third," he stated clearly. "And I'm going to get you down from here. You're going to grow up and live to be an old woman. And when you tell your grandchildren about this day, you're going to remember my name."

"What do I care about your name?" she argued. "I just want to know if you can catch."

"I can catch you," he repeated firmly. "You have to believe that. You have to have faith in me."

"I don't believe in anybody but myself. Why would I believe in you?"

"Look around, Sam. You're up against it here. It's just me and you. Faith is your only option."

The window on the floor below Sam—eye level with Ed—exploded, embedding Ed's face with glass shrapnel. Drops of blood gushed from dozens of tiny entry wounds, covering his face. Ed recoiled from the blast but clung firmly to the ladder as it began to sway once again, and he ignored the half-buried shards projecting from his exposed skin.

"It's time to go, Sam!" he commanded. Before she could submit a rebuttal, he told her how to do it. "If you jump with your arms and legs flying everywhere like a cat out of a window, it will be hard to catch you. I want you to stand up straight, face the wall, cross your arms in front of your chest, and grab your elbows. Then fall flat on your back, and I'll catch you in my arms like a log. Can you do that?"

"Of course I can do it. Are you asking me if I have the *courage* to do it?"

"Yeah, I guess that's what I'm asking, Sam. Do you have the courage?"

"I don't need courage. Courage is for people who care."

The immensity of the fire was thunderous, and Ed cocked his ear toward her as she spoke. Over the howling ruckus, he raised his voice and yelled defiantly, "Well I care, and I'm not going down this ladder without you!"

"Why not?" Sam demanded. "Why would you risk your life for me?"

"Because it's my job!" he yelled even louder. "Because it's my duty, and it's the right thing to do! Because you're young and have your whole life in front of you!" His voice cracked a little and he paused to look her over. "And because I have a daughter about your age. She has blonde hair and is kind of a tomboy. She even looks like you. And I would never leave her up here. I'm sure as hell not going to leave you!"

Sam stared at his big chin, his two-day beard, his bloody, glass-filled face, and whatever it was in those eyes.

Convinced of his sincerity and competence, Sam stood.

The crowd below began to point, and every eye was fixed on her. Jo watched breathlessly. The inferno whirled and danced and sucked vast amounts of air up from the ground, creating a roaring updraft. The smoke rose out of sight. Portions of the walls tumbled off in flaming sheets. The roof above Sam collapsed, and fireballs were ejected from the window, just missing both Sam and Ed.

Ed widened his base and braced himself, securing his grip on the ladder by hooking his feet in the angle between the rung and the sides. Then he raised both arms, palms up, forming two muscular hooks, and waited for her final decision.

Sam stood on the narrow ledge and faced the wall, her nose burning as it touched the surface, then crossed her arms in front of her chest and gripped both elbows like Ed had instructed. She walked her eyes up the side of the building straight over her head to the roof and leaned slowly back until she saw only smoke and sky and felt the pressure of her own weight gently leave her feet. The crowd below let out a cry and then froze in place. Free-falling blindly on her back, she maintained a horizontal posture and irreversibly assigned her destiny solely and faithfully to the arms of Ed Coltrane.

When she hit Ed's outstretched arms, they snapped shut around her like a steel trap. Sam was shocked at the force of the impact as both of them let out a "humpf." It was more like landing on a fixed object, and it hurt her upper back and thighs where she hit his immoveable arms. Her unsupported head whiplashed toward the ground. She had assumed it would be a soft landing, but she had grossly underestimated the structure of Ed's solid frame.

The ladder flexed toward the ground from the sudden load. As it sprung back, Ed let go of Sam with his right arm and grabbed a rung and pulled it toward himself with all his might, pinning Sam to the ladder like he had done his wrestling opponents. Anticipating the apex of the recoil, and to avoid being chucked from the ladder like the payload of a catapult, he maintained his hold on the ladder like he was waiting for the referee to slap the mat. Sam's rib cage was wedged between the ladder and Ed's crushing chest, and she could barely breathe.

The two of them remained locked together as the ladder bounced up and down, up and down, up and down. At length, Sam could feel the trembling in Ed's right bicep. But it didn't worry her. In fact, at that moment, a strange thing happened within her. Although forty feet in the air on a rickety, swaying ladder, unable to move her arms or take a deep breath, and just feet away from an all-consuming fire with flaming building parts falling around her, she had never felt safer in her life than she did in this man's arms.

Finally, the ladder stabilized, and Ed released his life-saving grip on Sam. The two of them climbed down the ladder amidst cheers and waves from the crowd. As Sam stepped from the ladder, photo flashes blinded her. Trying to remain incognito, she put her hand up in front of her face like an indicted politician. Jumping from the ladder truck, she scissored through the crowd and ran for Jo's house with Jo trailing behind.

"Wait up!" Jo yelled.

"We need to beat it before the cops catch us and start asking questions!" Sam yelled back. And the two orphans disappeared from the scene.

As the girls hurried their way through the streets of the city, Sam tried to keep a low profile and stopped frequently to make sure no one was following. The farther they got from the burning building, the greater the cloud of smoke appeared. Once inside the house, Sam checked the windows. Convinced they had not been followed and her identity remained concealed, she took a deep breath and plopped down on the couch.

Jo was stunned at what she had just seen Sam do. Sitting next to her on the couch, the smell of burnt building emanating from Sam's clothes brought the fire into the living room. Jo was in awe by Sam's display of nonchalance about what had happened. But what a sight she was. Her newsboy cap was dusted with ashes. Her shaggy blonde hair singed on the ends. Her face was blackened like a chimney sweep, but the bump on her forehead and the swelling in her left eye were still evident. Her off-white shirt was further off-white, and a few small holes were burned into her pants. A mangey, one-eyed, stray cat with a limp and a broken tail couldn't have looked worse. It was a pitiable image Jo would never forget.

"How did you do that?" Jo asked incredulously.

"Do what?" Sam said casually.

"Do what?" Jo repeated with slight agitation. "What do you think I mean by *how did you do that*?"

Sam, in her shockingly pathetic state, looked back at her and raised her eyebrows.

"How did you jump from the fifth floor of a burning building, on your back, into the arms of a fireman on top of a ladder? How did you do that?"

Sam waffled and stalled before saying, "Maybe someday I'll tell you how I did it, but not today."

Satisfied by necessity and increasingly comfortable in her role as hostess, Jo moved on. "Would you like to take a bath and wash your clothes? You are kind of stinking up the house."

Sam had not had a real bath in a tub since the frightening incident with Mr. and Mrs. Burrows. But after a look in the mirror, she consented. Jo pumped water from the hydrant in the kitchen sink and heated it on the stove, then dumped it into the galvanized bathtub. She put Sam's clothes in the sink to soak, then found Sam some soap and a towel and gave her a dress to put on—her only dress.

"You take your bath," Jo ordered. "I'm going to buy some milk. Steven would never let me buy it. He didn't want to spend moonshine money on milk. He said I could drink water for free. But that life is over, and now I'm going to buy some milk."

When Jo returned, Sam was finished with her bath and dressed in Jo's dress. Her hair, still wet, was a disregarded mat on top of her head. In addition to the gallon of milk, Jo was also carrying two hamburgers, a bag of French fries, and a box of Kellogg's Corn Flakes. The two girls feasted on the salty, greasy burgers and fries and savored the cold milk. Jo had been accustomed to drinking fresh whole milk when she lived on her aunt and uncle's farm. She had not had any since she'd moved in with Steven, and she really missed it. But milk was a novelty for Sam. It rarely turned up in her daily search for food. In fact, her most reliable source was milk stolen directly from the cow. Wherever her travels took her, if she could find a cow barn, she would sneak inside and milk a cow into a coffee can and drink it warm.

After their sumptuous meal, Jo finished washing Sam's clothes and hung them outside on the clothesline. By then the sheets were dry, and the two girls wrapped them in their arms and then worked together to make both beds. Sam sat on her bed and spread the fingers of both hands on the surface and caressed the smooth blanket, patting it and testing the firmness of the mattress. It had been two years since she had slept on a real bed.

"I couldn't save the pillow," Jo said sadly.

The next morning started out about the same as the day before. Jo was up first, rewashing her sheets, underwear, and bedclothes. Sam had awakened her in the night again with a nightmare. Jo had gone into her room to check on her, but instead of trying to wake her, she had simply waited until the shrieking had stopped and Sam had made her way blankly back to bed from the corner of the room.

After a breakfast of cornflakes and milk, Sam made an announcement.

"I have something to do!"

"What is it?" Jo asked.

"I have to go talk to that man."

"What man?"

"That fireman."

"Why do you want to talk to him?"

"I don't know. There's just something about him."

"Like, what do you mean?"

"Well, for one thing, he's the first grown-up in my life who kept his promise."

"What promise was that?"

"When I was up on that ledge, he promised he would catch me if I jumped. And he did! When I was looking down at him, his face was covered in blood; there were pieces of glass stuck in it from an explosion. It was windy up there and noisy, and there was smoke and fire everywhere, but when I looked into his eyes, he didn't seem to care about any of that. He ignored all that stuff and just looked straight at me, like I was the only thing in the world he cared about. Maybe that's what it looks like when somebody cares about you. I saw it in his eyes. Then when he was holding me in his arms on the ladder, I just knew that nothing bad was going to happen to me because *that man* was not going to let it happen. I need to look into those eyes one more time. I've got to see what's in there."

"Well, I'm going with you this time for sure!" Jo said resolutely. "You can't be trusted to stay out of trouble."

As the girls approached the fire station, the bay doors were open, and the firemen were hustling about, cleaning and polishing things, taking care of their equipment and killing time until the next call. Like all fire stations, it was neat and orderly. Everything in its place, ready to deploy. They were all dressed down in T-shirts, trousers, and rubber boots. The mood was light as they bantered back and forth, laughing.

Sam approached the first fireman and stated her business. "I want to see Edison Coltrane the Third," she proclaimed.

"Hey, Ed!" he yelled, "there's a kid here to see you."

Ed emerged from behind the very ladder truck that had saved Sam's life the day before. Dressed down like the other firemen, Sam could now appreciate his bulk. His arms bulged from the short sleeves of his T-shirt. So many shards of glass had been tweezered from his face that the tiny residual scabs had nearly coalesced into one, making him quite a frightful sight. She could now see his full head of blond hair just starting to recede in the corners. And his facial scrub had accumulated another day's growth.

When he saw her, he smiled broadly and said, "Well, if it isn't my little jumper!"

Sam didn't know what to say to that, so she just did what she came to do and looked straight into his eyes. He looked straight back, and she saw the same thing she had seen the day before. She wasn't sure what it was, but he looked at her like he meant it. It wasn't some trick he had used to get her off the ledge. It was real. He didn't discount her like an insignificant child. In fact, she felt like he honored her. That's what she was seeing in his eyes. She didn't know why someone like him would honor someone like her, but she liked the way it felt. So there they were, two tough guys, staring into each other's eyes.

Finally, Ed broke the ice. "What happened to you yesterday? You disappeared pretty fast. I turned around and you were gone."

Sam didn't reply.

"You know that you and me are kind of famous today, don't you?" He retrieved a newspaper from a nearby bench, unfolded it, and showed the two girls the headline. "LOCAL FIREMAN SAVES MYSTERY CHILD FROM LEDGE OF BURNING BUILDING."

Again, Sam failed to respond.

"The whole city is wondering who you are, mystery child."

Sam could not abide notoriety and certainly did not want to elaborate on the "mystery child" headline. "Listen, mister, I just have one thing to say to you." She paused and started nodding her head ever so slightly up and down like one does in agreement. She pursed up her mouth and pushed it to one side and said, "Nice catch."

Without another word, she turned and walked out without waiting for Jo.

Chapter 4

The Big Kid

Jo enjoyed her freedom and relative wealth for the next few days. Without the moonshine drain on the household coffers, there was plenty of annuity money for food. And not just food, but ample measures of milk and a few childhood luxuries as well, like root beer, licorice, and ice cream. She had money to buy Sam a new pillow as well. She started to feel comfortable and safe in the house with her new roommate. She knew it was too early to tell if Sam would become her friend. She didn't really know much about friends anyway. The mothers of other little girls had been reluctant to arrange playdates for their children with the likes of her mother. Besides, their itinerant lifestyle was incompatible with making friends. In truth, her only friend had been her cousin Rafe. She was sailing uncharted waters with Sam, making it up as she went. And Sam didn't give her much feedback to go on.

One day, as they crunched cornflakes and slurped milk at the kitchen table, Sam asked a surprising question. "How about we go see if those boys are playing baseball again?"

Jo looked at her with surprise. "Don't you think we'll have trouble with that Billy kid?"

"You let me worry about him," Sam assured.

A plan for the day decided, both girls pulled their hats on tight. Jo got her glove, and Sam got her bat.

As they approached the field, Jo could see that they were in luck. The same cluster of boys had reconvened, and they were about to pick teams. Stan and Billy were dueling with the sole bat—hand over hand like before—to determine first pick. This time Billy won. He stepped back and faced the unruly bunch as he prepared to make his first choice. The boys clamored for attention and lobbied Billy for selection with mouthy chatter and boyhood tomfoolery. The endlessly energetic Scotty Jones, ever astride his trusty Shiner, darted and flitted about the field like an electron in a quantum cloud.

Jo was nervous. They drew closer to the back of Billy's outline as he gestured one at a time to his carefully considered picks. Billy obviously couldn't see them coming, but Jo's anxiety escalated as each member of the preadolescent mob sequentially perceived their presence. She could see the shock and disbelief on their faces as the pre-game ritual crashed to a halt, and silence fell over the field. All eyes shifted to Sam.

Jimmy and Mike exchanged mutual looks. "Isn't that the kid with the bad haircut who hit Billy with the stick?" Mike said.

"Can you believe this kid showed up again?" Jimmy added.

Billy whirled to face the two girls. The rest of the boys froze like they had pockets full of nitroglycerin, as if movement of any kind would set off the unstable blend of Billy and Sam. The summer was a week hotter, the field a little drier, and the snowy fluff from the cottonwoods had all fallen to the ground. A slightly more sluggish breeze leaned but did not rustle the maple leaves toward left field. Sweat soaked through Billy's ball cap. He wore his mitt on the left hand and held the team's only ball in his right.

Sam stepped forward to face him like a volunteer. The residual green and yellow patches of a dissolving hematoma around her left eye attested to her history with Billy. And the matching green and yellow faded streaks on his cheeks attested to his history with her. All eyes shifted to Billy.

Sam's direct gaze was supported by the unreferenced thirty-one-inch club of hickory displayed restively on her right shoulder. Billy returned the gaze without expression.

"What's it going to be, Billy?" Sam challenged.

Billy was a more complex character than a garden-variety playground bully. For one, he was much smarter. So much so, in fact, that his bristling behavior was more motivated by annoyance with lesser mortals than anything else. That he nurtured a healthy disregard for others was self-evident, but he didn't seek self-aggrandizement through their denigration. Exertion of his dominance was more a casual restatement of the facts than required maintenance of his ego. As such, he could respect strength and substance when he saw it. And despite the assumptions of his peers, he was governed more by calculation than brute emotion, like revenge. Whereas the other boys gave every indication that a throw-down brawl was imminent, that's not what happened. Billy showed some of his true colors when he responded to Sam's demand with one of his own.

"You're on my team," he said matter-of-factly. "I'm not pitching to you."

With the tension resolved and the crisis averted, teams were chosen and the game commenced.

By the bottom of the ninth inning, Sam was reveling in the sheer joy of the game. She was pleased with herself, having crushed three long balls into the outfield in four times at bat. She had watched Jo confirm her prowess at third base, scooping grounders and diving to catch a blistering line drive by Billy. It was plain and simple fun. For the first time in a long time, she could relax and focus on the game without the uncertain scramble for a meal and a place to sleep constantly looming. And Jo seemed carefree as well, perhaps because she was at liberty to play ball as long as she wanted, with no expectation of returning to the dreary world of Steven Toone.

As Sam was waiting her turn at bat, little Scotty Jones sidled up next to her and finally came to rest. He was dressed in full Western regalia as always and had kept busy shagging foul balls and galloping about the field. But he had also been watching the action. He witnessed Sam smack those three homers, and despite his preoccupation with his stick horse and cap pistols, what he really wanted was to play ball. At age seven, he was deemed too little, and the other boys wouldn't let him play.

Looking up at Sam from beneath the brim of his cowboy hat, he shyly posed a question. "Hey, can you teach me to hit like that?"

Sam looked down at the inquiring little boy. She didn't know what to make of his question. She had spent the last few years of her life just trying to survive independently on whatever resources she could find. She lived in a world she did not help create. In fact, she more correctly lived *off of* a world she did not help create. She didn't contribute. She didn't have chores or a job to do.

She didn't make anything or provide a service. She was a parasite on society, and she knew it. And in almost all cases, she was the youngest person in her orbit. It never occurred to her that she might actually have something to offer someone else. That she might be that person to which other people look for help of any kind. And she was initially uncomfortable with Scotty's request.

"I don't know how to teach you to hit." She fumbled getting the words out. "You just hit the ball."

"I never saw anybody hit like you do," Scotty gushed. "I want to hit like that."

Sam wanted to get rid of him, but it was hard to say no to his pleading little face.

"Okay," Sam conceded, "come over here."

Pulling the little boy aside, she told him to drop the stick horse as she placed the bat in his hands and wrapped her arms around him from behind. "The first thing you have to do is hold the bat." She slid his hands together, and he hung on her every word. "This bat is too heavy for you, so you have to choke up on it."

She pushed his hands about three inches from the lip of the handle, then pulled the bat up over his right shoulder and raised his elbows away from his body. "Now your stance," she continued. "Spread your feet, bend your knees, and lean over the plate."

Scotty did as she commanded but ended up with his weight too far back.

"Scotty," she corrected, "you're not sitting on a toilet here. You need to get your weight forward, bend at the waist, and point your little butt in the air. Like this . . ." She demonstrated the proper position.

Scotty made the adjustments and started to look like a real hitter, albeit a tiny one. "Like this?" he said.

"Yeah, like that," Sam confirmed. "Then watch the ball all the way to the bat, push off of your back foot, and swing level."

Scotty took a few swings from his new stance and seemed pleased with the results. "If I do it like this, will I be able to hit like you?" he said expectantly.

"I don't know," Sam replied. "I don't know if you have what it takes or not."

"Well, what else does it take?"

"Here's the thing, Scotty." She got to one knee in order to meet him at eye level. "When you're big—like me and your brother Jimmy—baseball is about strength and speed and skill. But when you're small, baseball is about *courage*! You have to have the courage to stand at the plate while some big kid throws a hardball a few inches from your chest and not be afraid of it. You can't hit it if you're afraid of it. So you just have to be brave. That's the secret. Are you brave, Scotty?"

With the tutorial at an end, she took the bat from his hands and stepped to the plate to take her place in the lineup. Assuming the very stance she had just taught Scotty, she fouled the first pitch over the catcher's head and out of bounds. But before Scotty could retrieve it, a stray dog picked it up and ran off with it. Since no one could catch the dog, and they had no other ball, the game was called on a technicality.

As the game broke up, Jo quick-stepped in from third base to meet Sam, still milling about home plate. Her smile was full of delight. Because they were on opposing teams, she gave Sam a sporty, tongue-in-cheek, "Good game!"

Sam almost smiled back but kept her joy restrained. "Can you believe that damn dog took the ball?"

"I know!" Jo laughed with an even bigger smile. "If I ever catch that mutt, I'll wring his neck."

Sam almost smiled. Almost.

"Okay, let's go get a root beer at the drugstore," Jo proposed.

Each boy secured his own glove from whoever was using it last and lazily sauntered in the direction of his house. None seemed to be in a big hurry, as if there may have been chores awaiting them at home.

And that's when two more boys showed up. They were too late for the game, but neither of them had a baseball, a mitt, or a bat, and they weren't wearing baseball caps. Neither had been there the week before. One of them was tall and husky, even a little fat. He wore overalls with no shirt and a straw hat. He was dark-complected with a short haircut and a menacing expression. The other kid was smaller and hardly noticeable.

The big kid walked right up to Sam and Jo and planted his boxy frame in their way. "Are you that Sam kid?" he demanded, scowling.

"No," Sam said coldly, attempting to skirt his bulk.

The big kid stepped in front of her, preventing her escape.

Sam had lived on the streets for two years with no protection but her wits. She instantly recognized the situation for what it was and stepped back, weighing survival options.

Jo's smile vanished.

The dissolving band of boys began to reconstitute as a confrontation became increasingly evident.

"Oh, I think you are that Sam kid," he growled.

"You got the wrong kid," Sam countered.

"Do I? I heard this Sam kid was blonde with a bad haircut and a little newsboy cap." He paused and looked past Sam's face at her hair, letting it sink in that Sam had been caught. "I think that's you!"

"What do you want?" Sam said, knowing it wouldn't matter if she said it pleasantly or defiantly.

"I hear you beat up Billy Rose," he said, halfway between a question and a statement.

That's all it took for Sam to figure it out. She knew the hierarchy of the streets and realized what this kid wanted. But with her ever-ready equalizer in place on her right shoulder, she wasn't even scared. She had survived collisions with worse characters than this chump. Nevertheless, even a rattlesnake must be stepped around.

"You heard wrong," Sam corrected. "I didn't beat up Billy. Not in a fistfight. I just hit him with a stick."

"Oh, I don't care how you beat him up. Billy Rose is a tough kid. And if you beat him up, you must think you're pretty tough too. But I'm tougher. So now you're gonna have to fight me."

The imminent prospect of a scuffle caused the circle of boys to tighten. Even boys with no personal inclination to fight find it hard to turn away while two clucks bludgeon each other with their fists.

"I don't want to fight you," Sam proclaimed, then turned and walked away.

The big kid stepped after her and said, "You keep walking, and I'll hit you in the back of the head!"

Sam wheeled to face him. "Why? Why do you want to hit me in the back of the head?"

"Well, I'd rather hit you in the front of the head," he jeered.

"Why?" she repeated. "Why do you want to hit me at all?"

"That's what happens in a fight. Somebody gets hit."

"Well, I'm not fighting you."

"Why won't you fight me? Are you chicken?"

"If you say I'm chicken, I'm happy to be chicken," she conceded.

"So you're just too scared to fight me?"

"Yes, I'm too scared to fight you. Are you happy with that?"

"You know, it's a funny thing . . ." He put his fists near Sam's face and made small circles with them. "You don't look scared."

Sam knew the longer she kept this kid talking, the less likely she would end up hitting him with her bat. "The reason I don't want to fight you is that it's just no good for me. If we fight, only two things can happen. I could lose, or I could win. If I lose, I won't like that 'cause I'll get beat up. And if I win, I won't like that either, 'cause I don't care if I can beat you up or not. In fact, I don't care about you at all. Beating you up doesn't matter to me. So there's no reason for me to fight you."

"Well, here's a good reason . . . I'm going to start hitting you, and if you don't fight back, I'm going to keep hitting you until I get so tired of hitting you that I can't stand it anymore. How's that for a good reason?"

"Again, why do you want to hit me? If you start hitting me and you keep hitting me, here's what will happen. I'll get another black eye like the one Billy gave me. Or I'll get a broken nose, a split lip, or a loose tooth. When it's over, I'll be bleeding and swelling and in pain." Then she looked at the big kid with her arms extended to both sides and her palms up and shrugged slightly in the universal gesture for a question. "How will that help you?" She paused and opened her eyes wide, demanding an answer with her stare.

He seemed confused, bewildered even, unable to form words.

"How will that make your life better? I'll be the one bleeding and swelling and in pain. What does that have to do with you? How could my bleeding and my swelling and my pain possibly have anything at all to do with you?" She spoke calmly, with steel composure and fatal logic.

The big kid looked nervous. And then, in a twist of irony, he began to look like the scared one. The incredulous expressions on the faces of the boys forming the ring suggested they had never seen such a fight. The big kid's face turned pathetic and desperate. Snickers with no apparent origin emanated from the crowd.

"Come on," said the big kid's nondescript sidekick. "He's not going to fight you. Let's go."

But as would be expected of the hopelessly unevolved, a common-sense argument like Sam's found no purchase. "You don't really think you're going to talk your way out of this, do you, punk?" he bellowed at Sam.

"I kinda thought I already had," Sam answered despondently. "But I can see now that you like watching people bleed. Don't you? You like watching their faces bruise and their eyes swell shut. You like their pain." Then she reached into the crowd and grabbed little Scotty Jones with her left arm and picked him up off his feet and presented him to the big kid like a sacrifice, still holding her bat on her right shoulder. "Here," she said sarcastically, "punch him in the face! He'll bleed and bruise up, and he'll be in a lot of pain. You'll like that. With luck, he'll probably cry. You'll like that even more. Won't you?"

By now, the desperation in the big kid's face had turned to rage. The clench of his teeth was readily visible. His scowl squinted his eyes and bunched his brow. His nostrils flared and his exhale became audible. Little Scotty started vainly running in air as Sam held him tight, suspended a foot above the ground.

"Well, hit him!" Sam goaded.

"I don't hit babies," he said.

"Why not?" Sam pressed. "I would think hitting babies would be the best way to go. After all, they're easy to catch, easy to hit, and they can't hit back. They bleed good, they bruise good, and you know you've hurt them because they cry right away."

"I don't hit babies, but I'm going to hit you." He doubled up both fists.

Unable to escape, little Scotty's eyes grew wide as the big kid's right fist cocked back and his left foot stepped toward them in one motion. But Sam held her ground. At the last possible second, just before the big kid's fist flew over his head at Sam's face, little Scotty dropped a bomb! In the middle of all the big-kid drama, with black eyes, split lips, and chipped teeth at stake, he drew his cap pistol and aimed it at the charging brute.

"Hold it right there!"

The big kid pulled up as the snickering crowd burst into laughter at Scotty's quick draw.

The big kid froze in place with his arms straight down by his sides, elbows locked, and fists white-knuckled as he glowered at Sam. The boys continued to laugh at Scotty while he kept the big kid covered. They mimicked the way he had drawn down on the desperado and started pointing finger guns at each other and shouting, "Bang! Bang!" The big kid's face became redder as the humiliation dragged on.

Finally, he did the only thing he could do and lashed out at the crowd. "You all think this is funny?" he screamed. "You think you can laugh at me and live to tell about it? I'm going to slug the next kid who laughs!"

The laughter quickly petered out and was replaced by serious faces. Everyone was transfixed and the standoff resumed. Big brother Jimmy stepped up and collected Scotty from Sam's arms. "Come on, Scotty. Let's go home," he said, keeping an eye on the big kid.

"Now it's just me and you and we're going to get at it," the big kid said to Sam as he took a windup with his right fist and leaned toward her.

But Sam didn't prepare to take his punch. She didn't prepare to throw one either. Instead, she gripped the handle of the bat with both hands and lifted the meaty part a couple of inches off of her shoulder. She wondered why this kid would start a fistfight with someone harboring a baseball bat, but the big kid seemed unmindful of the danger. Perhaps he thought some kind of brawler's code would prevent her from using it in a well-declared fistfight. But he was sadly mistaken. Sam had every intention of using it on him, and she would do so without compunction. She had tried to avert the confrontation. She had lied about her identity and walked away. She had tried negotiation and diplomacy, even shaming. It was time to do what she had to do with her bat.

That's when Jo jumped in and stepped directly into the line of fire. "So, big shot, you don't hit babies, but what about girls? Do you hit girls? Are you a girl fighter?"

"What girl are you talking about? I don't see any girl," the bully shot back.

Then Jo did something no other third baseman has ever done in the history of baseball. She calmly turned her back on the big bully and faced Sam, pulled a comb from her pocket, yanked Sam's cap off, and began to comb her tangled hair—while still on the field of play, no less.

Every boy on the field went practically catatonic. No ball player had ever combed another ball player's hair.

Jo parted Sam's hair on one side and combed it up off of her forehead, detangling and fluffing as she went. She ran the fanned fingers of her left hand through Sam's hair from front to back against the grain to add further fullness and shape. For several captivating minutes, she teased her unruly hair into compliance. She was in no hurry to finish, much like a hairdresser honoring the fact that beauty takes time, and the men will just have to wait.

When she had done the best she could with Sam's unsalvageable haircut, she glanced over her shoulder at the dumbfounded bully, flashed him a wry smile, and then did the unthinkable. She licked her thumb and used it to wipe the smudges from Sam's cheek. Dirt had no place on the face of a gal getting dolled up.

Jolted into motion by horror and disbelief, the boys jumped back a step in full unison, like synchronized swimmers, including the bully.

Jo turned to the crowd of discombobulated boys and stepped aside as if to present Sam at a cotillion.

Sam surveyed the crowd slowly, sequentially catching the astonished gaze of Jimmy, Bart, Stan, and little Scotty. But the expressions were all the same. None of them moved, and Sam wasn't sure any of them were breathing. Finally, she asked the obvious question. "What's the matter? Haven't you seen a pretty girl before?"

With the spell broken, the boys looked at each other, then looked back at Sam, then looked at each other, then back at Sam. She could see the wheels turning as the scandalous reality crashed in on the discomfited boys. Her gaze came to rest on one slack-jawed Billy Rose. Of all the boys on the field, none had more skin in this upside-down game than Billy. She watched him replay the events of their short acquaintance in his mind. As her features refined before his very eyes, a slight shuffle of his head made it obvious that her transformation back to a girl was complete, despite all the internal resistance he could muster. His countenance shriveled and his trademark red face was practically glow-in-the-dark.

"What is this?" the bully said in disgust. "Trying to get out of a beating by pretending to be a girl? Now I've seen everything."

"She *is* a girl, you big dope!" Jo said as she pulled off her own hat and let her long dark hair tumble to her shoulders. "We're *both* girls!"

"Maybe *you* are," he retorted. "But he's not. You're just trying to save this coward."

With manifest exasperation, Jo turned to Sam. "He doesn't believe you're a girl. There's only one thing you can do. Take off your shirt."

"What?" Sam said, horrified. "How will that help? I can't prove I'm a girl by taking off my shirt. Fatty here has bigger ones than me!"

Jo looked directly at the chest of the shirtless and chubby prepubescent, his nipples only partially concealed by his overalls. Then she verbally clobbered the hapless twit. "I think you're right. His are bigger than yours!"

The snickers started up again as the big bully conspicuously avoided looking down at his own body.

"I'll tell you what we can do," Jo proposed. "Let's settle this with a screaming contest. After all, beating a girl in a fistfight should be easy for you, but out-screaming her, now that would be something."

"Go ahead, Sam," Jo encouraged. "You start."

In the eyes of all present, except for Jo, Sam had been a believable boy: athletic, rough-and-tumble, good at sports. But she was after all, a girl. And she had a set of pipes just like any other.

Sam took a deep breath, opened her mouth wide, and fired a decibel-packed salvo at a frequency that could shatter crystal.

The big bully grabbed his ears like they were on fire, and Sam held the tortured note until she ran out of breath. Instantly and without question, she was absolved of male status.

"Okay, your turn, big shot," Jo said tauntingly.

The big kid looked like a punch-drunk fighter, dazed and unable to find his own corner. Sam was satisfied that the fight was over. Jo had won.

Utterly vexed, furious, and nakedly impotent to do anything about it, the big kid pointed his finger at Jo and said, "This is the worst day of my life!"

"Just be glad I didn't let her kill you with that bat," Jo deadpanned. As a parting shot, she leaned into his face and slugged him in the eardrums with a long, shrill scream of her own! "Ahhh!"

Again, he reached for his ears as he spun on his heels and headed for the hills.

Without further explanation, Sam and Jo abruptly gathered their hats, bat, and glove and strolled off together, leaving the beleaguered boys in a stunned kerfuffle. But little Scotty Jones certainly had another story to tell his mother.

As they walked to the drugstore, Jo turned to Sam and said, "I have one question for you. Is there anybody who *doesn't* want to beat you up?"

"You'd think so, right? Now I have a question for you. Where did you learn to be so mean? You really should be ashamed of yourself for the way you picked on that fat idiot."

"The way I picked on him?" Jo said innocently. "What about you? 'Here, punch this baby in the face! You'll really like that! Here, babies bleed real good and they cry easy. You'll love that even more!'" Jo parodied. "You kicked him in the nuts before I even got started."

"Maybe," Sam admitted, "but you destroyed that kid!"

Jo's statement conjured up a flashback of that moment when poor Billy was suspended awkwardly in the air like a gangly sawhorse just before her line drive hit him in the groin. And for the first time since Jo had known her, she broke a smile. It was a weak, restrained smile without conviction or even much promise, but it was a smile nonetheless.

"What's with these boys and their nuts anyway?" Sam asked.

"No kidding," Jo agreed. "A boy gets even the tiniest tap in the nuts, and he acts like he's been shot with a gun. My cousin's black Lab wagged his tail once and hit him in the nuts, and he dropped like a sack of potatoes. After that, he practically walked backwards around that dog."

"Yeah, and you'd think if they call them nuts, they'd be protected by some kind of hard shell like a walnut or an almond," Sam added. "Instead, they act like they're made of glass or something."

"You ever seen a boy's nuts?" Jo asked with a wry smile.

"No, have you?"

"No, but one thing's for sure, they don't come with enough padding."

"I'll say. I'm glad we don't have those parts."

"Boys must walk around all day in constant fear that they'll run into a pillow or something." Jo laughed out loud at her own joke, and Sam threatened another smile.

"Just imagine if we were boys. We could never go to a dog show," Sam reasoned.

"Yeah, and how do they even ride horses? You'd think if the horse started trotting it would only take one bounce and all the boys would turn green, throw up, and fall off!"

Chapter 5

Howard

As the second week of their new living arrangements rolled around, Jo began to settle, like the sensation at the end of a roller-coaster ride when it comes to a complete stop but before the seatbelts are released. She didn't fully trust Sam yet, but she had begun to trust herself in front of Sam. The awkwardness was waning, even though she still found the depth of their conversations to be reversely ordered. When two people meet, they start out with light conversation and small talk. As risk is measured, they expose flesh accordingly. But in this case, Jo had disgorged her deepest, darkest secrets to Sam on their first day, and vice versa. Oddly, she felt more vulnerable with frivolous talk, in kidding and playing around. Personality was more fragile than history. Sam was especially withdrawn, perhaps not only from fear of exposure but also from the lingering numbness required to endure her nomadic lifestyle. Jo had been immersed in the darkness for a lesser period of time, so she adapted more quickly to the light. Their trial period was enjoying the promise of mutual incentive. They came to see that they needed each other.

And so there they were, on a Wednesday morning at nine o'clock, sitting at the kitchen table. The daily ritual of washing Jo's bed sheets had been accomplished, and they had just finished their breakfast of cornflakes and milk, which remained a novel treat.

"I have to tell you something," Jo started.

Sam looked at her, waiting attentively.

"After I tell you, then I want to ask you something." Jo's tenor was light and energized, less restrained, with a quality exuded by those who innocently assume they are universally loved. She hoped her demeanor would soften Sam.

"Go on . . ." Sam said.

"Have you looked in that drawer by your bed?"

"No, why?" Sam asked.

"Because there's a gun in there. I found it when I was cleaning out your room."

"Yeah, so?" Sam replied nonchalantly.

"Well, what do you think about that?"

"What do you mean? What am I supposed to think?"

"Do you know anything about guns?"

"Not really."

"Have you ever seen one up close?"

"Yes. Sometimes bums on the trains would have them."

"Did you ever see anybody shoot one?"

"Yes, a few times," Sam said hesitantly, as if there was more to that answer than she wanted to tell. "What about you?"

"I've never even seen a gun up close. I don't know anything about them."

"So, what are you getting at?"

"Do you think we should learn how to shoot it?" Jo asked. "I mean, we're here all alone, and just look at all we've been through. Maybe we could protect ourselves better if we knew how to shoot it."

"Okay," Sam agreed. "But who's going to teach us?"

"I don't know. We'll have to find somebody."

As the two girls washed their bowls and spoons in the sink, Jo asked Sam another question. "How come you never read any of my books?" It wasn't the real question, of course. Jo knew the answer to the real question. It was just a softer way of asking it.

Sam looked down at her feet with a deflated sigh and said nothing.

"When was the last time you were in school?" Jo asked.

"First grade," Sam admitted.

"So, you can read a little bit?"

"Not much. I couldn't read the headline of the newspaper that fireman showed us."

"Let's go to the library," Jo suggested. "They'll have a copy of the newspaper and some beginner kids' books. I'm going to teach you to read."

Jo put on her only dress and combed her hair. She pulled it to one side and held it with a barrette. Sam was still wearing the same clothes, but she did try to fix her hair as best she could and borrowed a barrette from Jo, leaving behind her newsboy cap.

The public library was an ancient stone and brick building surrounded by generations of tall, stately trees and limited parking. At the height of reading in America, before the distraction of radio and television, the 1920s paid due respect to paper libraries. In addition to stacks of books from all ages, it was a repository for the most prolific age of periodicals in history. Patrons of all sorts gathered to read and check out books. Sam had not been inside a library since the orphanage in first grade. As they entered, the lady at the front desk gave them a pleasant nod. There was an area of tables and chairs with a couple of well-worn soft couches surrounded by racks of magazines and newspapers. A few patrons of various ages sat quietly reading.

Jo walked over to the newspaper rack and found the date of the fire. She unfolded it and showed Sam the front page. "Here it is," she whispered. "It says, 'Local fireman saves mystery child from ledge of burning building.' That's you, Sam. You're the mystery child."

Beneath the headline was a picture of Sam jumping from the ladder truck with her hand in front of her face, the burning building in the background. Sam and Jo were the only two people in the world who knew the identity of the "mystery child."

"Do you want me to read the whole article?"

"No," Sam replied. "I'll come back when I can read it myself."

Jo left Sam with the newspaper and approached the librarian at the front desk. "Where can I find first, second, and third grade readers?"

"Do you mean instructional readers like school books?"

"Yes," Jo replied, "and some story books at the same reading levels."

"Of course, miss, right this way," she replied in a business-like manner as she led Jo to the shelves in question.

Jo and Sam picked out the books they needed and were heading to the check-out counter when they passed a boy sitting at a table by himself, surrounded by books and magazines, intently studying. Jo noticed a magazine called *American Rifleman*. Upon further inspection, all the books and magazines were about guns and ammunition. The boy was a tall beanpole with mousy brown hair and big ears who looked to be a couple of years older than the girls, maybe thirteen or fourteen.

"Look!" Jo whispered to Sam. "All those books and magazines are about guns."

"So?" Sam whispered back.

"Maybe he knows how to shoot guns."

"And you're just going to ask a total stranger to teach you how to shoot your own gun?" Sam said sarcastically.

"Look at him. He's all alone in a library on a Wednesday morning in the summertime, buried in gun books! Do you really think he wouldn't want to talk to somebody about guns?" Jo reasoned.

Annoyed by their chatter, the boy turned to the girls whispering behind him and asked, with thinly veiled irritation, "Can I help you two with something?"

"I'm glad you asked," Jo replied enthusiastically. "I'm guessing you know a little about guns?"

"No, I know *everything* about guns!" he said, sounding miffed.

"Could you tell us about that?" Jo said innocently.

Just then the librarian gave the girls the evil eye and shushed them from across the room.

"Maybe we could go outside and you could tell us all about your guns," Jo whispered softly.

"Why do you want to know about guns anyway?" he whispered back.

"Shhhh," Jo said as she put her finger to her lips and motioned him to follow them as she headed to the front desk.

Inexplicably, the boy promptly gathered his literature and followed them like a puppy dog, waiting patiently as they obtained a library card and checked out the books for Sam.

Outside on the steps, in the morning shade of the building, Jo engaged her new acquaintance at full volume. "So, what's your name?"

"I'm Howard."

"Where did you learn so much about guns, Howard?"

"My father taught me. He was a sharpshooter in the war and brought his rifle home with him from the Army, an M1903 Springfield .30-06 caliber bolt action with a five round magazine and an A5 Winchester scope!" Howard said in one breath.

A little stunned by the whirlwind, the two girls had no time to comment on the blast of information before he started in again.

"It has a twenty-four-inch barrel and shoots a 150-grain bullet at 2800 feet per second. And my father can hit a prairie dog at five hundred yards."

"That's nice. Do you have any other guns?" Jo asked.

"Of course!" he confirmed. "All kinds of guns. My father takes me hunting all the time. We go target shooting and skeet shooting as well."

"So, you know how to shoot a gun yourself?" Jo said, closing in.

He looked at her like she was insane. "Of course I know how to shoot a gun! Aren't you paying attention?"

"What about a pistol?" Jo posed.

"I have a .22 caliber six-shot revolver, and my father has a Colt M1911 .45 caliber semiautomatic with a 5.03 inch barrel and an eight-round clip. It was designed by John Browning himself. It shoots 830 feet per second and will fire bullets as fast as you can pull the trigger," he said, as if quoting the *Encyclopedia Britannica*.

"Would you show us how you shoot your guns?" Jo pleaded, sounding like a groupie.

"My father only lets me shoot a .22 or my 20-gauge shotgun when he's not around."

"But the .22 is a pistol, right?" Jo confirmed.

"Yes, that's what I just said," he scolded.

"Okay then. Where are we going to shoot?" Jo asked.

She was pleasantly surprised when the skinny firearm aficionado began to give them directions to his private shooting range. Sam gave Jo one of those *How did you do that*? looks.

"Do you know where that old building burned down last week?" Howard said.

"I think we can find it," Jo said wryly.

"Follow the train tracks away from the city for about four blocks," he instructed. "There's a spot down by the river where we can shoot. I'll go get my guns and meet you there in one hour." The gun nut turned slightly into a human when he added, "What are your names anyway?"

"I'm Jo and this is Sam," Jo said pleasantly. "We are going to take these books home and then meet you there."

As they walked away Sam said, "That was some piece of work you did on that kid."

"Not really. That kid wants to show somebody his guns."

"Okay, but I can't wait to see how you get him to teach you how to shoot your own gun."

At home, Jo opened the top drawer of the night table by Sam's bed and stared at the daunting weapon. She didn't want to touch it. But Sam was less squeamish and picked it up carefully, along with the box of ammunition, and slid it into her emptied pillowcase, then tied it in a loose knot as if she had a snake in a bag.

When they found Howard at the appointed spot, they were in an isolated river bottom surrounded by dense trees and undergrowth. A clearing next to the river with a sharp embankment on one end formed the perfect shooting range, as if it had been the product of careful city planning. Howard had meticulously laid out his guns on a blanket with boxes of ammo and earplugs next to them. As advertised, the first gun was indeed a six-shot .22 caliber revolver with a well-worn hand grip. The second gun was a .22 caliber lever-action rifle. And the third was a 20-gauge pump shotgun. Next to the shotgun was a stack of clay pigeons and a handheld clay pigeon thrower. Howard had placed some tin cans downrange on a log in front of the embankment.

"Where would you like to start?" he offered.

"Let's see you shoot the pistol," Jo said.

The two girls watched intently as Howard kneeled on the blanket, took the revolver in his hands, opened the action to expose the drum, and skillfully loaded the six cylinders. "These are .22 caliber, long rifle, rim fire, copper-coated, forty-grain shells," he lectured. "They travel at 1122 feet per second." He loaded earplugs into his ears as he had done the .22 shells into the gun and offered a pair to each girl. "Guns are loud." He stood and took a couple of steps in front of the girls, pulled the hammer back—*click, click*—and took aim.

Pop!

One can tumble from the log. He pulled the hammer back again, took aim, and fired with the same result. Four more times, four more dead cans.

"Wow!" Sam said. "That's some good shooting. Could you teach us to shoot like that?"

"I can teach you to shoot, but you'll never shoot like that." He spoke with such confidence that it didn't seem like bragging, just a declaration of the truth as he saw it. "And you have to learn the rules."

"Okay," Jo said, "what are the rules?"

"The first rule is never point a gun at anyone, including yourself," he said emphatically. "Not if it's loaded, not if it's unloaded, not if you don't know if it's loaded or not. Not ever! Is that clear?" He waited for the two girls to affirm understanding before he went on. "The second rule is keep the safety on at all times until you are ready to fire." Again, he waited for their nods of understanding. "The third rule is don't ever fire downrange until everyone is behind you." By now, the girls were nodding spontaneously. "And the fourth rule is you load your own gun." He looked at Jo and said, "Okay, tell me the rules."

Jo repeated the rules back to him word for word and received looks of surprise from both Sam and the pedantic young ballistics professor.

Howard then carefully handed the gun to Jo, making sure the barrel was always pointing away from the girls. "Normally I would have put the safety on before I handed you the gun, but this is a single action revolver and has no safety. The hammer serves as the safety because it won't fire until the hammer is pulled back."

He showed Jo the drum release and told her to open it. As the drum hinged open, the smoking empty shells fell to the ground, and Jo could smell the distinctive, and to some the intoxicating, odor of burnt gunpowder. "Now put a live round in each cylinder." After she had slowly and tentatively completed the task, he wrapped his hand around hers and helped her close the drum. "The gun is now loaded," he announced with the reverence of a priest.

Jo felt a twinge of excitement well up, something she had not expected. She took two steps downrange so that Howard and Sam were safely behind her. Then she raised the pistol in her right hand and broadly pointed it downrange.

"Okay," Howard coached, "now you are going to pull the hammer back with your left thumb."

Jo gingerly torqued the hammer back until it clicked.

"All the way back," Howard commanded.

Jo clicked it again, and the hammer laid back like the ears of an angry horse. The gun was heavier than it looked. The clicking of the hammer sounded solid, and she could feel the action in the bones of her arms. Knowing the gun was ready to fire scared her a little, and she began to question her decision to take shooting lessons. The barrel began to wobble as the uncertainty of a new experience dawned.

"Put your left hand on the handle of the gun to help steady it," Howard advised. "Then squeeze the trigger slowly." And with that, he left her alone in the tenuous silence just before a gun goes off. The silence was created by the concentration of the shooter and the deference of the observers. Shooting a gun, despite being coached and surrounded by onlookers, is ultimately a solitary venture.

Jo's slightly trembling hand cautiously squeezed the space between the back of the handle and the front of the trigger until . . . *Pop!* The gun twitched in a meager attempt to jump free of her hands. But she held it fast and marveled that an event of such anticipation was so suddenly in the past. It was thrilling. A power unlike anything she had ever known. The effects of the blast in her hands had taken result some thirty feet away in a fraction of a second. Her only experience with guns had taken place on the screens of silent Westerns and gangster movies. So the intensity of the blast, even with the earplugs, surprised her. The bullet had landed nowhere near the remaining tin can on the log. In fact, it had landed almost ten feet in front of the log.

Jo could not contain the smile on her face. It was as if this tiny victory expanded to fill the vacuum of her neglected life. Her glee was not lost on Howard.

"Okay, this time," Howard said calmly, "we're going to aim."

Now that she was no longer afraid of the recoil or the blast, she could focus on marksmanship.

"Cock the hammer back again," Howard said. "Close your left eye and put the top of the front sight in the bottom of the rear sight, then line up that point with the middle of the can."

Jo studied the geometry of his instruction until she felt it was just right. She lined up the sight on the red and white label of the lone Campbell's tomato soup can and squeezed off the second round. *Pop!* This time the bullet struck the ground five feet in front of the log. Jo was panting to catch her breath as she realized she had stopped breathing while she aimed and shot. Not waiting for further permission, she cocked the hammer back a third time and repeated the aiming procedure, this time with breath. *Pop!* She nearly hit the log that time and was openly pleased with her progress. None of the final three shots in the six-shooter hit the can, but two of them hit the log. Jo didn't care. She was exhilarated, both by the stirring nature of the new exploit as well as the self-fulfillment of measured advance.

"Now open the action again," Howard instructed. "Empty the spent shells from the drum."

Jo did as ordered, then handed the gun back to him with the drum hinged open and with requisite attention to the angle of the barrel.

"Not bad for a girl," Howard said.

Jo was elated, as evidenced by the irrepressible smile on her face.

"Can I try it?" Sam said excitedly.

"Maybe," Howard said. "What are the rules?"

Sam held up her right fist and sprung out her index finger for number one. "Don't point the barrel at anyone, ever." Then she sprung her middle finger out to join her index finger for number two. "Keep the safety on until ready to shoot." Then she added her ring finger for number three. "Don't shoot downrange until everyone is behind you." For number four, she added her pinky finger. "And I have to load my own gun."

Having produced the secret password, Sam was admitted into Howard's inner sanctum, and he walked her through the same process that he had done with Jo. Her results were similar; nothing close to hitting the cans, but a little better with each shot. When she turned to face Howard and Jo, there was an intensity of attention on her face like a bird dog getting that first whiff of a pheasant.

As Sam handed the empty revolver back to Howard, Jo produced the pillowcase and untied the knot. She slowly revealed the gun. "Do you have a gun like this?"

Howard looked a little surprised but remained unflapped. "No."

"Oh, then you probably don't know anything about it, do you?" Jo baited him again.

Howard took the gun from Jo's hand and precisely followed his own protocol. He kept the barrel pointed away. Kept his fingers away from the trigger and trigger guard. Pressed the drum release and opened the action, spinning the drum slowly to ensure all the cylinders were empty. When he was satisfied the gun was safe, he returned it to Jo. "I don't have one of these, but that is a Smith & Wesson Model 10 .38 Special. It has the standard four-inch barrel and shoots a .38 caliber bullet at a thousand feet per second. Unlike my .22 pistol, this gun is a double action. That means you don't have to pull the hammer back before you shoot; the hammer comes back automatically when you pull the trigger. So it has a safety."

"Do you know how to shoot it?" Jo asked, knowing the obvious answer.

Howard looked at her with contempt as if she was trying not to learn anything on purpose. "What do you think? Do you even have any bullets for that thing?"

Jo produced the tattered box that contained a dozen rounds.

Howard put the safety on and loaded the six cylinders and closed the drum with a snap. Then he turned to the girls and said, "You need to know this is a bigger gun. It's heavier, it's louder, it shoots a bigger bullet, and it kicks more. You'll have to hold onto it with both hands." Then he turned downrange and squeezed off the first round. *Pop!* The tip of the barrel hiccupped a little fire as Howard held it with both hands. He missed the can on the first two shots but hit it on the third.

He put the safety on and handed the gun to Jo. She noticed the weight difference between the .22 and the .38. This gun felt more serious. It felt like a gun with consequences, and Jo perceived the gravity. And she was right. The .22 was a gun used for target shooting and hunting small game, but the .38 was a service weapon used by police officers and soldiers. It was intended to be aimed at people and discharged in law enforcement and military action—and self-defense.

For the second time, Jo rethought her decision to learn to shoot. She had come here today to learn the mechanics from Howard and had practically seduced him into teaching her. Now that the simple but crucial mechanics had been addressed, she thought perhaps it was all for naught. What good would it do to know how to shoot a gun in self-defense if she didn't have the gumption to do it anyway? Swinging a bat at someone was one thing, but this was a gun.

Her internal struggle notwithstanding, Jo made no sign of hesitation as she deferred the weightier matter for another day. She flipped the safety, adjusted her feet to widen her base, wrapped both hands around the grip, extended her arms until there was only a slight bend at the elbow, closed her left eye, aimed for the center of the log, and pulled the trigger.

Pop!

This time the gun made a forceful effort to escape from her hands. The tip of the barrel jumped back as the gun pushed straight toward her, causing her nearly straight arms to hinge slightly up at the shoulders. The discharge was muscular and bold; the report filled the whole clearing and punched through the wall of trees.

The rumble in her bones was a deeper frequency, and she liked the feel better than the .22. She needed no time to recover or plan the next shot. Without pause, she fired the second round with equally thrilling results. On the third round, she hit the log and heard the low-sounding thud as the 125-grain bullet sank deep into the solid willow.

The six shooter was empty. Jo set the safety, opened the drum, and dumped the hot shell casings on the ground with the panache of a Western gunslinger.

This time she handed the gun directly to Sam, who stepped up and loaded her own weapon as required by the rules of "Howard's Range." Following Jo's example, she fired off three rounds, then put the safety on and handed it back to Jo. Although lacking a lavish smile like Jo, Sam's face was pure exhilaration. "I can't believe how fun that is."

Jo offered Howard another turn, and the three of them fired the .38 until they were out of bullets.

As the two girls bagged the revolver in the pillowcase, they were both still atwitter. "I never thought I would like shooting a gun," Jo said effusively.

"I know," Sam agreed with equal thrill in her voice. "It's just so fun."

"Maybe if we practice, we could actually hit a target," Jo said with a smile.

"Yeah, we should come back and do this again," Sam added.

As the two girls gushed back and forth over their newfound passion, they turned to find Howard staring at them in disbelief.

"What's wrong, Howard?" Sam said.

"Nothing," he said. "I just don't know any girls who shoot a .38 Special."

Jo laughed at him, and Sam managed a brief smile.

But Howard wasn't finished. He had brought two more guns. He set up the cans on the log again and showed the girls how to operate the lever-action .22 rifle, loading only one shell into the magazine. He demonstrated firing from the prone position, like a sniper, whacking the first can from the left. But shooting cans at fifty feet with a rifle from the prone position was no challenge for him. He handed the gun to Sam and observed carefully as she loaded ten rounds, levered the first one into the chamber, and assumed the prone position on the blanket. After releasing the safety, she took aim and fired. After a few shots, she began to hit the cans. Jo took her turn, and the two girls were hooked.

Then Howard loaded a clay pigeon into the thrower, instructing on the nuances of doing so without breaking the fragile clay disk. Then he demonstrated how to launch one using a delicately accelerating side-arm throwing technique with a little jerk at the end. The clay bird sailed toward the target log, rising at a five-degree angle.

"Think you can do that?" he asked.

"Jo has the arm," Sam said.

Howard handed the thrower to Jo and gave her a clay pigeon. "Just do it like I did."

She took a huge backswing and instinctively wrenched on it like she was gunning out a runner at first base. The clay pigeon exploded in the thrower.

"It's more skill than strength," Howard informed. "Think of it like throwing an egg."

Jo tried again, and this time it broke into only two or three pieces but hooked hard to the left.

"There's a little snap at the end," Howard said, motioning with his wrist.

On the third try, Jo wobbled one downrange, and somehow it managed to clear the log without breaking. She could feel it now. It was coming. Her young, plastic brain analyzed all the sensations and cobbled them together into a smooth, effective motion that sent the fourth attempt rising above the log on a straight line like the course of an alien spaceship.

Howard stepped slightly downrange with his loaded 20-gauge and said, "When I say pull, you let it fly." Then he widened his base, readied his weapon, directed his gaze downrange, and yelled, "Pull!"

Jo side-armed a clay bird with perfect direction and spin. Howard drew down on it with his front sight, anticipating its trajectory by a couple of feet, and fired as it passed over the log, blowing it to smithereens.

Two more times Jo threw clay birds into the air, and both times they were slain in mid-flight.

Howard gave the gun to Sam and watched closely as she loaded three shells into the magazine and then pumped one into the chamber. He told her to shoot a tin can on the log to get a feel for the kick of a shotgun. Then, in his meticulous way, he coached her through the intricacies of hitting a moving target. On her third shot, a single BB hit the clay pigeon, and a tiny fragment broke off. It was a hit! Sam was beaming as she handed the gun back to Howard.

Jo took her turn but was unable to hit one in the air. Nevertheless, she loved it, and she was quite confident she could get the hang of it with some practice—the same way she learned to field a grounder and throw a baseball.

With the clay pigeons gone and the cans full of holes, Howard began to gather up his small arsenal.

Jo didn't quite know what to think of this Howard kid. In her mind, she had tricked him into teaching them how to shoot the .38, which was all she really wanted in the first place. But so much more than that had happened. And he hadn't displayed his superiority for self-adoring purpose as some boys would have done. He hadn't discounted them because of their age and gender, or the fact that they were total strangers. He had genuinely and sensitively shared his passion with them, and they had embraced it. He seemed too smart to be tricked, yet he accommodated their agenda anyway. Why?

It was in the midst of this confusion that Howard more or less demanded a reckoning. With his pistol holstered on his hip and the two long guns wrapped in the blanket tucked under his right arm, he planted his feet in a broad base to signal he was not going anywhere until he got an explanation. He stared at the two girls, waiting.

Jo knew the jig was up but played the obligatory little-girl card anyway. "Hey, thanks, Howard, for teaching us to shoot. It was really fun. Maybe we could do it again sometime?"

But Howard didn't respond. He just stood there, facing them, waiting for more. Jo used her most innocent face to pretend she didn't understand his obvious intent and remained silent for some long, awkward moments. Saving face in the throes of manifest guilt was not her chief concern. She had secrets with consequences, so she wisely held her ground.

"Okay then," Howard insisted. "Who are you two?"

"We told you! I'm Jo and this is Sam," Jo said.

"What are your last names? And why haven't I seen you before? Why weren't you in school? And mostly, why do you have a .38 Special in a pillowcase?"

There it was. Laid right out for them. He waited for a reply, but none was forthcoming, so he continued his interrogation. "And why did you want me to teach you how to shoot it? Why didn't your daddies teach you?" He quickly answered his own question. "Because daddies don't teach little girls to shoot .38s! Also, little girls don't want to shoot .38s. So why do you two want to shoot one?"

Jo wiped the innocent look off of her face and let Howard see the scars. "Howard, Sam and I need a friend. We need someone to help us but not try too hard to know us." She paused to see how that would take.

Howard was a smart boy, and not just about guns. He had the kind of makeup that could abide a friend with secrets. He could mind his own business.

"Could we just be shooting friends and leave it at that?" Jo asked.

Howard paused for a moment, panning back and forth between the two girls. Jo stiffened and waited. He seemed able to read the pleading in their eyes even though he had no way of understanding it. And then he showed them he could be a friend. "You're going to need more bullets. The trick to handling a gun is practice. You have to feel at home with it. You have to handle the gun until your hands know what to do by themselves. Until it becomes second nature. Like tying your shoes. That's how you don't shoot yourself."

Jo unwound a little as the tension left her. "I think you're an amazing boy, Howard. You remind me of my cousin Rafe. He taught me how to play baseball."

"Baseball," Howard said, neither asking a question nor making a statement. "Your cousin taught you how to play baseball? Of course he did. I wouldn't be surprised if he taught you how to fistfight and ride bucking horses."

Again, Jo laughed out loud, and Sam cracked a weak smile.

The three new friends walked along the railroad tracks back toward the city. The June grass was dry, and its barbed shafts beckoned to the socks of every exposed ankle. Grasshoppers boinged from the weeds, and the sun glinted off the smoothed rail. The tar-like smell of creosote on the railroad ties hung in the air.

"I'll meet you back at the shooting range next Thursday at eleven," Howard said. "We'll exercise our Second Amendment rights."

"Our Second Amendment rights?" Sam said. "What does that mean?"

"It's just something my father says," Howard explained. "The Second Amendment to the Constitution says that every citizen has the right to bear arms."

Again, Sam looked lost.

"It means *shoot guns*," Howard said. "Everyone in this country has the right to own and shoot a gun."

Sam and Jo sat down at the kitchen table to begin Sam's foray into the world of literacy. Jo the teacher set out the pencils and paper and the books she had checked out from the library. Sam looked at the first-grade reader with the trepidation of meeting a long-lost friend after the friendship had ended in a fight.

"Are you sure you want to do this?" Sam asked.

"Do what?" Jo replied.

"Teach me to read."

"What do you mean? Why would you even say that?"

"Because it's going to be hard."

"It won't be hard. It might take a while, but it won't be hard."

"Yes, it will. Think about it. I'm in the first-grade, and you're in the sixth-grade. It will be hard."

"Let me tell you about hard," Jo said as she slid to the edge of her chair, planted her forearms on the table, and leaned in so that Sam could more easily read her face as she heard her words. "When my arms were ripped from around my mother's neck when I was eight years old and she said she didn't want me—*that* was hard! When I was kicked out of my aunt and uncle's house because I scarred my cousin's face—*that* was hard! Living with a mean drunk until I had to hit him in the head with a baseball bat to save your life—*that* was hard! This is not going to be hard. I can do this, and let me tell you why. Because I *love* to read. I love to read like Howard loves to shoot. I can't imagine my life without reading, and I can't imagine your life without reading either. If you and I ever have to choose between reading and eating, we're going to read! Do you understand?"

"Yes, ma'am," Sam replied, like she might have done to her teachers at the orphanage. "But—"

"But what?" Jo interrupted.

"But I'm scared," Sam admitted. "What if I can't do it?"

"So far, I haven't seen anything you can't do," Jo said as she stared into Sam's eyes with the faith of a convert. She held the stare until Sam believed her. "Now take this pencil and paper and write the letter *A* in uppercase and lowercase, then tell me its short vowel sound and its long vowel sound."

It didn't take long for Jo to become a teacher of literacy and for Sam to become a student with no excuses.

The summer sun had set on another day of Sam and Jo's improbable life together. The night air, with its slippery density and presumed secrets, called them outside. They succumbed to that irresistible childhood ritual of summer: laying on the grass and staring up at the stars. It was a clear night except for the fuzzy glow of water vapor in the air. The crickets provided the soundtrack, with the occasional help from a neighborhood mother summoning her children inside the house. The wind was asleep already. It was one of those nights that, despite a thousand attempts, could never be repeated. Sam marveled silently as she confronted the universe. Even though Jo was by her side, she always felt alone when looking up at the stars. The way she had many times through the doorway of a parked boxcar, even one filled with other vagabonds. It was like the night sky only let people in one at a time. You have to go by yourself.

"Why are you so good?" Sam asked, keeping her face directed at the sky as she spoke.

"What do you mean?" Jo responded with a quick start.

"I mean, why are you so good?" Sam repeated.

"Why would you say that? What makes you think I'm good?" Jo asked, confused.

"Because you are," Sam said flatly.

"You think I'm good after what I did to Steven?"

"What do you mean by that?"

"What do I mean? I hit him with a baseball bat and he died," Jo said despairingly.

"But you told me you did that to save my life. Are you sorry you saved me?"

"No, of course not. But I hit him in the head. I shouldn't have done that. I should have swung the bat at his arm. Or maybe I could have hit the knife out of his hand. I should have done something different."

"You just reacted, you didn't have time to think about it," Sam countered.

"Well, I've had a lot of time to think about it since, and he didn't deserve to die like that. Even though he was mean to me when he was drunk, I didn't hate him. I hated living with him, but I didn't hate him."

"I barely met him, and I already hated him," Sam said.

"That's just the thing. He was a stranger to you. But I've known him since I was five years old," Jo reasoned. "When he married my mother, he gave me this little teddy bear, and I slept with it every night." She paused, and when she tried to speak again, her voice was broken. "I loved that bear."

A few moments passed. Sam could tell Jo was fighting back tears, and she waited patiently. She let the stars work their magic.

Jo took a deep breath in and out and continued. "He wasn't always mean, and he was there for some of my earliest memories. I don't think he hated me." Her voice turned to disgust. "Then he died, and I threw him in the river like fish guts."

Sam could hear the self-loathing in Jo's voice. She wasn't good at this sort of thing, but she consoled Jo as best she could. "When you hit him with my bat, were you trying to kill him?"

"I would never!" Jo said.

"No, of course you wouldn't," Sam confirmed. "You weren't trying to kill him; you were just trying to stop him."

Jo neither agreed nor disagreed. "And what if they find his body? What will happen to us then? They'll probably put us in jail."

"No one is going to find his body," Sam assured.

"You don't know that. I've seen people fishing from that bridge. What if one of them hooks his overalls and drags him up? It could happen."

Sam knew Jo was talking out of guilt, and there wasn't anything she could say to make her feel better.

After a short pause, Jo continued. "I can't go to the drugstore anymore. We have to find a new one."

"Why?"

"It's the pharmacist."

"What about him?"

"He reminds me of Steven."

"Steven?" Sam said, confused. "He doesn't look anything like Steven."

"It's his voice. Every time I hear him talking to customers, I'm afraid if I peek around the shelves, Steven will be standing there behind the counter in his wet, muddy overalls, wrapped in that rusty chain, bleeding from his head."

"We did what we had to do, and I'd do it again," Sam said. "The reason it bothers you and it doesn't bother me is because you've got a good heart."

"I'm not any better than anyone else," Jo argued. "I'm not any better than you."

"Yes, you are," Sam confirmed. "And I'm wondering why you're so good when you don't have to be. I'm wondering how you got that way."

"I still don't know what you mean," Jo persisted. "What's so good about me?"

Sam raised her arms from the cool grass and tucked both hands under her head as a lone dog barked in the distance. "Look at everything you've done for me. You offered me ice for my eye on the first day we met. Then you saved my life when Steven was trying to kill me. Then you gave me a place to live and food to eat. And when I was covered in ashes and soot after the fire, you heated water for my bath and washed my clothes and gave me your only dress to wear. Now you're teaching me to read. And you've done all of that without knowing what kind of a person I really am. You still don't know me very well."

"Let me remind you that you saved my life first when Steven was choking me," Jo said, still facing the sky.

"But I would have never been there if you had not offered me the ice. And here's the thing . . . From what you've told me about your life, you never had anyone to teach you how to be good. You never knew your father. Your mother was a bad example. Your grandmother was unkind to you. Your aunt and uncle threw you out. And Steven was dirty mean to you. How did you end up being good when you came from so much bad?"

"You keep calling me good," Jo said, "so you must know something about it. Where did you learn about good?"

"Learning about good and being good are two different things. I *learned* about good, but you *are* good."

"And why do you think I am good but you are not?"

"I learned about good and bad and right and wrong at the orphanage. They taught us to be good. They taught us how it's good to be nice and better to be kind. It's good to tell the truth and to share. It's good to help each other. And it's bad to lie and cheat and steal and pick on people and call them names and be mean. When we were good, we were rewarded. And when we were bad, we were punished." Sam paused as she ran orphanage footage through her mind and was silent for a long time. "But that was all a lie. Once I left the orphanage, none of that was true. I wasn't rewarded for being good; I was punished. And I wasn't punished for being bad; I was rewarded."

"What do you mean?" Jo asked.

"When I went to live with the farmer, I worked hard and tried to be good. But I didn't get rewarded for that. I got starved. And when I shared that loaf of bread with those two boys, they didn't reward me; they tattled on me. The farmer was going to punish me with a whipping until I stole his knife and took off. And that's how it started. Ever since then, when I lie and cheat and steal, I get rewarded with food and other things I need. And I never shared my food with anyone. Whenever I got food, I would eat as much of it as I could, then I would hide the rest from the other bums. I never gave anybody my shirt or my coat. I never gave up my spot in a boxcar, and I never tried to protect anyone else with my bat. I've never had a friend, and I've never been a friend. I don't believe in good or bad or right or wrong. I believe in eating. I believe in being warm. I believe in sleeping where it's not raining."

Jo kept staring at the stars, and Sam still didn't look at her. Finally, Jo spoke. "You say I'm good. I don't make that claim at all, but maybe I've done a couple of good things. For you, maybe? I'm going to tell you why, and I'm going to tell you the truth. Not because it's the right thing to do or the good thing to do, but because it's the best thing to do. I've done things for you and helped you because it makes me feel good. It makes me feel important, like a grown-up. I like the way it feels. It rewards *me*. The fact that I have food and shelter to offer you, even though it was given to me by somebody else, makes me happy. Second, you know my situation. You know what my living options are. I don't want to live here by myself. It helps me to have you around."

Jo sat up and looked over at Sam. "When I first saw you on the ledge of that burning building, the firemen didn't know you were up there. I had to tell them. And when I ran over to the closest firemen I could find, I pointed up to you and I said, 'You have to save that girl. I need her!' I didn't plan to say it that way; it just popped out because it's true. I do need you. So when you say I must be good because of all the things I've done for you, that might not be true at all. Maybe all the things I've done for you, I really did for me."

Sam listened to every word, but she couldn't believe it. She began to shake her head back and forth ever so slightly. Then she sat up and looked straight at Jo, exclaiming emphatically, "Nobody goes around doing selfish acts of kindness!"

"Sure they do!" Jo shot back. "People do good things for all kinds of reasons, and some of them are selfish. Sometimes they do it to look good so others will think high thoughts of them and sing their praises. It makes them feel better than everyone else. And some people need that. There are lots of reasons."

Sam stared into Jo's eyes as she thought about her words. It didn't make sense to her. Why would people do that? "Even though I've never thanked you for one single thing?" Sam asked.

"What?" Jo said.

"It makes you feel good to help me even though I've never thanked you for one single thing?"

"You've thanked me," Jo assured.

"When?" Sam asked. "I don't remember ever thanking you."

"Maybe not in words, but you've thanked me."

"Like how?"

"Here's a for instance," Jo said. "After the fire, I left you in the bathtub, and then I came back with the burgers and fries and the milk and the cornflakes. It had been a long, scary day, and I was starving hungry. I was sure you were too. You were wearing my dress, but your hair was still wet, and you had not even tried to comb it. Probably because you were so tired and hungry and wrung out. And when I handed you that burger—that juicy, salty, greasy burger—you held it under your nose and breathed it in and closed your eyes like you were praying to the thing. And you didn't just take a bite of it; you plunged your face into it! Ketchup and mustard ran down both sides of your chin. When you stopped chewing to breath out, you made a sigh like you had never eaten anything so good. Even I could taste it! That's when you thanked me."

"You don't get it, do you?" Sam said impatiently. "If doing good things makes you feel good, then you're good. I guess it's that simple. You're a good person and there's nothing you can do about it."

"When I lived with my aunt and uncle, we would go to church sometimes. I remember once the pastor said, 'Most people are mostly good most of the time.' I don't know if that's true or not, but I know I want it to be true," Jo said longingly. "And I guess you're right. I do want to be good. I think that will make me happy. And I don't know where that came from. It's just in there."

Both of them resumed their former positions, their backs snuggling into their own templates in the flattened grass, seeking further understanding from the stars. Several minutes later, the divine stillness of the night sky was shattered by the last fizzling flash of a shooting star.

Jo resumed talking as if she had never stopped. "And I think we should go find those people who are mostly good most of the time. And I think we should go find all the good things we can, like baseball and reading and ice cream and shooting. I want you to know that you don't have to worry anymore about eating and being warm and sleeping where it's not raining."

The next morning Sam and Jo set out to find more bullets for their gun. Sam's hair had grown out a little, and so her borrowed barrette hairstyle made her look increasingly like a girl, despite her boyish clothes. Jo wore her dress and combed her long hair.

They walked several blocks from the house until they found Ferguson's Hardware. Entering the store, they passed the paint and wallpaper, then the nuts and bolts, brackets and hinges. As they rounded the corner to the outdoor section, they paid no attention to the picks, shovels, hoes, and rakes. But at the end of the aisle they came face-to-face with the wheelbarrows and heavy chains. Jo's eyes widened and she checked her step. But Sam grabbed her elbow and hustled her on through. Soon they reached the glass counter in the back where the guns were kept. The wall behind the counter was filled with various boxes of ammunition stacked on shelves. A middle-aged man with a stark pate and spectacles stood behind the counter, his soiled blue work apron doing a poor job of concealing his pronounced beer belly. He smiled condescendingly at the two girls as they approached his counter, as if they were in the wrong section of the store by mistake.

"We need some bullets!" Jo announced confidently.

His condescending smile broadened into a full-faced smirk. "Bullets?" he questioned in mild shock. "Did you say you need some bullets?"

"Yes, sir," Jo confirmed. "Bullets!"

"Well, what kind of bullets do you need? 'Cause I don't have no little girl bullets," he said mockingly. "I don't carry unicorn bullets, and I'm all out of gumdrop bullets." He tipped his head to the right and peered over the top of his spectacles.

Sam didn't think he was a bit funny, and she stepped abruptly toward the counter and blurted out, "We need a box of .38 caliber bullets."

"Oh, .38 caliber, you say? What are you two going to do with .38 caliber bullets? Rub somebody out?"

"We're going to shoot them," Jo replied in her no-nonsense way.

"Well then, do you two want the .38 Long Colts, the Short Colts, or the Specials?"

Sam was confused by the question. But then she remembered what Howard had said about the gun. "We want the bullets for a Smith & Wesson Model 10 .38 Special."

"So, you want the Specials?"

"Yes."

"Well, you can't have them," he scoffed.

"Why not?" Jo huffed.

"I can't sell live ammunition to a couple of little girls!" he barked.

"Why can't you?" Jo asked. "Just 'cause we're girls doesn't mean we don't know how to shoot a gun."

"Yeah," Sam chimed in, "we know how to load the bullets, take off the safety, fire all six, and take out the empties."

"Yeah!" Jo pointed to a handgun under the glass. "That gun is just like ours. You get it out and give me some bullets, and I'll show you I know how to load it."

"Listen, kid," he said with growing exasperation, "I'm not selling you live ammunition so you can go home and shoot your own foot off. And I'm sure as hell not giving you a gun *and* live ammunition in my own store so you can shoot *my* foot off."

"Well, you have to," Sam declared.

"What makes you think so?" he replied sharply.

"The Second Amendment!" she proclaimed, like an officer of the court. "Haven't you ever heard of the Second Amendment? We have the right to bear arms, so you have to sell us the bullets."

"Look, missy, there's nothing in the Second Amendment that says I have to sell live ammunition to baby girls! Now why don't you two get something more fitting of your age and delicate gender, like that skip rope over there?"

"But we need bullets," Jo pleaded.

"Well, you're not getting bullets. Do you want the skip rope or not?"

Sam and Jo looked at each other dejectedly. The anger boiled up inside Sam. Not only had she been abused and neglected by the adult world, but now that same adult world, in a face-value claim of protection, was obstructing her efforts to take care of herself. She wanted to take it all out on this man and scream some really big swear words in his face. She wanted him to feel the wrath of her frustration.

He interrupted her self-roiling with a plea. "Tell you what. If you'll just get out of my store, I'll give you both a skip rope."

Sam wanted to tie his apron in a knot around his neck. But that's not what she did. Through gritted teeth and labored composure, she said, "Yes, I would very much like a skip rope. And so would my friend. Is there another hardware store around here?"

"Sure is. My cousin Harry has a store over on Oak Street. But he's not going to sell you live ammo either."

As they left the store with the skip ropes and no bullets, Sam's wheels were turning. She hadn't survived on the streets for two years by a lack of resourcefulness. "I have an idea. Follow me." Sam darted across the street to the drugstore where she searched the shelves for a pencil and some paper.

"What are we doing?" Jo asked.

"You'll see," Sam answered.

As they paid for the pencil and paper, Sam asked the clerk for directions to the restroom. Once sequestered inside, Sam said, "Now take a piece of paper and write on it 'SMITH AND WESSON MODEL 10 .38 SPECIAL,' then trade clothes with me. I need your dress."

The two girls swapped clothes, and Sam primped a little in front of the mirror, adjusting her barrette and fluffing her hair, such as it was. "Let's go!"

They barged through the restroom door and headed for the street.

"I still don't know where we're going," Jo said.

"Trust me," Sam assured.

About a block down Oak Street, the girls found Harry's Hardware, just as Mr. Ferguson had said. The store looked quite similar, the aisles filled with all manner of items for home and garden. On the wall to the right, Sam spotted the familiar glass case where the guns were kept. Behind the counter, on shelves just like Ferguson's, were boxes and boxes of ammunition. Between the glass case and the ammunition stood the figurative and literal obstacle to their objective: Harry, of Harry's Hardware.

This time, instead of marching directly to the counter like Sherman on Savannah, Sam sauntered, taking time to admire wallpaper samples and paint colors. Jo silently but attentively watched. But she could never have guessed what was about to happen.

Harry struck a shockingly similar appearance to his irascible cousin, more like brothers, including the soiled blue shop apron and the wire spectacles. As she approached the counter, Sam shifted her gaze back and forth and up and down as if lost or confused. Finally, her wandering eyes came to rest on Harry, who smiled briefly.

"May I help you ladies?" he asked politely, but with slight tedium.

Then Sam dropped the most unexpected bomb. "Pawdon me suh. Awe you the proprietuh?" She spoke in a deep Southern accent as sticky as a baby with an all-day sucker.

Jo's jaw dropped. She glanced over at Sam as if she were peering over her own spectacles.

"Yes, ma'am," he responded formally.

"Well," she continued, "could you be so kind as to direct me to the fiyuhawms and ammunition depawtment?"

Standing over a glass case full of handguns, with rows of rifles and shotguns chained together on his flank, and in front of a veritable wall of ammunition, he appeared baffled by the question. "Ah, miss, the firearms and ammunition department would be right here," he said with grace—her very unobservant question notwithstanding.

Glancing about, pretending to finally notice the obvious, she cast her face with mild surprise followed by an ever-so-faint smile of harmless embarrassment. "Why of coawse it is! How silly of me." She blushed. "Well puhaps you can help me then." She pulled the paper on which Jo had written the information about the gun from her pocket and presented it to him like a prescription to a pharmacist. "My daddy sends me all ovuh town on these insufferable chowuhs. He's powuhful busy, you know. He's a lawyuh and has no time to take cauh of his own affaiuhs. So I end up in this stouh and that stouh all ovuh town doing this and that. It's quite tiuhsome indeed. He sent me in heuh to get bullets fouh his pistol. He told me what kind of bullets to get, but I have no recall fouh those kinds of technical things. Now you ask me one of my mamma's recipes, and I can tell you every little pinch of salt. And my mamma says I have uncanny recall fouh pawluh gossip and such. But you ask me to repeat something like a calibuh of a fiyuhawm, why I'm no good at all. That's why he wrote it down fouh me so I would be shouh to get the right thing."

Then she paused like a stage actor waiting for the applause to die down. Jo was in awe of her performance.

Harry studied the paper briefly and then asked, "Where do you come from, miss?" an obvious reference to her pronounced drawl.

"My people come from Mobeel, Alabaaama," Sam said. "Why evuh do you ask?"

"Just noticing your accent," he replied innocently.

"Why mistuh Harry," she asserted, "I'm afraid you awe the one with the accent."

He smiled in deference to her clever response.

"Now could we see about those bullets?" Sam inquired.

"Certainly," he said as he wheeled around and pulled a box from the shelf behind him. "Here you go."

"And awe you shouh these awe the propuh bullets fouh what evuh my daddy wrote on that papuh?"

"These are .38 Specials. That's what he wrote on the paper," he assured as he handed her the box.

But before taking the box, Sam withdrew both her hands and held them up in a defensive position. "Could you put that in a papuh bag, please? These little things give me a powuhful fright. I don't even want to touch them. My mamma told me that no woman in the entiuh Portuh line has evuh touched a fiyuhawm!"

"That will be a dollar fifty," he said, handing her the paper bag containing the prize.

She pinched the very uppermost edge of the bag between her thumb and middle finger in order to give the appearance of keeping the scary bullets as far away as possible. Holding the bag at arm's length like a stinky diaper, she swung it toward Jo, stopping abruptly when the bag was directly between their two faces, but much closer to Jo's. She held it there as the weighted bag swayed back and forth like a pendulum. No words were necessary.

As they walked out of the store and onto the sidewalk with bullets in hand, Sam skipped along as if the ordinary events of another day had just occurred. There was no explanation, no acknowledgment of the unexplained, and no victory dance, not even a shitty little grin. Just her usual nonchalance.

"Are you seriously not going to tell me?" Jo finally said.

"Tell you what?" Sam responded innocently.

"Are you not going to tell me where you learned to talk with that accent?"

Sam looked at Jo, wondering why she would ask a question with such an obvious answer. Without even the tiniest smirk, she responded, "Why Mobeel, of coawse."

Chapter 6

Madam Kaminska

With no jobs, no school, and no one to tell them what to do, Sam and Jo often wandered the streets of the city in search of new adventures, which they usually did not find. But that was not the case on this particular evening. At the intersection of Fable and Park, they came across the Stone Theatre, a locally famous landmark at the center of the city's culture district. The marquee displayed, "Madam Natalia Kaminska and the Warsaw Philharmonic Orchestra."

Patrons, mostly couples in fine dress, were filing inside. Jo read the poster in the window to learn who the featured woman was: "World famous concert pianist from Poland, Madam Natalia Kaminska. Wow, a world-famous person in this town."

"What is it?" Sam inquired.

"She's a famous piano player from Poland," Jo answered. "And the Warsaw Philharmonic Orchestra."

"What does that mean exactly?" Sam asked.

"I think it means she plays piano with a whole orchestra. You know, violins and clarinets and French horns."

"Should we go in?"

"We don't have enough money to get in, and we're not really dressed for it. Look at all these fancy people."

"Fancy shmancy!" Sam said as she headed for the alley. "Come with me."

"Where we going?"

"You'll see."

Sam led Jo to the stage door in the alley, but it was locked. There was a tiny light above the door. Looking past the door into the alley was total darkness, like the bottom of the sea. The alley was littered with debris and dry mud puddles. "Help me with these cans," Sam said as she approached some garbage cans nearby. Pulling the cans close to the door, Sam crouched in the shadows and disappeared.

"What are we doing?" Jo asked.

"Just get over here and hide," Sam commanded.

Jo took her place next to Sam behind the stinky garbage can. "Now will you tell me what we are doing?"

"We're waiting for someone to open the door."

"Why?"

"You'll see."

They waited in the dark for about fifteen minutes. The smell of fetid juices in the garbage can made Jo hold her nose, but Sam was used to it. Suddenly the door swung open, and a man came out and lit a cigarette. He was in his twenties with dark hair and a few days of scruffy beard. He wore suspenders over a T-shirt with no sleeves. Sam and Jo were silent and still as he puffed away on the cigarette and loudly passed copious amounts of gas. When he was finished with both, he went back inside. But as he walked through the doorway, Sam scurried up behind him and grabbed the outside doorknob and turned it just as it closed, preventing it from locking, then held it shut until the man walked away.

When the coast was clear, she opened the door and presented the free entry to Jo.

Once inside, Jo turned to Sam and said, "Didn't we have a talk just the other day about lying and cheating and stealing?"

"Didn't we also have a talk the other day about finding the good people and the good things?" Sam shot back. "This could be both!"

Jo agreed but appeared reluctant as they proceeded into the hall. Passing some empty boxes, Sam picked one up and handed it to Jo. "If we see anybody, just pretend we work here and we're delivering these boxes." As they fished their way through the back passages of the building in search of the stage, Jo heard the dissonant sound of tuning instruments. They turned a corner and a stagehand brushed by, ignoring them in his hurry. Then an elegant woman in a long black dress carrying an oboe emerged from a dressing room and walked quickly away from them. As they followed her, the dissonant sounds grew louder and louder, and the lights grew brighter and brighter, until suddenly the stage appeared before them, and the woman took her place in the winds section.

Sam searched for a place to land before opening a nearby door and discovering a dark stairway. Slipping quickly inside, the sounds of tuning faded as the door closed behind them. They inched through the darkness, feeling the wall as they went. At the top of the stairs, they bumped into another door. Opening it slowly, the tuning instruments sounded as light shot through the crack. The door opened onto a high platform above the top of the curtain that led to a narrow walkway directly above the orchestra with a perfect bird's-eye view of the piano.

"Wow," Sam said, "I never saw a piano that big before."

"I think it's called a grand piano," Jo said.

The two girls sat on the walkway, each of them straddling her own handrail post, their feet dangling over the edge, and waited for the curtain. The stringed instruments in various tuning stages petered out, and the hall became deathly quiet.

"This is kind of exciting!" Jo whispered into Sam's ear.

But Sam was way ahead of her. And she noticed everything. She noticed the beautiful gowns worn by the women, and the tuxedos and black ties worn by the men of the orchestra. She noticed the long tail of the coat worn by the conductor and his white gloves. She counted eighteen different instruments and seventy-two musicians. She noticed the beautiful, deep-red curtain and marveled at its size.

"How much do you think that curtain weighs?" Sam whispered back.

Jo responded with a blank stare and a subtle head shake.

The curtains parted and the announcer proclaimed, "May I present the Warsaw Philharmonic Orchestra!" The crowd clapped briskly as the conductor turned to face the audience and bowed graciously at the waist. Before the applause had extinguished, he continued. "And please welcome special guest Madame Natalia Kaminska!" The applause built to a crescendo as a tiny woman in an exquisite ball gown appeared on the other side of the stage and floated over to the piano beneath them as if on wheels. She sat at the piano and nodded slowly to the audience until the applause was over.

Then there was silence, like a submarine crew avoiding an enemy ship. The orchestra froze in place. Not a whisper, a cough, or a shuffle could be heard from the audience. All eyes were on Madam Kaminska, who stared straight into the music stand on her piano as if studying the notes of her first selection, but there were no pages. Sam couldn't help but recall the anxious interval the moment before a gun goes off, and she almost held her ears.

And then it began. The supple fingers of the great Madam Kaminska began to softly caress the keys. The first penetrating notes from the skillfully crafted and immaculately tuned Steinway grand piano rose to meet the searching ears of the two girls. And the genius of Bach filtered up from the stage like heat through a transom. For ten minutes, her fingers gently teased from the keys the soothing beauty of the masterful composition. Sam was hopelessly seduced by the willowy melodies.

At length, she slowed to a stop, but on a note that did not sound complete, then placed her hands in her lap. Sam was ready to burst into applause but held her hands at the last second as she realized the audience was still. The great pianist suddenly raised her hands from her lap and lunged at the keys with the claws of a lioness. Whereas before she had coaxed the beauty from the keys, now she demanded power and majesty from them.

The conductor slowly raised his arms toward the orchestra and held his baton at the ready. He made a furtive flick of the wrist upward, and on the downstroke the orchestra began to play. The stage was charged with sound. The girls were utterly transfixed by the moment, by the grandeur, and by the resonating volume. For two hours they sat on the wooden walkway while the orchestra played masterpieces by Chopin, Mozart, Beethoven, Bach, and Handel. From her singular perch, Sam could see the motion of every finger of the great pianist's hands as she sculpted the keys into a work of art. Her fingers scampered across each one like a chipmunk.

Sam was light-years away from a boxcar and an abandoned building. The chaos of her disjointed life was in stark contrast to the order and synchrony of a symphony. She was drawn to it. It was fine and elevated. And somehow, she recognized in the symphony something that was as it should be. During the length of the concert, tens of thousands of notes were played without a single detectable mistake. And this was not lost on Sam. She marveled at the expertise of the musicians and instantly respected them. She felt like these were people who could be trusted. These were people who did what they said they would do. They were disciplined and responsible and appreciated beauty.

When it was over, Madam Kaminska took her bows and left the stage on the opposite side. Sam leapt to her feet and said, "Come on! Let's follow her!" as she bolted down the walkway into the darkness toward the other side of the stage. A matching staircase on that side led back down to the stage floor. Fumbling in the dark, they made their way to the door at the bottom and opened it just as Madam Kaminska turned the corner down the hall.

"Hey, where are we going?" Jo said to the back of Sam's head.

"We're going to talk to her. I have to see those hands," Sam explained.

As they hurried to catch her, Madam Kaminska opened a side door and disappeared inside. Sam kept her eye on the door to make sure she had the right one. Once Jo had caught up with her, Sam raised her fist to knock on the door.

"What are you doing?" Jo said as she grabbed Sam's hand before it could hit the door.

"You want to talk to her, too, don't you?" Sam replied.

"Yes, but we can't just barge into her dressing room!"

"We're not going to barge in. We're going to knock," Sam explained.

"I don't know," Jo said as the hallway filled with other members of the orchestra who were speaking in Polish and gesturing to each other as they passed by.

"When are we going to have another chance like this?" Sam reasoned.

After a little hand-wringing and some facial angst, Jo relented. "Okay, let's go."

Sam gave three sharp wraps on the door. A voice inside responded, but Sam couldn't make out the words. So she slowly opened the door and they inched their way in.

As the two girls entered the upscale dressing room, Sam instantly had the feeling she shouldn't touch anything. The floor was finely carpeted, the walls appointed with paintings and photographs of famous performers. The wallpaper was expertly applied and suffered no fading or blemish. There was electric lighting around the mirror and cosmetic table, which was not illuminated. Only a single ceiling light was on, rendering a soft, relaxed atmosphere. The great pianist, lounging in an overstuffed chair, sipped red wine from a glass goblet.

She was wearing a navy blue satin gown with a snug bodice, slightly out of style for the day, but reminiscent of a more elegant time. Her hair was pulled up and wrapped in a stately bun, further adorned with a few well-placed ringlets. Her thirty-seven-year-old features were a little rounded, asymmetrical, and not classically beautiful. From the rafters she had appeared smartly petite, but up close she was practically childlike in stature.

Sam and Jo, not at all dressed for such an occasion, waited for an indication to proceed.

"Come!" Madam Kaminska said to the girls sternly, more like a command than an invitation, while motioning with her free hand. "Come!"

As the girls sheepishly approached, she sat up straight in her chair as any proper lady would to receive guests. "And who are you?" she asked, rolling her Rs like a purring cat.

"I'm Sam, and this is Jo," Sam said timidly.

"And what can I do for you?" Madam Kaminska asked.

"Can we see your hands?" Sam replied.

"My hands?" she questioned, looking surprised.

"Yes, your hands," Sam said. "We watched you play, and we've never seen anything like that before. It was like your hands were magic or something."

The elegant woman set the wine glass on the vanity and presented her hands to the two awestruck girls. Her dainty hands boasted a sensible but elegant French manicure. Her fingertips bore no calluses despite years of tapping the keys, but her veins bulged like those of an older woman.

"Can I touch them?" Sam asked. Jo shot her an unapproving glance.

"But of course, my little darling," Madam Kaminska replied as she reached out her left hand to Sam.

Sam softly palpated the tiny, magic fingers in a futile attempt to discover their secrets.

The kind woman smiled at Sam's naïve search, then redirected Sam's wonder. "But as you can see, they are just hands. There is no magic, only hard work. If you want to see what is so special about my hands, you must look here." She pointed to her eyes. Then she looked directly at Jo. "Tell me what you see."

Jo studied her eyes but looked baffled.

"I will tell you what you see," Madam Kaminska offered. "You see conviction. You see discipline. You see determination and sacrifice. You see confidence and some victory. Some people say I have gift. That God gave me gift. But he play trick on me. He bury gift under ten thousand hours of practice. For thirty years I dig." She smiled wryly and motioned with both hands like she was shoveling. "I dig."

"Where did you learn to play like that?" Jo inquired.

"Sit." Madam Kaminska gestured toward a floral divan against the wall. "I tell you story."

Jo and Sam sat on the edge of the divan and leaned intently toward Madam Kaminska, enamored by her Polish accent. They had trouble understanding her at first. Little was *leetle*, darling was *darlink*, hands were *hants*, and that was *tat*. Never before had they encountered such an interesting woman. She was like foreign royalty to the two Midwestern American girls.

"When I was little girl in Poland, I see famous pianist, Wanda Landowska, in concert. She was magnificent! I go home, I tell my mother, 'I want to play piano.' She say, 'I am so sorry, sweetheart, but we have no piano.' We are very poor and live in small village. I am disappointed but I do not give up. There is no piano in my village, so I walk two miles to next village where I learn of woman with piano, and she teach lessons. I knock on her door, but when she answer she look over my head and not see me. I am eight years old and small for my age. I say to her, 'Hey, I am down here!'" She chuckled, raised her right hand, and waved it at the two girls as if hailing a cab.

Sam and Jo smiled at the quirky gesture.

"'What do you want, little girl?' she say to me. I say, 'I want job. I sweep your floor.' She is kind woman and she smile at me and tease me a little. She say, 'How much do you charge for your work?' I say, 'I sweep your floor, and you pay me with one piano lesson.' She laugh and say, 'Come in.' So I sweep her floor and she give me first piano lesson. It was very exciting, and I get warm feeling inside. When we are finished she say, 'You go home and practice every day and come back in one week.' But I say, 'I have no piano at home.' She say, 'Then you come here and practice every day.'

"So for six years I walk two miles to her house. I sweep floor. I practice. She give me lessons, and I walk two miles home. My piano became the joy of my young life. One day when I am fourteen years old, I play for her Beethoven's *Moonlight Sonata*, a very difficult piece. When I finish, she cry. I say to her, 'Why are you crying?' She say, 'I cry because I am happy, and I cry because I am sad.' I say to her, 'Why are you happy?' And she say, 'I am happy because you play like angel. You are genius. Even the heavens weep when you play.' I say, 'Why are you sad?' She cry harder and she hold me in her arms so I cannot see her face when she tell me, 'I am sad because I must let you go.' I am confused. I don't know what she is saying, so I begin to cry myself. And she say, 'I must not be your teacher anymore.' This is like arrow through my heart because I love her. She is like mother to me. I say, 'But why?' And she say, 'I have nothing more to teach you. I cannot teach you something I do not know. You have passed me up. I am of no more use to you. You must now have a master teacher.' And I say to her, 'No! You are my teacher. You will always be my teacher. I cannot play without you.' And she say, 'Listen to me carefully. It is your destiny to become great pianist, and it is my destiny to make sure you become great pianist.' And so she hold me in her arms and we cry together."

Madam Kaminska took a sip of wine and let the images of the story distill on her rapt young audience of two. "Finally, I say to her, 'But if I have new teacher, where will I practice?' And she say, 'You will practice on my piano, and I will sit and listen to you and thank God for the privilege.' Then she say, 'And you do not have to sweep my floor anymore.' But I say to her, 'No, it is my privilege to sweep your floor, and I will do it as long as I play your piano.' Four more years, I sweep her floor and I play her piano. She have cleanest floor in all of Poland.

"When I am eighteen I go to Chopin University of Music. I learn from the best teachers in Europe. But they tell me I can never be a serious pianist because my hands are too small." She showed them her hands once again, hands that were no bigger than theirs. No bigger than an average eleven-year-old American girl.

"I cannot play some chords with four notes because my fingers are too short. I cannot even reach a full octave from middle C to high C. But I do not give up. I do not listen to them, and I develop my own style of playing to accommodate my tiny hands. I become a success on my own terms. I do not take no for answer." She paused and took a slow drink of her wine and appeared to be contemplating her own story while Sam and Jo remained entranced by her presence.

"I do not take no for answer, and neither should you, my young friends. Whatever you will do, you must become bully."

Sam wasn't sure what she meant and looked at Jo for clarification. But Jo only returned a puzzled look.

"I do not mean you become bully to other people. You become bully of your own life. You take what you want because you are strong. You do not wait your turn. You do not ask for permission. You do not be kind to it. You are the master, and it will obey you. And sometimes, like your great American boxer, Jack Dempsey, you must punch it in face!" She clenched her jaw and shot her tightly sealed but bony little fist into the air like an upper cut and shook it ever so slightly at the startled girls. "Punch in face!" she repeated emphatically.

In response to Madam's little outburst, wholly at odds with her delicate demeanor, the girls pulled their chins back in unison.

Then she stood abruptly and announced, "I must leave you now, my new American friends. I have place to go."

As if on cue, the girls also stood. Jo said, "Thank you, Madam Kaminska."

"Yes," Sam joined. "Thank you for playing for us and for letting me touch your hands."

"It is my pleasure," she responded graciously.

"What are those instruments in the orchestra that look like a violin but bigger?" Jo asked.

"Those are cellos," Madam Kaminska replied.

"I think the cellos are my favorite," Jo responded.

"Cellos are very beautiful. If I did not play piano, I would play cello."

As Sam and Jo walked toward the door, Jo hesitated, then turned back to face the pianist. "Madam Kaminska? I also want to tell you that we are sorry."

"Whatever for, my dear?"

"Well . . ." she started, obviously embarrassed. "You see, we didn't buy tickets to your concert. We snuck in, and then you were so nice to talk to us, and now I feel bad about it."

"Do not worry yourself." A mischievous grin crept across her mouth. "How do you think I got in to see the great Madam Landowska?"

The next morning the girls were sitting at the kitchen table for Sam's reading lesson. As Sam finished the last sentence, she looked up from the page seeking Jo's approval. But Jo seemed to be somewhere else.

"I can't get over how amazing that concert was last night," Jo said. "How could that much sound be crammed into one place. How did it fit?"

"I don't know," Sam said. "And I don't know why it made me want to cry, but it did."

"I didn't see you cry," Jo said.

"I didn't cry. I just felt like I wanted to."

"So why didn't you?"

"Because I can't."

"What do you mean *you can't*?"

"I mean I just can't. Nothing makes me cry. It doesn't matter how sad or happy I am. It doesn't matter how bad it hurts. It doesn't matter how many times I get socked in the eye. I don't cry. In fact, I haven't cried for two years."

"What happened to you that you can't cry?" Jo said.

"Do you remember when I told you about the night I got kicked out of the Burrows' house and found a little shed to stay in?" Sam asked.

"How could I forget?" Jo said compassionately.

"Well, I cried the whole night. I couldn't stop. I just kept crying and crying. But in the morning, nothing was better. I was still alone. I was still cold and hungry. I still had nowhere to go. When the sun came up and I felt a little heat on my face, I just stopped crying. And I haven't cried since."

"Well, I sure did," Jo admitted. "I think it was hearing the cellos. But Madam Kaminska was great too. How did she play like that? I know she told you her hands weren't magic, but I don't believe her. And they were so tiny." She held her right hand up and stared at her palm. She rolled it over slowly and looked at the back. "How big is your hand, Sam? Let me see it." Caught off guard, Sam cautiously raised her left arm and extended her hand until it matched up with Jo's. As their fingertips pressed together, Sam had a strange feeling. Jo was pushing slightly to make a tight seal between their hands. Sam realized she couldn't remember the last time she had touched the hands of another person. She had no reason to hold hands with anybody, and there was certainly no polite handshaking in her world.

"Our hands are about the same size," Jo said, summing up the comparison. "But my fingers are kinda skinny."

"Maybe mine are too fat," Sam countered.

Jo raised her other hand and Sam followed her lead. Now, both hands were pressed together, as if they were holding each other up. Perhaps they were, more so than either of them realized.

"Hey, do you know 'Say, Say, Oh Playmate'?" Jo asked.

"We used to sing it at the orphanage," Sam said. "But I don't remember all the words."

"It goes like this . . ." Jo started the hand-clapping sequence and began to sing slowly.

"Say, say, oh playmate,
Come out and play with me,
And bring your dollies three,
Climb up my apple tree.
Slide down my rainbow,
Into my cellar door,
And we'll be jolly friends
Forever more, more, more, more, more."

As Sam bobbed her head along with the rhythm, she mumbled through the words and fumbled with the hand slapping until she started to get it. Before long, they were ripping through it at full speed, hands flying, voices in unison. The cheerful morning sun enhanced the lightness of the song, and the kitchen came alive with the energy of little girls. They stared into each other's smiling eyes as they sang and danced with their hands. Over and over, they repeated the song. Each time growing more distant from their troubles.

Jo stopped and wiggled excitedly in her chair. "I have an idea! Let's make up our own song about magic hands." After a brief but intensive creative writing period, they had fashioned their own version of the song.

"Oh, oh, magic hands,
Though tiny may they be
Play something nice for me
Flying across the keys.
Tell me your secrets,
I beg you for your grace,
Play the music lovely,
Or punch my face, face, face, face, face."

They replaced the hand slapping of the last line with fist bumps as they alternated right, left, right, left, right while singing face, face, face, face, face. Sam could not help but recall the way Madam Kaminska had shaken her tiny fist at them. It was an image she would never forget. And she would also never forget the delight in Jo's eyes as they sang it together.

Chapter 7

The Fornoffs

Inspired by their new Polish pianist friend, the girls set out in search of a cello and a piano. They wandered around town until they stumbled across Fornoff's Music Store. As they walked through the front door, Sam whispered, "I've never been in a music store." Jo realized she hadn't either. The place was filled with instruments of every variety, and an entire wall was papered with sheet music. Every corner of the store was well-lit, dust-free, and heavily immersed in the musty odor of the spit valve of a French horn. Music books, numbered in levels of mastery, lined the shelves.

The proprietors, a silver-haired couple, were perusing the score of a symphony together when the girls entered. In her usual fashion, Sam charged unabated toward the couple and stopped abruptly. Their conversation broke off midsentence as they lowered the score with a start. They smiled cordially and greeted the girls.

"How can I help you two ladies?" the clean-shaven gentleman with a bow tie said.

"We're looking for cellos and pianos!" Sam announced matter-of-factly.

"How many of each?" the man teased.

"Just one cello and one piano," Jo chimed in.

"Which one of you wants the cello, and which one of you wants the piano?" he asked.

"I want the cello, and Sam wants the piano," Jo said excitedly.

"Mrs. Fornoff," he said, gesturing toward Sam, "would you show this young lady the pianos?" Then he turned to Jo. "And let's see about a cello for you, young lady." He quickly wheeled about and marched toward the back of the store, passing shelves of violins, flutes, and clarinets. Rounding the corner of the final rack of shelves, the cello suddenly appeared. It was leaning against a stand next to a chair in the middle of what looked like a tiny amphitheater carved out of the wall. An overhead lamp beamed down on its lustrous finish like a spotlight. Jo was a little starstruck to see the instrument she had admired from a distance at the concert now within reach.

"Do you play it?" Jo queried.

"For sixty-one years," he replied.

"Would you play it for me?" Jo pleaded.

"I would be happy to. First, let me introduce myself. I'm Franklin Fornoff." He gave a slight pause, signaling to Jo that she might recognize that name. "That cello was made by the famous Italian craftsman, Domenico Montagnana, more than two hundred years ago. I have played it for kings and presidents," he said grandiosely. He looked deep into Jo's eyes as his countenance softened, and she perceived not only a kindness, but a respect she was not anticipating. "But it will give me equal pleasure to play it for you." He removed the stand and sat on the edge of the chair behind the cello and held the neck of the instrument in his left hand. With his right hand, he skillfully aimed the bow across the strings, and the ancient cello began to sing. The sonorous tones rumbled through the store, engulfing it in music. Something distantly soothing and vaguely intimate reached deep inside of Jo. She could not quite identify its blurry significance, but she was drawn to it, even mesmerized by it. She stared at the instrument without blinking. After he had finished the short piece, she was unable to move.

The voice of Mr. Fornoff broke the trance. "Are you quite well, miss?"

Ignoring his question, she asked, "What was that song?"

"That was a brief version of Johann Pachelbel's Canon in D. It is two hundred fifty years old."

Jo reached out and pointed at the third string from the left. "What note does this string play?"

"That is the D string," he replied.

"Could I try it?" she inquired boldly.

The kindly but fastidious Mr. Fornoff was generally loath to permit any sticky-fingered child to touch his beloved antique cello. Jo would only much later come to know just how uncharacteristic it was when he conceded to her brash request.

"Surely," he agreed.

Jo sat behind the polished instrument and held the neck with her left hand. In her right, she pinched the seemingly delicate bow. Mr. Fornoff correctly positioned her left hand on the neck and helped her compress the string as he told her to place the bow on the string and draw it across as he had done. The finely tuned instrument did exactly as commanded and admitted a wobbly D note into the air as Jo's untrained bow apprehensively skidded across the third string. It didn't sound that great, but Jo began to feel the vibrations through the fingertips of both hands just as she reached the end of the bow. Much like shooting her .38 Special, she didn't wait for permission to take a second shot. This time she gave a slightly nuanced command, and the cello responded with a full, rich, and resonating D note. The vibrations from her fingertips ascended each arm until they hit a resonance in her center, and she jerked the bow from the strings as if she'd been shocked.

"Are you all right, miss?" the wide-eyed Mr. Fornoff asked.

Again, she ignored his question and returned the bow to the string and played the D note steadily and with great clarity. She held it until she ran out of bow. At once, she felt a thrill and a serenity for which she had no explanation. She didn't know what was happening to her.

"I've not seen a young person quite so affected by a cello before," Mr. Fornoff stated.

"I must learn to play," Jo said as if she had no choice in the matter. "Do you teach lessons?"

"Yes, I do, but I'm afraid I only take advanced students," he said apologetically.

At that moment, Sam and Mrs. Fornoff returned from the piano room. "Dear, Sam here has made us a proposition. In exchange for music lessons and the use of our practice piano, she has offered to sweep our floors."

"But we don't take beginners, my dear," he reminded her.

"Girls, please excuse us for a moment while we confer." Mrs. Fornoff beckoned her husband to the back room.

Once out of earshot, Mrs. Fornoff began to plead her case. "I know we don't take beginners, but just look at those two girls. They came here without their parents. How often does that happen? I'm not even sure they have parents. Well, I'm certain little Sam has no mother. If she did, she wouldn't be running around in boy's clothes with that hideous haircut. I think these are some girls who could use a little help. And I want to help them. Besides, has a child of any age ever walked into our store and offered to exchange work for music lessons? I think not. We should give them a chance. I'm certain they don't have any money."

"We both know that even children with the utmost parental support rarely last more than a few weeks before they tire of practicing and give up. What chance do these girls have?" Mr. Fornoff reasoned.

"They have the chance that I'm going to give them," Mrs. Fornoff said with a tone of finality, indicating the conversation was over.

When the Fornoffs returned, Mrs. Fornoff began her speech. "What is your name, dear?" she asked Jo.

"I'm Jo."

"I am Mrs. Fornoff, and this is Mr. Fornoff. Here, Sam and Jo, is our counter proposal. You will clean the store twice a week. That will include not only sweeping but dusting and wiping down surfaces, washing the windows, taking out the garbage, and anything else that needs cleaning. In return, we will lend Jo a practice cello to take home, and Mr. Fornoff will give her a lesson once a week. Sam will come to the store to practice the piano Monday through Saturday at ten a.m., and I will give her a lesson once a week. We will expect you both to do a good job, and we will not tolerate tardiness." She paused to let the girls consider her offer. "Do we have a deal?"

The next morning, Sam and Jo arrived at the music store to begin their new job and take their first music lessons. They eagerly attacked the sweeping and cleaning and made quick work of their duties. Then Jo went with Mr. Fornoff to the cello amphitheater, and Sam went with Mrs. Fornoff into the piano practice room. It was a small, isolated space behind two doors in the back of the store. But it had a window and was well-lit, painted in warm colors and adorned with the images of the great composers of history. It was a tiny musical sanctuary.

Mrs. Fornoff was a thin, elderly woman of average height. Her hair was a stunning silver and still surprisingly full of youthful body. Her clothes were stylish, spotless, and freshly pressed. She had an intelligent look about her with a slightly imperious air. She was articulate and spoke in complete sentences. She might have even been somewhat intimidating to other children.

Of course, Sam was as oblivious to her manner as she was immune to such concerns. She sat down on the bench in front of the piano.

Her casual demeanor belied the excitement she felt to begin playing. It was almost like stepping up to the plate.

Mrs. Fornoff looked Sam over a few times before taking her place on the bench next to her. "I shall call you Samantha," she announced. "That is your name, is it not?"

"Yes, ma'am," Sam responded hesitantly. "But I've been just plain Sam for a long time now."

Mrs. Fornoff studied the earnest child some more. "I can't really put my finger on it, Samantha dear, but I get the most suspicious impression that there is nothing plain about you at all." Then she continued with a point-blank question. "Why do you want to play the piano?"

"Because I saw the concert at the theater."

"What concert was that, dear?"

"Madame Kaminska and the Warsaw Philharmonic Orchestra."

"You saw that concert?" she questioned, with visible shock.

"Yes, ma'am."

At first Sam wasn't sure Mrs. Fornoff believed her. She seemed perplexed as she continued the inquiry. "May I ask with whom did you go to the concert?"

"Jo."

"Just the two of you?"

"Yes, ma'am."

"The two of you," she repeated, "went to the Warsaw Philharmonic by yourselves?"

"Yes, ma'am."

"And where did you get the tickets?"

Sam didn't want to answer that. Mrs. Fornoff waited for a response and then finally restated the question by adding further explanation. "The tickets were very expensive, and they were sold out months in advance. We only got them ourselves because the conductor owed Mr.

Fornoff a favor. How on earth did you get them? And whatever did you wear?" she sputtered.

Sam had spent most of the conversation staring forward at the keys of the piano, but to answer this question, she turned toward Mrs. Fornoff and looked her straight in the eye. "I'd really rather not say."

"No," Mrs. Fornoff said, clearly understanding what Sam was pointedly not saying. "I bet you wouldn't. So, what did you think of Natalia?"

"Who?"

"Natalia Kaminska, the pianist."

"You know her by her first name?"

"Of course. Natalia was my student."

"But I thought she was from Poland, all the way across the ocean."

"She is, but I was a visiting professor at the Chopin University of Music when she arrived there at the age of eighteen. I was one of her teachers."

Sam's eyes grew wide. She looked Mrs. Fornoff over a couple of times in the same way Mrs. Fornoff had looked her over. She knew, of course, that Mrs. Fornoff, being a piano teacher, would certainly be a good piano player, but she had no idea that the woman sitting next to her on the bench could possibly be in the same musical universe as the great Madame Kaminska. And had, in fact, been her teacher.

"So you know Madame Kaminska?" Sam repeated, just to be sure she was understanding correctly. "And can you play like her?"

"Natalia is a genius. No one can play like her. She developed a unique style that no one in the world can copy. I helped her develop that style when she was a teenager. But even though I was the teacher and she the student, I could never play it like she did. Not only is she a musical genius, but never before in the history of the world has more ferocity been cast into such a tiny package." She briefly stared off into the decades of the past and left Sam in the present.

After some time, Mrs. Fornoff continued. "Then there are these." She reached her hands out toward the keyboard but left them suspended in air where Sam could study them. Sam was shocked at the condition of her hands. Her joints were red and swollen, and the four fingers of both hands were grotesquely angled outward, making them look more like the flippers of a sea lion than the hands of a concert pianist. "I'm afraid rheumatoid arthritis has taken my hands. I can still play a little, but not much and not for long." She retracted her hands back into her lap. "So what did you think of Natalia?"

Sam thought for a moment. "I don't know how to say it. I don't know what I was feeling. I can't make it out in my mind, let alone try to tell someone else. But it was kind of like this. I fell off a train once and hit my head on the ground. When I got up, I couldn't see straight. Everything was blurry and rounded, and I couldn't make out the edges. One thing became another thing before the first thing ended. I was dizzy and felt like everything was spinning. I had to hold on to a sign post so I wouldn't tip over. It went on and on, and I started throwing up. And just when I thought I was dying, the edges came back.

"When I was at the concert and Madame Kaminska began to play, somehow it was just like that moment when the edges came back. And it was so strange because I never realized I had been living in a world without edges until then. During the whole concert, it was like I was making my way around an exciting new town or someplace I had never been before and discovering all new things. Things with edges. And when it was over, the edges were gone again."

Sam paused and looked over at the transfixed Mrs. Fornoff. "I guess I'm not making much sense, am I?"

"On the contrary, my dear Samantha, that may have been the most eloquent essay on the essence of music I have ever heard." Then it was Mrs. Fornoff's turn to look Sam straight in the eye. "I believe what you are describing is *beauty*. Your edges perhaps represent the clarity that comes when something beautiful enters your life. I don't know anything about your young life, Samantha, but through your journey it's possible you have been unable to embrace the beauty until that moment when you heard Natalia play.

"When we are better acquainted, you can tell me about your life, and I will share with you about mine. But I promise you this: Life without beauty is a grueling struggle. But together we will find it. That is my promise to you. We will find the beauty. And I want this to be the day that changes your life. Let us start with your hands."

"My hands?" Sam questioned.

"Yes, dear, let me see your hands."

Sam tentatively raised her hands and presented them to her. Mrs. Fornoff carefully inspected each hand, turning it front to back and then back again. Then she squeezed the supple palms and flexed the limber joints. She spread the fingers widely, then wrapped them into a fist. She reopened the hands and positioned them with palms together for comparison. "These are beautiful hands," she proclaimed. "Divinely shaped and perfect in symmetry. They are flexible yet strong. Most of all, they are endowed with that singular virtue of promise: youth. They are young, Samantha, and if properly exercised and skillfully tutored, they shall absorb instruction with endless capacity. You must never take them for granted."

Mrs. Fornoff gave Sam's hand a squeeze, then placed a beginner book on the piano, opened it to the first page, and showed Sam middle C.

Later that evening, Jo was still fussing with her new cello. It wasn't new, of course, but it was new to her. It was no two-hundred-year-old Montagnana, but rather an appreciably beat-up off-brand that the Fornoffs had rented to dozens of kids over the past three decades. Some had taken it for only a few days, others for a few weeks or even months, before abandoning it for a diversion that did not require hours of practice. Only the rare student had kept it long enough to achieve a proficiency deserving of an instrument of higher quality and had returned it for an upgrade. Now it was Jo's. And it was a perfectly sound cello for a beginner, especially a beginner without a parent's signature on the rental agreement. But it was a cello. Mr. Fornoff had tuned it expertly, and it played all the notes. Jo became instantly infatuated with it.

The waning summer sun having long since set, Jo was playing her newly learned scales practically in the dark. Sam entered the living room from outside and stumbled toward the sound without turning on the light. "You've been playing that thing all day!"

"I know. I have to stop. The fingertips of my left hand are killing me and are nearly worn through!" She put the cello in the case and sat on the couch next to Sam in the dark and milked some blood flow into the sore fingertips with her other hand. "Mr. Fornoff gave me that cello and said, 'When you are a good player, this cello will sing for you. And when you are a great player, she will weep.'" Jo turned to Sam, able to make out only her profile in the foggy light. "Someday I'm going to make her weep."

"You really love that thing, don't you?" Sam said.

Jo didn't immediately respond to the question. It didn't seem to her like the type of question for which an answer was really expected. Not only that, but she was harboring a secret from Sam. A secret she wanted to share but wasn't sure it was the right time. She was afraid of what Sam might think. She agonized over her decision. She didn't want to put Sam off, but she was desperate to confide in her. She was ready to commit to a friendship, risks or not. But this might be too much for Sam. At length, she took the plunge. "I want to tell you something, but it's going to sound a little strange. Maybe even weird. Promise you won't laugh, and you won't think I'm crazy?"

"Promise," Sam said.

"Okay, here goes." Jo took a little breath. "When I play the D note on my cello, I can hear my mother's voice."

"That's not so weird," Sam said softly.

"That's not the weird part," Jo said. She was glad the room was dark so she didn't have to look at Sam's face. "The D note on the cello is much lower than my mother's voice. She has a pretty high speaking voice. When I play it, I don't hear her voice the way it was the last time I heard it. Something deep inside of me can feel the vibrations, and I have the strangest feeling that I can hear her voice the way I would have heard it just before I was born."

Sam remained quiet. Her shadowy profile didn't move.

Jo cautiously continued. "Deeper. The sound is even deeper, and it's not just something I hear with my ears. I can feel it gently shaking my bones. When the string vibrates, I can hear her voice, and I can feel her voice all around me, but I can't make out the words. The cello doesn't play words, of course, only music. But it seems like she is saying something very familiar to me, something I should remember and understand. It is so soothing, like when you sink into a warm bathtub and the water goes all the way up the back of your neck. It's her voice. I just can't make out the words."

They were silent for several minutes as they sat on the couch in the dark. Through the open windows, a summer breeze flowed in from the freshly cut alfalfa field behind the house. The moon cast a faint shadow of the window panes on the far wall. The crickets filled the silence with their chirpy calls.

"Do you love your mother, or do you hate her?" Sam asked.

"I don't know. Can you love someone and hate them at the same time?"

"I don't think so," Sam reasoned. "But I'm pretty sure you can love someone and be angry at them at the same time. But then, I've never had anyone to love. So what do I know about it? Maybe you shouldn't listen to me about such things."

"I don't know if I love her or hate her," Jo conceded. "The only thing I know for sure is that I loved her when I was little."

"Well, do you think about her very often? Would you want to see her?"

"I think about seeing her, but every time I do, I ask myself the same question. What is the first thing you say to someone when the last thing they said to you was, 'I don't want you?'"

Again, Sam said nothing.

"Something about the sound of that cello makes me want to love her again. And I'm just going to stick with that." She realized that speaking her feelings out loud had given her clarity and satisfaction. And she was glad she had told Sam. "What about your parents? Would you ever want to meet them?" Jo wasn't sure what to expect from Sam's answer. After all, she had never met her own father. But she could never have predicted what Sam would say.

"My mother has always been imaginary. There is no father."

Chapter 8

Mrs. Jones

It was Monday, baseball day. The morning schedule had been completed. Jo had washed her sheets and tutored Sam in reading. Both girls had practiced their music. Jo at home on her cello, and Sam on the piano at Fornoffs music store. It was now afternoon, about the time the game usually started. The girls hadn't been back to the field since the encounter with the big kid—and the subsequent gender reveal. Sam wasn't sure the boys would let them play since they had admitted to being girls. It shouldn't have made a difference, of course. After all, they were the same baseball players when they were boys as they were when they became girls. Ultimately, it would all depend on the constitution of Billy Rose. How would he react this time?

As they approached the field, Jo with her mitt and Sam with her bat, the boys were picking teams as usual. The girls were sporting their boys' attire and had stuffed their hair into their hats, even though the jig was up. They marched up to the selection pool and joined in like everyone else. Jo gave Sam a hopeful look as the captains made their choices. Then, without calling her name, Billy motioned Sam over to his side. Stan followed suit, giving Jo the nod. And that was that.

But there was one thing different. The familiar 1925 Chevrolet sedan driven by the mother of Jimmy and Scotty, Mrs. Jones, was already parked on the street opposite the third baseline. Mrs. Jones had taken up residence in the splendid shade of a large maple tree on the first base side of the field. She was surrounded by some paraphernalia stacked on a spread quilt and was setting up an easel.

As the game proceeded, she held her palette of oils in her left hand while brushing strokes on the canvas with her right. She quietly blended into the scene and was more or less ignored by the ball players. That is, until a whizzing foul ball hit the trunk of the maple tree, then ricocheted into the branches, and came to rest on the quilt next to her easel. Without the slightest hesitation, she slipped the handle of her paintbrush between her teeth, picked up the ball with her right hand, and, while still holding the palette in her left hand, threw the ball on a line back to the pitcher. Then she resumed her painting without missing a stroke. Her aplomb in managing the errant baseball did not go unnoticed by Sam.

As the game matured, the girls did their usual things. Sam blasted a couple of homers, and Jo vacuumed up all the grounders on her side of the infield, each followed by her signature throw to first base. The rest of the boys more or less treated them like one of their own. Except they were curiously more polite to them than before. But not too polite, of course.

In the bottom of the ninth inning with two away and a runner on first and third, and the batting team down one run, the game ended anticlimactically when the fifth batter, Dougan no less, hit a ten-foot pop fly blooper to the catcher. A dispirited groan by the bench and scattered victory whoops from the field melded into the inevitable sound of sport. The home team rushed the plate with cheers all around and mitts flying high into the air.

When the groaning and the celebrating were over, Mrs. Jones made her presence known with an announcement. "Boys!" she yelled out across the field. "I have lemonade and soft pretzels for everyone."

Another cheer arose from the crowd as Mrs. Jones was swarmed with hungry, thirsty, and sweaty boys. She pulled two one-gallon jugs of lemonade from a cooler and began pouring it into cups and passing it out. When everyone had a drink, she opened a big bag of homemade soft pretzels studded with large salt crystals and gestured to the ravenous crowd to come and get them. Hands flew into the bag with the speed of cats. Mrs. Jones could only hold the bag at arm's length and turn her head from the onslaught.

"Boys! Boys!" she scolded playfully.

And that's when Sam and Jo met Mrs. Jones. Like ladies, they waited until the carnivores had left the kill. Then they each politely took a pretzel and thanked Mrs. Jones. Sam could not help but notice that the lemonade was not only sweet and delicious, but Mrs. Jones had obviously packed it on ice. The salty hand-twisted pretzels were the ideal complement to the lemonade on this hot day of baseball.

As they ravenously ate and drank, Mrs. Jones looked at Stan. "Stanley, when is your mother getting out of the hospital?"

"My father went to get her this afternoon," he responded.

"You run home and tell your father that I will bring dinner over at six-thirty."

"Yes, ma'am," he replied enthusiastically, an erstwhile benefactor of one of her luscious meals.

Then she pulled a book of art from her bag and handed it to Bart. "Bart, your sister Clara asked if she could borrow this book. Please take it to her."

"Okay," Bart said blandly as he took the book.

"Okay *what*?" Mrs. Jones said pointedly.

"Ah, okay. Yes, ma'am," he corrected.

"That is so much better. Thank you," Mrs. Jones replied.

It was at that moment that little Scotty, who had been running circles around the gathering at the maple tree on Shiner, suddenly appeared at his mother's side, covering his right eye with his hand. "Mommy, I have something in my eye!" he said urgently.

"Let me see." She peeled his hand from his face and gently pulled down on his lower eyelid. "I see it," she said calmly. "It's a bug."

"Get it out! Get it out!" he yelled frantically.

"Don't panic, sweetie. I'll get it out," she assured.

Sam watched as she sat down on the quilt with her legs outstretched and pulled a cotton ball from her purse. "Lay down here, sweetheart." Sam was immediately drawn to this woman. Her every movement was deliberate and precise. She took charge like she knew exactly what to do. Sam stepped closer to get a better view. Little Scotty lay on his back on the quilt with his head cradled in his mother's lap and looked up at her face. He was instantly calmed. Sam was stunned by the effect her lap seemed to have on the little boy. It occurred to her that she didn't know what it felt like to lay her head in a woman's lap. She wondered if it was as soft as it looked. It was probably something little Scotty did all the time. Mrs. Jones made it appear routine and second nature.

Once he was situated and still, she lovingly wiped the copious sweat from his brow with her bare hand as mothers do. She took the cotton ball and tore off a wedge and rolled it into a tight cylinder. Then she wet one end with her mouth. Carefully pulling down on the lower lid, she surgically removed the bug with the moist cotton in a single stroke.

Little Scotty blinked tentatively a couple of times and then sprang from her lap, remounted Shiner, and resumed making laps around the tree without so much as a thank you or even the slightest acknowledgment of her skilled efforts on his behalf.

"And he's off!" Mrs. Jones exclaimed with feigned exasperation as she glanced down at her empty lap and mutedly threw her arms in the air.

With the lemonade slurped and the pretzels devoured, there was nothing further to keep the primordial mob, and they began to scatter, but not before "thank you Mrs. Jones" erupted in response to the catalytic first "thank you" proffered by the one boy in the crowd with actual manners.

Sam, despite the lack of example in her life, but more so by common gender, felt compelled to thank Mrs. Jones in person. As she approached her to do so, Mrs. Jones arose from the quilt to greet her.

At five feet eight inches, Mrs. Jones was a tall woman. She was thin, shapely, and athletic with brown eyes, a dark complexion, and light brown hair the color of a patiently toasted marshmallow. She had a mouth full of perfect teeth and was beautiful by the standards of any day.

Sticking her hand out to Sam, she introduced herself. "I'm Caroline Jones." She took Sam's hand in hers and squeezed it firmly but with no shake. "You must be Sam." Then she offered her hand to Jo and said with equal confidence, "And you're Jo." She disarmed them both with a warm smile and soft eyes. "I've been dying to meet the two of you!"

"Why would you want to meet us?" Jo asked shyly.

"Oh, I've heard some tall tales about you two from my little Scotty. At first I thought he might be getting a little carried away, but when Jimmy pretty much confirmed everything he said, I decided I had to see for myself." She paused briefly to study the two girls from top to bottom. "My, my! Such ball players! From what I've seen today, the legend appears to be true!"

"What legend?" Sam asked.

"The legend of two girls who play baseball. One who hits like Babe Ruth, and the other who plays the infield like Joe Dugan."

Seeing the puzzle on Jo's face, Sam said, "Joe Dugan is the third baseman for the New York Yankees."

"Why, yes he is," Mrs. Jones confirmed enthusiastically.

By then all the boys had left except for Jimmy and the still-orbiting Scotty. "Jimmy, you and Scotty take all of my things to the car and wait for me there. Except for the easel. I'll bring that along myself."

As Jimmy and Scotty trudged toward the car lugging her stuff, Mrs. Jones turned back to the girls. "Would you like to see my painting?"

As she turned the canvas toward them, Jo studied it intently, her eyes slowly widening. Sam was startled by the image as she stared without blinking. The painting was a mixed reference style with close-ups of selected characters in the depth of a larger field. It was, of course, a painting of a baseball game, but all the players were small, generic male figures except for two. The batter was an enlarged image, and it was Sam's image. It was Sam's dirty shirt, her ratty pants, and a zigzag of blonde hair jutting from her newsboy cap. She was hitting a baseball in mid-swing. Her anchored, broad-based feet were well represented. The rotation in her hips was evident, her bat level, arms at ideal extension. But it was the expression in Sam's face that stood out: eyes intently focused, jaw clenched, lips slightly separated and curling away from her teeth. The minimal flare in the nostrils hinted of rage.

"Is that how I look?" Sam said, astounded.

"That's how you look to me," Mrs. Jones said.

The other enlarged image was of Jo fielding a grounder from third base. She was shown in a frozen, braced fashion in anticipation of the ball. Her mitt was extended to the ground, her exposed face stone-like with immovable eyes. Mrs. Jones captured that split second between securing a final position to field a grounder and the actual impact of the ball. It was ingeniously perceptive, and Jo instantly ran her hands down the sides of her overalls to wipe the sweat from her palms.

"How can you do that, Mrs. Jones?" Jo asked as she stared deep into the painting.

"I can do that because I have been working at it for twenty years. This painting is not finished, of course, but when it is, I shall have prints made for both of you. If you wish, that is. Would either of you like to learn to paint? I would like to get to know you two better. Perhaps we could do that over some art lessons. I would be delighted to teach you. And besides, I've just got to hear how you clobbered Billy with Scotty's stick horse in your own words," she said to Sam. "And how you wrecked that mean Reynolds kid," she said, looking at Jo and smirking mischievously. "How about it?"

Sam and Jo conferred briefly in the form of a blank stare at one another, then Jo said, "Sure, we would love to do that."

Mrs. Jones handed Jo a slip of paper, which she had obviously prepared in advance, and said, "Come to my house at this address at ten o'clock tomorrow morning."

"Oh, we can't come at ten," Sam said. "I have piano."

Mrs. Jones opened both eyes widely, cocked her head slightly to the left, and withdrew her chin sharply. "You have a piano lesson?"

"Not exactly a lesson," she explained. "I don't have a piano, so I practice every day at ten o'clock at the music store."

"Well, then come over after your practice. We'll paint, we'll chat, and we'll have some lunch." She gave another of those butter-melting smiles and looked directly at each girl separately, such that there could be no question as to the sincerity of her invitation.

As the charming and gracious Mrs. Jones walked away with her easel and her unfinished painting, her dynamic aura gradually dissipated, and the girls were left in the empty space of her absence. A cloud wafted in front of the sun, casting a pall of dreariness over the sultry haze of midafternoon. Sam barely had the energy to stand. Jo gave her a forlorn look.

"I think I hate that woman," Jo said flatly.

"Not me," Sam said. "It's Jimmy and Scotty I hate."

The next morning, they knocked on the door of the Jones home. It was the nicest house on the middle-class block, solid brick with a large front porch and a yard that looked like a flower farm. Mrs. Jones greeted them enthusiastically and welcomed them into her home. Having lived on the streets for two years, Sam was thoroughly unprepared for the inside. The entry was paved with a glistening hardwood floor. Tasteful furniture lined up in perfect order, like drilling soldiers. The paint on the walls looked barely dry, and the wallpaper appeared ironed on. The rooms seemed to magnify the natural light, giving the house an airy, bright, even cheerful vibe. Her beautiful paintings were prominently displayed throughout. There were photographs of her family and individual baby pictures of her boys. On one wall next to the kitchen was a large cork-fronted bulletin board plastered with reminder notes, assorted postcards, shopping lists, a family calendar, and several of the boys' recent school papers—all with high grades marked in red.

As Sam beheld the ambiance created by Mrs. Jones, a random thought popped into her head: *I bet there are no rats in here!*

The art room was on the south side of the house and had two large windows, making it the brightest room of all. But there was more to the art room than just art. Wherever there was not a window or a door were shelves of books. Art books, to be sure, but also history, architecture, economics, and classic fiction by Dickens, Bronte, Emerson, Hawthorne, and Mark Twain, among others. An entire shelf was devoted to children's books suitable for all ages. Jo appeared starstruck as she gazed about the room. Three easels were set up, each supporting a blank canvas.

"Shall we begin?" Mrs. Jones said as she handed them each a smock. The irony of protective clothing to wear over her tattered fare was not lost on Sam. Slightly embarrassed as she took the garment from Mrs. Jones, she recognized the gesture of courtesy for what it was. As she wrapped the smock around her shoulders and her own clothes disappeared, she felt an unexpected surge of respect and inclusion. Like it was a uniform.

The two reverential girls took their places, and Mrs. Jones began by drawing simple shapes on her canvas and gesturing to them to do likewise. Jo tentatively plucked at the canvas in short, slow, and dainty strokes. Mrs. Jones watched intently, but for only a quick moment. "Jo," she whispered with a twinkle of a smile, "no one has ever been attacked by a canvas!"

Jo offered a weak smile in return as she let her breath out, then painted a bold and deliberate line.

"That's much better," Mrs. Jones beamed. "And don't feel bad. Let me tell you what happened to me when I was a budding art student. One day in class, we were supposed to paint a cartoon animal. So I painted a goofy, buck-toothed bunny rabbit. It was supposed to be fun. But I couldn't get the teeth right. When the art teacher saw it, he said, 'Miss McLoud, bunny rabbits do not have fangs! Were you trying to paint a killer rabbit?' The other kids teased me about it, and from then on, they called me Killer McLoud."

Her self-deprecation, in the face of obvious mastery made Jo chuckle and put Sam at ease. She coached them along and encouraged them at every step as they fought through the initial awkwardness of learning something new. Then she put her hand over Jo's. "I want you to feel this part. Just relax and let your hand follow." She skillfully drew a long ellipse in a smooth, continuous motion. Then she drew a shorter ellipse with the same height inside the first one. Then another and another, each time shortening the ellipse until she had drawn a perfect circle in the middle.

Sam watched as the satisfaction of the process and the successful result were evident on Jo's face. Then it was Sam's turn. Mrs. Jones's hand over hers felt like a warm glove. She followed in tandem as the woman repeated the exercise through the ellipses and into the circle. But Sam wasn't thinking about art. She was thinking about the safe, warm hand connecting with hers. The touch.

As the lesson progressed, Mrs. Jones started up the personal conversation again. "Sam, you said you practice the piano at the music store. Is that right? Because you have no piano at home?"

"Yes, ma'am," Sam replied.

"And would that be in the back room of Fornoff's Music Store?"

"How did you know?"

"Oh, it's not too hard to figure out. A particular young girl such as yourself, who has no piano, so she is permitted to practice at the music store. That has Mrs. Fornoff written all over it."

"So you know the Fornoffs?"

"Of course. They sold me my first violin. How long have you played the piano?"

"Four days," Sam said concretely.

"Four days?" she repeated, a little confused.

"Yes, ma'am," Sam said. "I just started."

"That's interesting, because the Fornoffs only take advanced students. How is it that Mrs. Fornoff accepted you?"

"I don't know," Sam puzzled. "I told her I didn't have any money to pay her, but I would sweep her floors if she would teach me the piano."

"Of course you did," Mrs. Jones said, as if she had just been defeated in some way. "I can certainly see Mrs. Fornoff making a bargain like that."

"It wasn't just me. Jo and I both work at the store. I get piano lessons, and she gets cello lessons."

"Cello lessons from Mr. Fornoff?" Mrs. Jones replied, her shock evident. "And did you also start four days ago?"

"Yup," Jo said sprightly.

"Wow! However did you manage that?"

"Well, he didn't seem to want to at first. But then Mr. and Mrs. Fornoff went into the back room to discuss it, and when they came out he had changed his mind."

"Yes, I'll bet he did," Mrs. Jones exclaimed. "Mrs. Fornoff can be quite persuasive that way."

She left the girls to practice painting while she fixed lunch in the kitchen. The menu included ham sandwiches, pickled beets, potato chips, and a pastry dessert.

As Sam bit into the delicious sandwich, she couldn't help but recall all the times she had pilfered through a restaurant garbage can for cold scraps. Although Jo had only intermittently been in want of food, her interest in the ham sandwich was evident.

"This bread is so good, Mrs. Jones," Jo said.

"Oh, don't call it bread, dear," she corrected. "These are *croissants.* I learned to make them in Paris when I was there studying art."

"Is this some kind of special French ham too?" Sam asked.

"This is *prosciutto.* It's Italian," Mrs. Jones clarified.

Then the dessert came out. Sam had never encountered the ecstasy of French pastry. After only the second chew, she had to stop and wait for her senses to verify the unbelievable signal hitting her brain. She closed her eyes to savor the luxurious texture of puff pastry and smooth custard as it swirled around her mouth. The slightly understated sweetness of the chocolate frosting crescendo left her instantly craving more. She marveled that anything could be so good. "Mrs. Jones, what is this?"

"French pastry. It's called *mille-feuille.* It means *a thousand leaves.* It has two layers of puff pastry crust filled with light custard and topped with thin white frosting and then decorated with chocolate frosting in a pattern that looks like leaves. See?"

"I've never tasted anything like it," Jo gushed.

"French pastry is not merely tasted, my dear." She raised her right hand whimsically in a faux regal gesture intended to poke fun at snooty French chefs. "It is a gustatory sojourn! A symphony of oral sensation! A marriage of texture and taste destined to produce the offspring of delight!" Then her expression gave way to a broad smile and a brief chuckle.

Without understanding all of her words, the girls smiled in kind.

"The secret to French pastry is subtlety. Do you know what *subtlety* means?"

"Not really," Sam said.

"It means being less noticeable, less obvious, less bold. French pastry is deliciously mild in texture and taste. American pastry is usually gobbed with sugar, like a frosted doughnut—rich and satisfying to be sure. French pastry tantalizes and teases but never quite satisfies—and always leaves you wanting more."

As they finished the gourmet meal, there was a lull in the conversation. The kitchen was quiet, and Mrs. Jones made no effort to interrupt the silence. During that brief interval, the mood of the occasion imperceptibly shifted. Her cheerful smile morphed slowly into a smile of concern. Then she asked Sam a carefully worded question. "Sam, do you think your mother would mind if I fixed your haircut?"

Sam was caught off guard by the loaded question. She was at once conflicted between her guarded street smarts and the unexpected feelings of trust she had developed for Mrs. Jones. She didn't want to lie to her, yet she didn't want to tell her the truth. She compromised with, "I'm sure my mother wouldn't care." A statement that was, in all probability, true.

Mrs. Jones paused, as if waiting for Sam to try again. But Sam, of course, held her ground.

"You don't have a mother, do you, Sam?" Mrs. Jones said delicately, with a measure of kindness unknown to Sam.

"Everybody has a mother, Mrs. Jones," Sam replied. Again, she was technically correct.

"But you don't know where your mother is, do you?"

"No. No, ma'am, I don't." Sam wasn't trying to be defiant. She wasn't looking for pity or help. She certainly wasn't making an admission of failure or guilt. Sitting in Mrs. Jones's spotless kitchen in her tattered boy clothes with a self-performed haircut, she simply gave a straight answer to a straight question and let the chips fall where they may.

Mrs. Jones studied her for a few moments and appeared to be contemplating her answer, then transformed her face by adding a cheerful smile. "Well then, I think we should see what we can do about that haircut."

She sat Sam on a stool and wrapped a sheet around her neck. With a comb and scissors, she began clipping away. Snippets of blonde hair tumbled down the slope of the sheet and floated to the floor.

"Are you a barber too?" Jo asked.

"Well, I'm no practitioner of *haute coiffure*," she explained, "but I can fix this mess."

"What does that mean?" Jo asked.

"Haute coiffure?" she repeated.

"Yes," Jo said.

"It means *fancy haircut.* Tell me, Sam, did you cut this yourself?"

"Yes, ma'am," Sam admitted.

"Did you use sheep shears?" she asked playfully.

"Pocket knife," Sam corrected.

"Ahhg!" Mrs. Jones screamed with feigned horror.

Again, the girls smiled at her.

When the job was finished and Sam's haircut had been miraculously resurrected and smartly styled, Mrs. Jones removed the sheet. As Sam stood, Mrs. Jones popped a hand mirror in front of her. Although still quite short for a girl's cut, it turned her back into a girl for the first time in two years. Sam couldn't believe it was her face in the mirror. She stared at herself and tried not to seem affected. But she didn't hold out much hope that she could conceal her joy from the likes of Caroline Jones.

"There's my beautiful girl!" Mrs. Jones effused as she took Sam in her arms and gave her what was, by all pretext, a playful, congratulatory hug.

Sam's face fell into the upper chest of the tall brunette as her arms tightened around her. A hug was a foreign language to Sam, and she didn't speak it. She didn't know what to do with her arms, so she left them hanging limply at her sides. She could feel Mrs. Jones's hair on her neck and her moist breath on top of her head. She could smell the pleasantly unique scent of her body. And despite the firmness of her embrace, there was a softness like Sam had never known. A wholly surrounding softness that made Sam feel like she was sinking in. And she was warm. So very warm. It was this warmth that carried Sam away, delicious and irresistible. Sam wanted it to never end, so she froze in place to make it last. And didn't move.

It was in the revelry of this softness and warmth and Mrs. Jones's delicate scent that the uninvited memory of the night she was kicked out of Mrs. Burrows' house barged into this peaceful moment. Sam was back in that little shed where she'd spent that first night on her own, crying. At once, she was both frightened and comforted, hungry and full, shivering and warm, alone and embraced, upset and consoled. In the anguish of this stark conflict, with her ear pressed tightly to the chest of Mrs. Jones, Sam slowly became aware of the sound of a human heartbeat. The living, affirming, deep, rhythmic pounding of this kind woman's vibrant heart.

And that's when Sam, the granite girl, cracked. Her throat seized, and her left eye punched out a single tear that streaked down her cheek and into the corner of her mouth. She took a tiny gulp of air as she did the unthinkable and wrapped her arms around Mrs. Jones, making the embrace complete. Mrs. Jones instinctively responded with an even tighter hug. And Sam, as if she had been struggling to push an impossibly huge boulder up a steep hill for a very long time, finally let it go and began to sob. Tears drained from both eyes as her face reddened, her nose ran, and the back of her neck moistened with sweat. She made no attempt to wipe away the tears or the snot. She let it all fall on the front of Mrs. Jones's dress and clung to her for dear life.

Mrs. Jones also made no attempt to wipe away her tears. Nor did she offer words of consolation. She simply held Sam tight and let her cry her eyes out.

"Are you okay, Sam?" Jo asked gravely as she placed her hand on Sam's back.

Sam continued to sob.

Mrs. Jones extended her right arm toward Jo, inviting her into the embrace like a hen gathering her chicks under her wings.

Jo stepped closer as Mrs. Jones pulled her in. It didn't take long for Jo to get caught up in Sam's storm of emotion, and she began to cry too.

Sam felt Jo's head press tightly up against hers as Mrs. Jones wrapped them up together. She was glad Jo was here, but mostly she was glad she could cry. She knew something was wrong with her. She knew little girls cried and that she should be able to as well. It felt so good to cry. The sobbing of both girls continued, interrupted intermittently by shaky gasps for air.

Mrs. Jones held them close. Little could she have known what frightful torment they had endured. What kind of wretched lives they had lived. The true extent to which they had been abandoned, neglected, beaten, abused, chased off, starved, and betrayed. The extent of the violence in all of its forms. She bit her lip, but no amount of personal fortitude could protect a woman of her sensibilities from the effects of this gut-wrenching purge—which, of course, had nothing to do with a haircut. Within moments, she began to weep as well.

The three of them huddled together and cried until the girls ran out of tears. As they held each other, no words were spoken. Only the occasional sniffle broke the intimate silence.

Sam sensed tears filling her right ear and pulled back from Mrs. Jones's chest enough to drain it. That's when she noticed that the entire front of the woman's dress was soaked to the skin with tears, snot, and slobber.

As Jo also pulled away, she began to apologize. "Oh, Mrs. Jones, your dress is soaked. We're so sorry."

The indomitable Mrs. Jones at once put them at ease and wedged some levity into the event. "Don't be silly! I've had two babies. I'm just glad it's not barf!" She slipped into the kitchen and returned with three freshly laundered dish towels. She looked a fright, with swollen eyes, a sweaty brow, red lips, a snotty nose, and tears still dripping from her cheeks. She handed a towel to each girl. "Here, you two are a mess! Clean yourselves up!" Then she took her own towel and wiped her face and futilely patted at the front of her soggy dress.

The girls each reached for one, and Sam made an instinctive move to blow her nose, then stopped.

"Go ahead. Just blow it into the towel," Mrs. Jones said.

The girls' eyes grew wide in disbelief and then they shrugged. In unison, the three of them honked the residual snot from their respective noses into Mrs. Jones's very fine, white dish towels. Looking up at each other upon completion of the ill-mannered deed, they all began to giggle like little school girls—even Sam.

"Well!" Mrs. Jones took a deep, cleansing breath. "Now that that's over, I have a little surprise for you two."

She led the girls into the back bedroom. Clothes and accessories of various colors and styles were neatly laid out on the bed, chair, dresser, and even on the floor. Dresses, play clothes, underwear, socks, shoes, hats, barrettes, ribbons, scarves, sweaters, and winter coats. "My sister has five daughters. The youngest one is just older than you two. Her husband owns a bank, and those girls have always had fine things. So early this morning I went over there and cleaned house with my sister. Her girls have outgrown all of these things, and I want you both to have them."

Sam looked about the room in amazement. A gesture of such magnanimity—especially from a veritable stranger—simply had no register in her world. Until recently, the full force of her brief existence had been consumed with clawing away at basic survival. Thoughts of niceties, fashion, and luxury were too grand, too remote, too far-flung. The sudden confrontation with it all left her blank and wordless. She simply stared at what could only be described as the starkest reminder of the vast distinction between her and other girls of her age, spread out neatly before her.

Jo also had no words as she beheld the colorful spread. She looked at Mrs. Jones in disbelief.

Finally, the standoff between the two dumbfounded girls and the room full of fine attire was broken when Sam slinked forward and plucked a beautiful blue dress from the bed like she was stealing eggs from the hen house. She held it up against her until it covered her tattered pants and her wrinkled and dingy boy shirt. The delicate lace collar framed her face and made her appear angelic. The blue satin ribbon trailed to the floor, and she could envision tying a perfect bow at her waist.

Jo was drawn to a bright-yellow dress with white polka dots. She stood in front of the mirror and smiled at herself for the first time in years. Then she kicked off her shoes and tried on a pair of white Mary Janes and ruffle socks.

Sam turned to face Mrs. Jones, the blue dress following like a dance partner.

"How did you know that we don't have any other clothes?" Sam asked.

"Oh honey, the same way I know when the pastry is done. The same way I know when my boys are fibbing. The same way I know when a painting is finished."

Chapter 9

Mr. Taylor

Remarkably, and against all odds, the girls had found a groove. Despite the absence of adult supervision, and possibly because of it, they had cobbled together a suitable life for themselves. They had seized control of their own destiny in a fashion as unlikely as it was dramatic. They had become their own little masters. They had figured out not only how to survive, but how to prevail. They had a clean, safe place to live, all the food they could eat, and thanks to Mrs. Jones, all the clothes they could wear.

For the next couple of weeks, they settled into a schedule that would have been the envy of the most energetic summer camp director. In the mornings, Jo washed her sheets and then they ate breakfast. Then Jo tutored Sam in reading. At nine thirty, Sam left for piano practice and Jo played her cello. Two days a week they cleaned the music store and took lessons on Saturday. Monday was baseball. Tuesday was art day with Mrs. Jones. And Thursday was shooting practice with Howard. Unstructured time was usually spent reading. As Sam began to recover her early reading skills, she became increasingly engaged and could not get enough of it. She was thrilled with each new word learned. Luckily, in keeping with her personality and her own love of reading, Jo thrived in the teacher role.

The formerly root-bound girls were blossoming. They were proof that youth fostered resilience. They were consummate examples of the simple idea that most kids, if cultured in proper medium, will flourish. But the big event was their discovery of each other. During the critically formative and tenuous period of their relationship, they had miraculously met Caroline Jones. For all intents and purposes, she had taught them intimacy. She had taught them how to connect. She made them believe in her, trust her. Each week when they arrived at her home for their art lesson, she greeted them with a hug. Not a cursory hug of formality, but one of those great big, deliberate, and sweet-smelling hugs. A signature Mrs. Jones hug.

One night, at the end of their busy day, Sam went into Jo's bedroom wearing her gifted pajamas. Jo was just ready to slip into bed. "Do you love Mrs. Jones's hugs as much as I do?"

Jo thought the question oddly random. She wondered where it came from. She searched Sam's expression and manner for a hint and paused to consider the conversations of the day, but to no avail. "I adore her hugs! She makes me feel like I'm the most important person in her world."

Sam, the stone-faced little rail tramp, showing no particular emotion and without great fanfare, wrapped her arms around Jo's neck and gave her a tight squeeze. "I probably can't hug like Mrs. Jones, but you are for sure the most important person in my world."

Jo melted a little inside. Tears welled up, but she got control just before they could spill out. She hugged Sam back, her nose and mouth up against Sam's ear, and wondered what she would do without her. "You're the most important person in mine too. We're friends forever, okay?"

Sam pulled away and nodded sincerely, then sat on Jo's bed. "I've been meaning to tell you something for awhile now, but I could never find the right word."

"Why do you need a special word to tell me something?" Jo asked.

"I guess I really didn't know what to say until I figured out how to say it. But now I know the word."

"Okay," Jo said, her interest peaked. "What's the word?"

"When I was riding the rails," Sam began, "there was this bum who spoke English. Not American English but English English. He was a professor of English literature at a university in England called Oxford. He kept saying he came to the United States on *sabbatical*, but I don't know what that means. Anyway, he was a teacher at a place in New Jersey called Princeton. But he got fired because he drank too much and ended up homeless on the rails. He used to say the word *lovely* all the time. In our country, when someone says *lovely*, they usually mean *beautiful*. Like a lovely woman. But to English people, I guess it means more than just beautiful on the outside. He would put a can of beans on the fire and say, 'What a lovely tin of beans.' Or he would call another man 'a lovely gentleman.' Or he might say 'this lovely boxcar.'" Sam paused and looked at Jo as if she didn't know where to go from there. "I don't know . . . *Lovely* just seems like a good word for you."

One Saturday morning after her piano lesson, Sam ran into an old friend. She was hanging around the sheet music shelf waiting for Jo to finish her cello lesson when she heard a familiar voice on the other side of the aisle.

"How much is this one?" the voice said.

Sam peeked around the corner. Mrs. Fornoff was showing a violin to a customer. Sam couldn't see the customer's face, but his blocky frame was unmistakable. It was her fireman hero, Ed Coltrane.

"Is this for your daughter?" Mrs. Fornoff asked pleasantly.

"Yes," he said, deflated. "She's been pestering me to get her a violin since her cousin got one. But I don't know why. Her cousin has been taking lessons for a year, but every time she plays that thing it sounds like she's torturing an animal. The Great War didn't hurt my ears like that girl can. I can't imagine Hannah is going to be any better. I'm dreading the whole thing—the practicing, the recitals. Then when school starts, she'll be in the seventh grade orchestra, and they have concerts for the parents. I hope there's a big fire on *that* night so I'll get called into work."

Mrs. Fornoff smiled at his grousing. Sam couldn't see Ed's eyes, but she could certainly see that Mrs. Fornoff's eyes were lit up by his charm. "You're a fireman, I presume?"

"Yes," he admitted. "But that doesn't mean I wouldn't *start* a fire if it got me out of a seventh grade orchestra concert."

Mrs. Fornoff chuckled briefly, beaming at the handsome young man as he made jokes. "But you are going to buy this violin for her, aren't you?"

"Of course," he said, like it was a foregone conclusion.

"Because you'll do whatever it takes to make her happy, won't you?"

Ed paused and looked at the kindly woman. Then he won Sam's heart with his answer. "Whatever it takes."

Sam so wanted to talk to him. She wanted him to make jokes for her, to call her his little jumper, and smile as he stared at her through those blue eyes. She wanted to follow him home to watch him with his daughter. To see his face when he gave her the violin. But she was afraid. She was afraid he would ask her questions. So she stayed hidden behind the shelf and let him go.

The morning started out normal enough for Sam. She went downstairs to eat breakfast at the kitchen table. But Jo wasn't there. In the four weeks or so they had lived together, Jo had been up first every single morning. But this morning there was no Jo. Sam thought perhaps she was in the backyard, hanging her sheets on the clothesline. She opened the kitchen door and popped her head outside, but no Jo *and* no sheets.

As she returned to the kitchen table, she heard an ear-piercing scream descending the stairs!

"My bed is dry! My bed is dry! I'm dry!" Jo screamed as she sailed down the stairs in her pajamas and spilled into the kitchen. Sam scooped her up in her arms and hugged her as she had done the night before, and they held each other tight. Jo kept whispering in Sam's ear over and over, "I'm dry, I'm dry, I'm dry."

"Congratulations, Jo! I'm so happy for you!"

"You know that first day we met, when you hit Billy Rose with the stick and knocked the wind out of him?" Jo began.

"Yeah, of course I remember."

"Do you remember the look on Billy's face when his wind came back and he was finally able to get a breath? That's how I feel right now!"

Jo practically floated back upstairs and got dressed. She made her bed but did not remove the sheets for the first time in four months, then returned to the kitchen. During breakfast, she could not contain her elation. She giggled until she bubbled over. "I'm so happy! I'm so happy! I'm so happy!" she repeated with the delight of a small child.

"Take it easy, Jo," Sam said calmly.

"I love corn flakes! I love corn flakes! I love corn flakes!" she went on with loud and silly glee.

"Jo! Stop!" Sam pleaded as she began her own little chuckle. "You're embarrassing yourself!"

"I know! Isn't it great?" Jo exclaimed as she giggled some more.

Then there was a knock on the front door, and the giggling stopped. Sam knew there was no reason for a visitor. No one ever came to the house. They had been very careful to ensure that no one in their new circles knew where they lived. So who could it be?

Jo put her right index finger to her lips and gave Sam the quiet sign, indicating they would pretend nobody was home and just not answer the door. They sat in silence, but the knocking continued.

Then the knocking stopped and a man's voice erupted from behind the door. "Jo? Are you in there? I can hear you in there, little Jo! Open the door!"

Jo stepped cautiously to the window and peered through the glass.

"Who is it?" Sam asked.

"It's Mr. Taylor. Steven's moonshiner," Jo said with consternation.

"What does he want?"

"I don't know! But he knows we're here. Should I answer the door?"

Sam scrambled to devise a plan, but her scheming proved worthless. Mr. Taylor suddenly appeared in the living room window and locked eyes with Jo. "Hey, open the door, Jo. I want to talk to Steven," he yelled as he motioned to the front door.

"Steven's not here!" Jo yelled back.

"Where did he go?"

"He didn't say!"

"Jo, could you open the door so we could talk without yelling?"

"I'm not supposed to open the door to anyone when Steven's not here."

"But I'm not a stranger. You've known me for months! What's going on in there anyway?"

Jo gave Sam the sign that she was going to talk to him. She opened the door but stood in the doorway and did not invite him in. Mr. Taylor was an average-looking forty-year-old without much description to his features except for his noticeably weak chin. He seemed peeved, quite understandably.

Sam followed Jo to the door and stood behind her nervously as she confronted this potential threat to their independence. It was critical that Jo kept her cool.

Before he could speak, Jo calmly repeated her earlier declaration. "Like I said, Steven is not here."

"That's curious. I happen to know he hasn't left this house for months. That's why you come and get his hooch, isn't it? Because he never leaves the house?"

"Well, he's gone now. Sorry, I can't help you." Jo attempted to close the door. Sam thought the encounter was over, that he was satisfied with her answer and would go away.

But just before the door closed, he pushed it back open slightly with his right hand. "Hold on there. I haven't seen you come around for a long time either, more than a month. Why is that?"

Sam's heart began to tick faster as she stood behind the door next to Jo and tried to think of answers in case Jo faltered.

"Steven doesn't send me to get moonshine anymore," Jo said.

Sam liked that answer and hoped it was enough.

But he continued his line of questioning.

"And why not?"

Jo paused, and Sam's heart ticked even faster as she frantically concocted an answer for Jo. But she couldn't think of anything, so she decided on a diversion instead. It wasn't a good plan. It wasn't her best work. But it was all that came to her in that desperate moment. She decided she would pluck his hat from his head as she ran past him. He would chase after her, and she would lead him away from the nest like a mother killdeer faking a broken wing. Jo still didn't speak, and Sam didn't think the situation could abide further delay, so she prepared to act. But just as she started to push Jo out of the way to execute her ill-advised plan, Jo came through.

"Because he quit drinking," Jo said.

Mr. Taylor was visibly shocked. He literally stepped back and grabbed the door jamb with his left hand so as not to tip over. "You're telling me that Steven Toone stopped drinking?"

"That's right."

"I don't believe it. I don't believe it for a second. You know, it's not like Steven is just another customer. I've known him for ten years. There's no way he could ever stop drinking. It would kill him."

"Well, that's the truth," Jo said. "He stopped drinking, and I won't be coming around to buy any more of your moonshine."

Unable to argue against Steven's supposed sobriety, Mr. Taylor left. Jo had acquitted herself with the guile of a politician by technically not lying to him but clearly deceiving him. Sam hoped that would be the end of the man.

"You were great, Jo," Sam said. "I was starting to panic a little, but you really came through."

"I don't know," Jo said. "Mr. Taylor worries me. Probably because he's one of the few people who knows Steven. If he goes snooping around, he might figure out that Steven's not here. And if someone finds the body, how are we going to explain it? What are we going to tell the police?"

"No one is going to find it," Sam said. "We've been over this a dozen times."

"I want to go to the bridge," Jo said. "I want to see for myself, in the daylight."

Ever since the night they tossed Steven's body from the rusty steel bridge into the gloomy water, they had not been back. Although Sam didn't share Jo's guilt, the thought of returning to that bridge gave her the willies. She instantly recalled the putrid smell of Steven's unwashed and alcohol-saturated body. She could hear the clanking of the chain on the bridge siderail and the sickening flop of Steven's torso as it hit the water. She could see his bloody face in the moonlight.

"Are you sure?" Sam questioned.

"Yeah, I'm sure."

Sam looked away so Jo couldn't see her face. "I'm kind of scared to go back there."

"Because you're afraid of what we'll find?" Jo asked.

"No," Sam said. "Nightmares."

"But you haven't had one for weeks."

"That was a terrible night, Jo. I don't want to relive any of the details."

"Okay," Jo said. "I'll go by myself."

"No!" Sam said firmly. "I can't stand the thought of you going by yourself. I'll go with you. I'll be fine."

As they retraced their steps of the night that started it all, Jo seemed to be in a hurry, but Sam felt sick to her stomach. They walked through the neighborhood and into the woods without speaking, each silently battling her own demons. The end of the bridge came into view and Sam's mouth went dry as she struggled with rushing flashbacks. She remembered the overhead portion of the structure to be a dark, forbidding tangle of shadows looming over her, as if waiting to pounce. She remembered the sweaty feel of the steel.

But this time was different. The bright morning sun told the whole story of the bridge. Old and rusty to be sure, but straight, solid, and symmetrical. They walked to the center and peered over the siderail on the upstream side. The gently strolling river, murky as always, told no tales of mischief as it passed under them. Tall, beautiful trees lined the banks and hosted flocks of flitting and chirping birds. A small deer on the far bank drank from the river and twitched its tail nervously. Jo checked the downstream side of the bridge, peering into the water intently. But there was nothing. Nothing except the serenity of slowly moving water surrounded by nature in all its forms. Sam soon realized it wasn't the same place in the daylight, and the dread gradually left her stomach.

Jo checked everything. The water, the banks, the bridge. Finally, she turned to Sam. "There's nobody to tell. You know that, don't you?"

"What do you mean there's nobody?" Sam said, confused.

"I mean Steven's parents are dead. He doesn't have any brothers or sisters. If he has any family, I've never met them."

The two girls stood side by side and watched the sun reflect off the water as the river flowed away from them. "I guess he's like me," Sam said pensively. "But at least he knew his last name and his birthday."

"You don't have a last name?" Jo said.

"I have the one they gave me at the orphanage, but it doesn't mean anything. It could be Jones or Smith or Johnson, any old name."

"What about your birthday?"

"They picked one of those for me too. They told me my mother left me at a fire station. I guess I've been saved twice by a fireman. But they didn't know how old I was. So they guessed my age and gave me November ninth for my birthday."

It was Friday, July first, annuity day. On the first of every month, Jo went to the bank to get the allowance that Steven was supposed to use to take care of her. The bank was a mile from the house—a good twenty-minute walk if there was no dawdling. It was a brick, steel, and glass building like all other banks with echoing tile floors, heavy mahogany desks, and paintings of past bank presidents on the walls. The tellers were all busy helping customers. Fridays were the busiest banking days, so there was a long line, and it wasn't moving.

As they waited, there was a man sitting behind one of those big desks, shuffling papers and writing notes and stuffing folders. He was about forty-five and wore glasses and a three-piece suit. He was clean-shaven except for a prodigious jet-black mustache. He was intently working away when a teenage girl, probably about fifteen years old, slightly pudgy with long blonde hair, sidled up to him. She hooked her right arm around his neck and laid her head on his left shoulder. His countenance instantly softened, and he abruptly stopped his work and reached somewhat awkwardly with his right hand to pull the back of her head tighter up against the top of his shoulder.

"Hi, sweetheart. I didn't know you were coming."

"Hi, Daddy. I just came to see how your day was going."

"Well, it's going a lot better now that I got to see you," he said with a bright smile. "Tell me about your day."

"Not that much to tell. Just another summer day. I pedaled my bike down to the stable and rode my horse in the arena. He did really good today, but he threw a shoe on the front left foot. Think you can put another one on for me after work?"

"Sure, we'll both go down after dinner. Did you go to ballet today?"

"Yes . . ." she said leadingly.

"Well, how did it go?"

"There's a new girl. She's skinny and pretty and dances better than anybody in the class. I hate her guts!"

"Now, now, you know we don't say *hate*!" he chided mildly.

"Okay, I *dislike immensely* her guts! Is that better?"

"That's my girl," he said with a wry smile. "But you know, she'll probably become your best friend."

"That's the worst part! After I saw her dance, I was hoping she'd turn out to be a real snot so I could dislike immensely on her with full satisfaction. But she's sweet and nice and even told me I have beautiful form."

"How dare she!" he teased.

"I know! So I invited her over to dinner."

"What's Mom cooking tonight?"

"She's making a chicken and stuffing casserole and an apple pie."

"That sounds delicious! I can't wait."

"You mean for the apple pie, right?"

"Of course. Your mother's casseroles are torture. This isn't a new recipe, is it?"

"'Fraid so!" the girl said with the timbre of an inside joke. "She got it right out of the *Ladies Home Journal*."

"You have to tell her you don't like those insufferable casseroles!" he said in pleading fashion. "The dog won't even eat them."

"You tell her!"

"I'm the husband. I can't tell her something like that."

"What makes you think I can?" she retorted.

"You're a teenage girl. She expects you to be bratty, critical, and ungrateful."

The girl lifted her head and smirked at him as she punched him on the shoulder.

"Besides, I'm shoeing your horse. You owe me a favor." Then he hooked her with his left arm, smiled adoringly, and pulled her in close.

At last, the line to the teller began to move, and Sam and Jo stepped forward. But Jo kept her eyes on the girl and her father.

The girl pulled a chair up next to him and sat down. He handed her a stack of envelopes and a roll of stamps. Together, they sealed and stamped the already addressed envelopes and placed them in his outbox. Then she opened the bottom left drawer of the desk and rummaged through its contents until she found a lollipop, which she grabbed by the stick and then quickly stabbed the candy end into her mouth. Once her lips were sufficiently wet and sticky from the sucker, she stood and grinned with the scantest of mischief. Then, as a course of apparent ritual, she kissed him on the cheek.

When she walked out, he didn't immediately return to his work. He watched her walk away until she disappeared through the front door of the bank. Then he pulled a hanky from his pocket but kept staring at the door.

As Sam and Jo left the bank with the annuity money, neither of them spoke. They walked in silence for a couple of blocks before Sam said, "You aren't thinking about that girl at the bank, are you?"

"No, of course not," Jo said with a hint of annoyance.

"Yeah, me neither," Sam replied.

It was the Fourth of July in middle America. The celebration activities promised to fill the day with fun and excitement. Sam and Jo each picked a fashionable ensemble from their shared wardrobe, which included a dress with matching shoes and hat.

They had discussed the upcoming event with Howard at their last shooting lesson, and he had offered his father's services to give them a ride to Hyrum Park—the epicenter of the celebration and the best place to watch the parade. Deep in the downtown area, the park was quite some distance from Jo's house. They had agreed to meet Howard at the train tracks, which is where they were standing when a car pulled up, driven by Howard's father. The girls smiled in expectation of the day ahead as the car slowed and they recognized Howard in the back seat.

However, their mutual buzz was immediately doused when Howard opened the door and announced, "Hey, I'm really sorry, but we can't give you a ride to the park. My cousin is running in the five-mile race, and I told him we'd give him a ride to the starting line. But it's in the opposite direction from the park. I hope that doesn't put you in a bind."

Sam was disappointed and promptly prepared for a long walk.

But the look on Jo's face made it clear she was having none of that. "Put *us* in a bind? Let's review this. Did you or did you not offer us a ride to the park?"

"Well, yes I did," Howard admitted. "But—"

"And then you offered your cousin a ride at the same time to a different place?"

"Ah, well, yeah. I guess so, but—"

"So you made commitments to be in two places at the same time?"

"Yeah, I guess that's technically true."

Jo gave him a slightly piercing look as she flipped both hands palms up and said, "Then I'd say *you're* the one who's in a bind, Howard."

Howard's father laughed at his hapless son. "Howard, you're in way over your head. Slide over and make room for the little district attorney and her co-counsel."

Howard tentatively moved over as Jo piled in the car, satisfaction on her face, and punched him in the arm.

The day delivered as billed. The crowds were huge, and the air electric. Nineteen twenty-seven was a heady time in the country. American Charles Lindbergh had just flown the Atlantic from New York to Paris. Babe Ruth was on track to set the single season home run record. The economy was booming. Average people had discretionary income and leisure time, and they came out to celebrate both with exhilaration and fervor. Activities in the park took on carnival flare.

Looking fancy in a pink gingham dress, Sam tightened the satin ribbon of her sun hat under her chin so it wouldn't fall off. Then she stepped into the batting cage and faced the two-wheeled pitching machine—a popular novelty of the day. By the time she had clobbered about ten pitches, a large crowd had formed. As she continued to hit successive pitches, the crowd cheered with each one.

"Turn it up!" came an anonymous yell. "Let's see what she can do!"

The attendant looked at Sam. She nodded him on, so he turned up the speed. The crowd grew restless as she stepped to the plate, took her signature stance with her dress-covered little butt pointing into the air, and eyed up the machine. The first pitch whirred in at waist height and right over the middle of the plate. Sam chased it to her bat, as she always did, and sent it straight back to the machine, bouncing it off of both wheels to the astonishment and jubilation of the crowd.

Then she hit the second pitch! By the third pitch, the crowd was counting.

Whir! Crack! Roar! "Three!"

Whir! Crack! Roar! "Four!"

Whir! Crack! Roar! "Five!"

With the fifth hit, the machine stopped pitching balls as the crowd broke into applause and whistles.

"Crank it up again!" came a voice from the crowd.

The attendant looked at Sam, then said, "It only goes up one more speed. Are you sure you want to try that?"

"Let me see it!" Sam yelled as she stepped back from the plate.

The attendant flipped the switch and loaded a ball. It whizzed over the plate in a flash, scarily faster than the previous pitches. The crowd recoiled as women covered their mouths and men opened their eyes wide and laughed that low-pitched "ho-ho" man-laugh at the speed of the ball. Jo stared ahead in consternation.

Slowly and deliberately, Sam stepped to the plate. She held the bat in her left hand by the handle with the meaty end practically on the ground. Then she looked over at the pitching machine and gradually raised the bat until it pointed to center field. She held it there for five full counts as the cheers from the crowd grew louder and half an octave higher. It wasn't hubris on her part; it was convention. That's just how they did it in the Bigs.

She took her stance and prepared for the ball. The attendant fed the beast, and the ball hurled toward her. The condensed interval between the time she first saw the ball and the time it hit her bat was lost to the universe. Gone. Never to be retrieved. But hit it she did. With a crack, the ball shot into the left upper corner of the cage, indicating she had actually been a little early with the swing and had probably hit the ball over third base. The crowd went nuts.

The attendant rushed into the cage like the bench charging the mound and gave her a five-dollar prize and a huge stuffed polar bear. Every man and boy in the crowd, and some of the women, lined up to try their luck.

Sam and Jo moved on to the next attraction. This time it was Jo drawing a crowd as she killed ducks in the shooting gallery. First, she won the small stuffed animal, then the medium size one, then the big one. She was going for the grand prize when a boy in the crowd yelled out, "Check out Annie Oakley!" As Jo shot, the crowd chanted, "Annie! Annie! Annie!" Having achieved high marks at Howard's shooting academy, these short-range targets were easy pickings. Howard, of course, would never have demeaned himself with a tawdry shooting gallery, but Jo thought it was great fun. And she won the grand prize: a stuffed brown bear of such proportions as to rival Sam's polar bear.

It was time for the parade. Sam and Jo secured a prime piece of real estate on the parade route beneath a broad-leafed sycamore planted in the grassy strip between the sidewalk and the street. Uncle Sam on stilts was the lead entry, followed by a marching band and then the grand marshal. It was all quite splendid.

Then they heard the sirens. Shortly thereafter, the fire engines appeared, including the ladder truck—Sam's ladder truck. As it approached, Sam could not help but notice a familiar hulking figure perched conspicuously on top, waving at the throngs.

Without speaking, Sam grabbed Jo by the elbow and pulled her into the street.

"Hey, where are we going?" Jo demanded. But as the ladder truck drew closer, she could see the reason. "Is that your fireman?"

"That's Edison Coltrane the Third!" Sam said emphatically.

When the ladder truck reached them, they were standing well out into the street. Ed's gaze swept slowly across them but, to Sam's surprise, it didn't stop. Sam stared up at him. The scabs on his face had healed, and she could see the clear outline of his clean-shaven mug swaged onto his thick neck. But he wasn't looking at her. He wasn't looking at Sam in her dress with her smart new haircut and lady's hat. He appeared to be moving on as he nodded to the crowd.

In desperation, Sam whipped her hat off and waved it at him. He glanced down and there they were again, staring into each other's eyes, all alone, the surrounding thousands notwithstanding. Sam's world ran in slow motion as a broad, delighted smile spread across Ed's face. In the midst of the parade cacophony—running engines, honking horns, clomping horses, crying babies, blowing brass bands, and cheering crowds—Sam could hear nothing, and the surreal, time-suspended moment fell silent.

She saw Ed mouthing the words, "Wow! Look at you!" as he raised his right arm and pointed his index finger at her like a statue. She recalled the feeling of safety in those burly arms even as they had squeezed the breath out of her. She could smell him and again see the bloody shards of glass in his face. He gave her a gracious salute, then blended into the celebration and was gone.

Sam's hearing awakened abruptly to the ambient noise, her world returned to real time, and the ethereal encounter was over.

She megaphoned her left hand around her mouth and leaned toward Jo's ear. "I really like him!"

After the parade, the girls hit the food vendors. Hot dogs, root beer, snow cones, and cotton candy. After that, more attractions. Games and contests, water fights, arts and crafts of all mediums. It was as they stood admiring some oil paintings that Sam noticed four girls a couple of years older, who seemed to be staring at them from across the way. The foursome was all dressed up in their casual finery. They were pretty girls with cute haircuts, fancy headwear, and clique-ish teenage swagger.

Before long, the apparent leader marched headlong toward them, still staring. As she approached, with her three lieutenants in tow, she appeared to be studying Jo's dress, then Sam's dress, then back to Jo's dress. "That is really odd!" she said without any sort of introduction, as children tend to do to younger children of lesser rank. "I had a dress just like this one," referring to Jo's dress. "And I had one just like that too." She nodded toward Sam's dress.

A question had not really been asked, so Sam and Jo gave no answer.

"What are the chances I'd run into two girls together wearing dresses just like two of my old ones?"

Again, Sam and Jo said nothing and offered only the tiniest shrugs in response.

"Did you get this dress at Shari's boutique?" she asked Jo.

"No," Jo answered.

"Let me see that top button," she demanded. Jo turned her back slightly, and the bossy girl inspected the button in question. "This *is* my dress! I know because I had to replace this button! I can tell because it doesn't quite match the other three." Then she turned to Sam. "And that's my dress too! Where did you two get my dresses? I threw those away. Did you go through our garbage or something? Is that what you do? Go through people's garbage like rats or something?" She put her hands up to her face and shortened her arms, making clawing motions with her fingers while sticking her upper teeth grotesquely out over her lower lip and began to gnaw like a rat. The three other girls giggled and copied, as they were destined to do.

Sam could see the slow boil on Jo's face. She wondered if this might be one of those moments that made Jo want to rethink her pacifist tendencies and scratch this kid's eyes out.

But Jo spoke with rational appeal. "Your mother gave these dresses to your aunt Caroline, and she gave them to us."

"Yikes! How embarrassing. How double embarrassing. Not only are you wearing worn-out hand-me-downs to a public place, but you can't even hide that fact because you're so lame that you ran into the previous owner. How humiliating." The girl's followers piled on giggles and snooty looks.

But then there was Sam. Nobody could do it like Sam. She stepped up to face the leader of the apprentice coven with no fear. "If I *had* seen this dress in the garbage, I would gladly have pulled it out because this is the most beautiful dress I've ever worn." Then Sam paused and looked at the four spoiled girls and let them think about that.

The giggling went away and the snooty looks faded. "But I didn't have to do that because a kind person who doesn't owe me anything, and who knew without ever being told that I didn't have a nice dress, or any dress, gave it to me." Then she pinched the fabric of her dress on both sides and raised it slightly to show it to the four now-solemn girls. "You said this dress is a worn-out hand-me-down. If that's true, I'd sure like to have seen it when it was brand new on the day that you got it." Sam took a step closer and met the girl's eyes. "Tell me, what was that like?"

Chapter 10

Mr. Jones

It was Tuesday. Art day. The highlight of the week. Although Jo certainly enjoyed her artwork, the actual purpose of the visit to Mrs. Jones would have been quite inconsequential to her. She would have used any excuse to visit, and she was sure Sam felt the same. As she stepped up on the porch with Sam, wearing her donated clothes, she anticipated Mrs. Jones's greeting. She knocked.

Sure enough, Mrs. Jones answered the door and shined that big smile, followed by one of those delicious hugs for each of them. The consummate hostess, Mrs. Jones radiated that ingenuous grace that convinced Jo she was thrilled to see her. Perhaps she was. But something was different this time. The warmth and inviting nature of Mrs. Jones's home was even more overwhelming due to the smell of something cooking in the kitchen. Every other time Mrs. Jones had served cold lunch foods, usually some type of sandwich. But this time she had something already in the oven. And of course, it smelled delectable.

They donned their painting smocks and took their places facing their respective easels. Mrs. Jones instructed them on the objective of the day's lesson, and they began. She complimented them on their progress to date and encouraged them with her energy and passion. Jo so wanted to please her.

Over the past few weeks, Mrs. Jones had made a host of careful attempts to pry loose any insights into the lives of the two girls. But they had kept their cards close to their vests. So she remained largely ignorant of their history, and certainly of their current living situation.

As Jo painted and Mrs. Jones hovered about, she couldn't help but think about the girl at the bank. Something about the encounter between the girl and her father had affected her in a way she did not understand. "Mrs. Jones," she began, "what do parents think?"

"What do parents think?" Mrs. Jones repeated. "Whatever do you mean?"

"About their kids, I mean," Jo continued.

Mrs. Jones looked carefully at Jo. "In what context are you referring, honey?"

"I'll have to tell you a story so you'll know what I mean." Jo continued dabbing at her painting as she began, as if she did not want to look at Mrs. Jones while she told the story. "Friday we were at the bank. It was crowded so we had to wait in line. There was a man sitting at a big desk. He looked very busy with his papers and such. Then this teenage girl walked up behind him and put her arms around him. It was his daughter because she called him daddy.

"They talked and smiled a lot, then after a while she pulled this lollipop out of the bottom drawer of the desk and put it in her mouth. Then once her lips were all wet and sticky, she kissed him on the cheek. I could tell he knew it was going to be sticky because he winced a little, but he let her do it anyway. Then she left. I thought he would return to his paperwork right away, but he didn't. He watched her walk all the way across the lobby and out the door. After she was gone, he kept staring at the door. Then he pulled a hanky from his pocket and put it toward his face like he was going to wipe the sticky away. But it never touched his cheek. He dropped the hanky on the desk and kept staring at the door where she had disappeared. I wondered what he must be thinking. Why did he keep staring? Why didn't he wipe his face?" Jo looked directly at Mrs. Jones, making inescapable eye contact.

Mrs. Jones looked like she had swallowed a walnut, and Jo knew it was going to take her a minute to answer.

Jo granted her a short reprieve by continuing. "It was the same thing the first day we met you at the ball field, when Scotty got that bug in his eye. He was lying on that blanket with his head in your lap, and you looked down at his face and wiped the sweat away with your hand. It was the way you were looking at him. It was the same look as the man at the bank, staring at the door when his daughter left." Then she paused, her eyes repeating the question before she spoke the words. *What are parents thinking during those moments?*

Mrs. Jones eventually composed herself and answered the question. "It's *cherish*," she said. "The word to describe those moments is *cherish*."

Jo still wasn't sure.

"Do you know what that word means?" Mrs. Jones asked.

"I thought I did," Jo said.

"Parents cherish their children. They don't just love them, they treasure them! They adore them! And they marvel at how lucky they are to have something so precious in their lives.

"When Jimmy was born and I got my very first look at his face, I was instantly smitten with that beautiful boy and convinced he had just come from the very presence of God. I had been making art my whole life, but the first thing that occurred to me was, *This is my masterpiece.* Immediately, I wanted to protect him and care for him, and I wanted him to graduate from college first in his class and invent the telephone and discover insulin. Nursing him became the most absorbing joy of my life. He would nurse until his tummy was so full and round that he could only take grunty little breaths. I had never known such perfect satisfaction. My favorite part was when he would fall asleep with a mouth full of my milk and it would drool all over his face. He looked like a tiny drunk, lying there in a stupor, intoxicated by the warm, sweet milk that came from my breast.

"I used to go into his room at night just to watch him sleep. And that went on until he was embarrassingly old. As he grew, I stopped caring about having my own fun. I only cared about his fun. When he broke his arm, my own arm hurt for a month. When he would get a terrible leg ache from growing pains, I secretly cheered because then I could rub his little legs and soothe him. It still thrills me when I first see his face after he's been at school all day, or first thing in the morning. I sit on the edge of his bed and stroke his forehead until he wakes up. And when he looks at me, I'm already smiling at him. And even if I wanted to, wild horses couldn't wipe that smile from my face. It's been eleven years, and it's still a thrill!"

Mrs. Jones opened her brown eyes wide and cupped Jo's cheeks in her hands—her strong, warm, and sensitive mother's hands—in a palpable gesture of inclusion. Although she may not have known it at the time, she was the only woman in the world with the credentials to make such a gesture. "The man at the bank . . . me at the ball field. That's what we're thinking . . . *cherish*!"

Jo believed her. How could she not? She nodded slightly and returned to her painting. Mrs. Jones, looking curiously spent, let out a tiny sigh. But eventually, Jo had to ask the inevitable next question. An infinitely more difficult question. The kind of question a child in her position was exquisitely entitled to ask. "But not all parents cherish their children, do they, Mrs. Jones?"

Mrs. Jones, obviously crestfallen, gave Jo a look like she wanted to apologize for everything wrong in the world. But Jo knew she couldn't do that. And she knew Mrs. Jones couldn't hold her in her lap and pluck the bug from her eye. There was a long, empty silence. When she finally answered, Jo sensed the surrender in her voice.

"No," Mrs. Jones said sympathetically. "I suppose not all of them do."

But Jo was less interested in sympathy than she was in understanding, and at that point she let Mrs. Jones off the hook. Refocusing on her art piece, she asked, "Do you think I should I go with more brown here?"

Mrs. Jones called the girls for lunch. As they approached the kitchen table she announced, "I have a surprise for you two."

Sitting at the end of the table was a tall, handsome man with dark hair wearing a business suit. "This is my husband, Mr. Jones," she proclaimed proudly.

"How do you do, ladies?" he offered in debonair fashion as he rose like a gentleman to greet them.

"This is Sam, and this is Jo," Mrs. Jones said, presenting the girls to him.

Mr. Jones took off his suit coat and draped it carefully over the shoulders of an empty chair. "I've never heard more about two little girls in my whole life," he said with a polite but loaded smile as he shot a furtive glance at his wife.

"Mr. Jones is an engineer. He designs bridges and structures of all manner. I asked him to come home from the office for lunch to meet you."

Jo felt slightly invaded as she looked at Sam for support. They usually had Mrs. Jones all to themselves. Even Jimmy and Scotty rarely made an appearance during their visits. And they were automatically leery of men.

The girls weren't accustomed to formal introductions, and both of them lacked the social skills to manage the setting with any decorum. Neither of them said anything to him and stood there timidly.

He gestured to the table. "Please sit down, ladies," he said respectfully.

Mrs. Jones pulled from the oven a magnificent meat pie topped with her signature puff pastry cooked to a flawless golden brown. She cut it into steaming wedges and served Mr. Jones first, then the two girls, and finally herself.

As they all veritably assailed the savory pie with its flakey crust, tender beef chunks, soft vegetables, and delicately spiced gravy, Mr. Jones opened the conversation. "So is it true that you two ladies have charmed all of those sweaty boys into letting you play baseball with them?"

"Yes, sir. I guess so," Sam said reservedly.

Turning to Sam directly, he asked, "And even the cantankerous Billy Rose not only lets you play but insists you play on his team?"

"Well, he doesn't really like to pitch to me."

Mr. Jones, apparently aware of the famous line drive to the groin, laughed heartily, practically spraying meat sauce all over the table. "No! I'll bet he doesn't at that!"

"And what about you?" he asked Jo. "Little Miss Joe Dugan of Maple Street Stadium?"

"Yes, sir," she said. "I play third base on Stan's team."

As she answered his question, he looked at her carefully as if taking a picture. He paused, like a person thinking of two things at once. Jo began to feel slightly uncomfortable. "I think that's just marvelous," he said with a congratulatory nod at each of them.

As the meal progressed, Mr. Jones bantered playfully with his wife, and they discussed the goings on at his office and other adult things, but constantly circled back to the girls, keeping them engaged in the conversation. Jo's inhibitions slowly melted in the presence of this charismatic figure. She couldn't help but warm, if ever so slightly, to the male intruder.

The next afternoon Sam and Jo were sitting on the couch reading when Jo suddenly announced, "Sam, I think we need more color."

"What are you talking about?" Sam asked.

"Come with me," Jo commanded playfully.

Jo led Sam to her bedroom. "Take a look around. What do you see?"

Puzzled by the question, Sam gave her a curt shrug but said nothing.

"Now think of Mrs. Jones's house, then answer the question."

Sam looked about the room. This time she noted the faded and peeling paint. She realized the walls were blank and the room had no life. There was no energy, nothing of beauty, nothing created, nothing that suggested a human being lived there. There was nothing drawing her in. Nothing attracting her, inviting her, centering her. Oddly, in a room she had seen many, many times, she suddenly felt cold and empty. The room had no pulse.

"See what I mean?" Jo asked.

"Yeah, I get it now," Sam conceded. "But what are we going to do about it?"

"We're going to paint this room!" Jo declared. "Then we're going to paint your room!"

Sam was immediately on board. "But where are we going to get the paint?"

"Ferguson's Hardware."

"I don't like that guy!"

"Me neither, but his store is a lot closer than Harry's Hardware."

Sam relented, and they set out for Ferguson's.

As they entered the store, Sam hoped for another attendant besides the disagreeable Mr. Ferguson. But no sooner had they found the paint department when they were accosted by the bespectacled irritant in the sloppy blue shop apron.

Maybe he won't remember us, Sam thought.

But that notion was dismissed when, upon seeing them, he immediately broke into what can only be described as a shit-eating grin. "Well, well! If it isn't the Capone sisters."

Jo shot him a look of disgust.

"You two come back for a Tommie gun this time? Maybe you need more firepower than the thirty-eight? Somebody muscling in on your territory? You gotta lean on 'em? Feed 'em a lead sandwich?"

The witless oaf appeared so pleased with himself he was practically smacking with glee.

Jo gave him a look as serious as a heart attack. "Are you finished?"

"Okay! Okay!" He laughed.

Sam was not amused. And Jo still had a look of disgust on her face.

When Ferguson had composed himself, he took a deep breath and said, "What can I do for you two prepossessing ladies?"

"We need some paint," Jo stated.

"Now we're talking," he replied with enthusiasm. "What color?"

"Yellow," Jo said. "Yellow like the sun."

Mr. Ferguson searched the shelf briefly and selected a can of bright-yellow paint. "This is a very good exterior paint," he said confidently. "It will last for years."

"Exterior?" Jo said. "I'm painting my bedroom."

"Oh, you can't put this color in your bedroom!" he warned as he put it back on the shelf.

"Why not?" Jo said defensively.

"It's too yellow," he informed. "On the outside of the house, compared to the sunshine, this is a compelling color. But inside, this color would be a violent, screaming yellow," he said with hyperbole. "You'll hurt yourself with this color. I can't sell you this paint in good conscience any more than I could have sold you those bullets you wanted."

Sam, in defense of her friend, piped up. "You know, Mr. Ferguson, you're not nearly as nice to us as your cousin Harry!"

"That's because he doesn't have any kids!" he snapped. "He doesn't know any better." Then he pulled another can from the shelf and pried it open with a screwdriver. "Look at this one. This is a tamer, softer yellow. This is what you want in your bedroom."

Jo studied the color but seemed unconvinced.

"Trust me. When a little girl wakes up in the morning, she wants to see something bright and beautiful. She wants it to be fun and cheerful and warm. But she doesn't want something that burns her retinas and muddles her little brain."

"And how would you know what little girls want?" Jo said with disdain.

"Because I *have* a little girl who wanted a yellow bedroom," he said matter-of-factly.

Jo's face revealed that she might be thinking the same thing Sam was thinking. That perhaps Ferguson might be a colossal phony. A colossal, bald, phony crustacean with a coarse shell but a soft, fleshy center.

She asked the obvious question: "And does she *have* a yellow bedroom?"

"Of course she does!" he retorted sharply.

"Okay then," Jo said. "I'll take it, but you have to show us how to do it."

"What is this?" he said, mildly flabbergasted. "A purchase with conditions?"

"I've never painted a bedroom before. I've never painted anything before."

"Well can't you ask your mommy?"

"I don't live with my mother."

"Then ask your daddy."

"It's my stepdad, and he will not help me. I can promise you that."

"Well, who's paying for the paint?"

"I am," Jo said. "With my own money." She pulled a crinkled five-dollar bill from her pocket.

And that took all the gruff out of him.

Sam was excited to get started on Jo's bedroom. Ferguson had revealed his soft center when he spent twenty minutes giving them detailed instructions on how to accomplish the task, which included the use of a brand-new product recently introduced by the 3M company that promised to make the job much easier, especially for a couple of amateurs: masking tape. Then he loaned them a step ladder, a drop cloth, a paint roller with a long handle, a roller basin, an old coffee can in which to clean the brushes, some mineral spirits, and two paint scrapers. He even gave Jo a fifty percent discount on the paint. Not such a shmuck after all.

The girls set to work with the full energy of youth. They scraped, they wiped the walls with a damp cloth, they taped and draped, and they mixed and stirred. Then they rolled and brushed and fussed meticulously with the edges. They dabbed at the runs and kept checking over and over for drips, like Ferguson had taught them.

When they were finished, the drop cloth and masking tape remained in place until the paint was dry, per Ferguson's orders. Jo's mattress was leaning against the wall in the hallway, and the room smelled heavily of paint. It was late, and they were tired.

"You can sleep with me tonight," Sam offered.

"I can?"

"Sure."

Jo looked at her incredulously. "Aren't you afraid I might have an *accident*?"

"What do you mean? What kind of accident?"

"You know, the kind I had every night for four months."

"You mean like a pee accident?"

"Yes, like a pee accident!"

"You haven't had an accident for a couple weeks, have you?" Sam said, starting to feel some early concern.

"No," Jo assured. "But I guess there's always some chance the accidents will come back."

"But you're over it, aren't you?" Sam said, hoping for clear confirmation.

"I think so, but I did have two root beers while we were painting."

Sam felt a little sick, like a guy in no-man's land having second thoughts but realizing it was too late to do anything about it.

"I think you have to ask yourself the question, 'Could I still be friends with this girl if she pees on me?'" Jo said.

Sam looked over at her relatively clean, pee-free, and aromatically neutral bed, then turned back to Jo. Teasing each other had not really been a part of their relationship. The circumstances under which they had met, and the subsequent events, had simply been too grave and the stakes too high. It took a few moments for Sam to notice the subtle eversion in the corners of Jo's mouth and her wide-open eyes. But gradually, it dawned on her. "If you're trying to scare me," she said calmly, "remember, I'm the girl who stepped off the fifth-story ledge of a burning building—backwards!"

Both of them giggled as they put on their pajamas. They gave each other a good-night hug, as had become their routine. The night was muggy. Even with the window open they were too warm, so they each stayed on their own side of the bed.

When morning came, the room had cooled, and Jo awakened to find herself snuggled up against Sam.

"You're so warm," Jo said.

"You feel warm to me too," Sam replied.

"Why is that?"

"What?"

"Why is it that we're both cold, but we feel warm to each other?"

"I don't know, but answer me this. How come if you get into water that's the same temperature as a warm room, it feels freezing? And air that is the same temperature as warm water feels like you're cooking?"

"I don't know," Jo said, deferring the mysteries of physics and physiology for another time as she bounded from the bed. "But I have to go see my room!" Together they frantically pulled off the tape and rolled up the drop cloths. Once they had cleaned up all of the construction mess, Jo stood back to admire their work.

The room had undergone a celestial transformation. Light shining through the window sparkled and popped as it reflected off of the renewed walls, ordaining the space with vitality. None of this newfound energy was lost on Jo. And Ferguson was right; the room was warm and cheerful.

This was about more than having a nicer room. Had Jo just won the Olympic gold medal in bedroom painting, she couldn't have felt more spectacularly fulfilled. Having conquered an endeavor universally confined to the adult spectrum by themselves was a monumental victory for two eleven-year-old girls. If they could do this, they could do anything.

"We did it!" Jo said, beaming with pride. "It's gorgeous! Caroline Jones herself couldn't have done a better job. I sure wish we could show it to her." She stood in the doorway, watching the morning sun give life to the room.

"Want some help moving your bed back in?" Sam asked.

"No. I can't put that stinking mattress back into this splendid room. It would feel unholy or something."

"Okay, then you can sleep with me until you get another mattress. I mean, if you dare."

"What do you mean *if I dare*?"

"Well, you know, we could get you a helmet or something."

"What helmet? What are you talking about?"

"You know, like an army helmet. The kind with a chin strap so it won't fall off."

"Again, what are you talking about?"

"A helmet for your head in case I have more of those bat-swinging nightmares."

Sam, as could be expected, was much better at deadpan humor than Jo. She could tease with a total absence of facial clues. Stone-cold killer.

"All right, all right," Jo said. "Very funny. I'll take my chances."

"Just trying to look out for you, Jo," she said sarcastically. "You know, with the—"

"Yeah, the helmet. I get it. Now let's do your room! Do you want the same color or your own color?"

Sam looked about the room and began to nod in rhythmic fashion. "I'll take this color."

And the nesting began.

Once Sam's room was painted, they hauled Jo's malodorous old mattress to the street. As they threw it discourteously on top of the garbage cans, a more symbolic gesture of the ignoble end to a wretched phase of her life could hardly be imagined.

"I want to buy you a new mattress with the money I won at the batting cage," Sam announced.

"Wait, what? Who said that?"

Sam looked at her coldly. "What do you mean *who said that*?"

"I mean was that the little boxcar girl who never shared her food or her warm clothes and only ever thought of herself? Was that her offering to buy me a new mattress with the first five-dollar bill she's probably ever held in her whole life? Was that her?"

Jo was at it again.

Sam stared at her briefly, again with the flat face. "Yes, mother, it was."

Then the smiles came, then a little giggling, then the obligatory hug.

They searched the furniture stores in their walking radius but couldn't find a new mattress for five dollars. But they hit the jackpot when they discovered a thrift store with a respectable selection of used mattresses free of stains and able to pass Jo's stringent sniff test. In addition, they found some delightful blue and green curtains in paisley mounted on spring-loaded rods. The clerk was kind enough to demonstrate how to install them without tools or know-how. The girls made quite a sight team-lugging the mattress down the street, propped up on its edge like a pane of glass.

With Jo's new mattress stationed on the bed frame and the bedding tucked in, they turned to the window. Sam took the leftover masking tape and patched the hole in the glass made when Jo had thrown the butcher knife through it. Replacing the pane would have to wait. Then they installed the curtains in both rooms and piled their stuffed animals on top of the beds. They adorned the walls with their early masterpieces from Mrs. Jones's art school, and before long their decorous little sanctuaries flourished with eleven-year-old flair.

The Saturday after the Fourth of July, Sam and Jo cleaned the music store, then sat for their lessons.

Sam took her spot on the piano bench and opened her level-one book to her assigned piece in preparation for playing it for Mrs. Fornoff. The morning sun shining through the window brightened the tiny room. The upright piano had become her second best friend, after Jo, and the wood bench her favorite fixture. The stern, if not glaring, portrait of the famously ill-tempered Ludwig Von Beethoven hung on the wall above the piano peered down at her. At first intimidated by the sullen genius, she now pretended that she could cheer him up if she played well enough. And that was her goal each day: to make Beethoven smile.

Mrs. Fornoff, elegant and grand as usual, took her seat beside Sam. Ever since getting her unsolicited haircut from Mrs. Jones, Sam had been especially taken with the lustrous silver hair of Mrs. Fornoff, and she really wanted to touch it. But she was far too timid to request such an impertinence.

Mrs. Fornoff began the lesson with, "I noticed you didn't practice on Monday."

Sam thought for a minute, slightly alarmed, then remembered. "Monday was the Fourth of July. I thought the store would be closed."

Mrs. Fornoff smiled sheepishly as she wrapped her left arm around Sam's shoulder and squeezed softly with her gnarled hand. "Of course it was, my dear. I'm just teasing. You have not missed a single day in the last month, nor have you been late. And you and your compatriot have kept the store spanking clean. My congratulations to you both. You should know that you girls have been instrumental in preparing the humble pie I have been feeding Mr. Fornoff."

"I don't know what that means."

"It means that Mr. Fornoff did not think you both would last this long. Don't get me wrong. He hoped you would, and he was cheering for you two. He just didn't think it was very likely to happen."

"Why wouldn't it happen?" Sam said incredulously, if not marginally offended.

"Because, my dear, when it comes to the piano or the cello, everyone wants to play, but no one wants to practice."

"But I love to practice!" Sam said emphatically. "I love the sound of every note, and I love to put the notes together to make a song or a piece of music. I love that the sound coming from the piano is my sound. And I don't care if it's a simple sound because it's *my* sound. I created it. I have control over it. I can make it loud or soft, fast or slow. And when I force my fingers to do something they don't want to do, and the piano makes a beautiful new sound, I like that too."

"You and me both, kid!" she said with uncharacteristic gusto. "Now let's see what ya got!"

Sam played all of the assigned pieces without mistake or hesitation. Then, to the surprise of Mrs. Fornoff, she played the rest of the pieces in the book too.

When finished, she turned to Mrs. Fornoff and said, "I need another book."

"You certainly do." She opened the second book in the beginner series and placed it on the music stand. "Try this."

Sam sight-read the first piece flawlessly. Then the second, then the third. Mrs. Fornoff kept turning pages, and Sam kept playing. Soon they were finished with the second book. Mrs. Fornoff pulled out the third one. "This book introduces some terminology and includes text and music. We will read and learn as we go."

Sam didn't like the sound of that, not one bit.

"Start here, and read this paragraph out loud."

Sam looked at it, but most of the words on the page were not in the readers Jo had given her, and she couldn't make out the first word. She looked over at Mrs. Fornoff blankly, then began to play the music at the bottom of the page perfectly.

When she was finished with the short piece, Mrs. Fornoff intervened. "Samantha, dear, are you telling me you can sight-read music but you can't read words?"

"I can read a little. Jo is teaching me."

"And why can't you read?"

"Because I haven't been in school since the first grade."

"And why haven't you been in school?"

"I've kind of been moving around a lot." She drew her arms close to her body.

"Samantha, do you have a mother?"

"No, ma'am." She curled her legs back under the bench.

"Do you have a father?"

"No, ma'am." She lowered her chin, stared at her lap, and stiffened all over.

"So you're an orphan?"

"Yes, ma'am," she said softly.

"Do you live with Jo?"

"Yes, ma'am," she said even softer.

"And why is Jo the one teaching you to read?"

No answer.

"And what about her parents?"

By then, Sam was rolled up like a potato bug. "I just want to play the piano," she whispered.

Mrs. Fornoff replaced her arm around Sam's shoulder and pulled her in close. "Of course, dear, and so we shall. I will read this paragraph to you, and then I will help you read it back to me. Once you understand what it means, we will play some more. Sam relaxed ever so slightly but kept her head down.

Mrs. Fornoff reached over with her right hand and gently lifted Sam's chin from her chest and rotated her head until their eyes met. "But know this, Samantha, I don't teach music. I teach young people. As your teacher, I'm going to share in your discovery of something sublime. But only a small part of that beauty will ring from the piano. Most of it will radiate from within you. And I cannot remain unaffected by that marvel. I want to be there for that. So you have to let me in a little. If I only give you technical training, you'll only ever play notes. But I want you to make music."

Mrs. Fornoff held her piercing gaze. Sam looked deep into her light-green eyes and believed her like she had never believed anyone before.

"I've taught hundreds of children in my career. But none have affected me like you have. Perhaps because none have been such a spectacular underdog. There is something so believably genuine and substantive about you. You're a girl with but one face."

She released Sam's chin and glanced forward at the lesson book. Sam thought she was finished, but she had more to say.

"As for your playing, you are certainly talented, possibly gifted. It's still too early to tell. Your progress through the beginner books is uncommon but not rare. We shall see. But one thing is for sure. Not since Natalia Kaminska have I seen a girl with such grit."

When the lesson was over, Mrs. Fornoff turned to share something personal and sacred. "Samantha, dear, I want to tell you about my life. I asked you some questions about yours, so it's only fitting I tell you about mine. Would that be all right?"

"Sure," Sam said.

"But be aware, I'm going to tell you things I've never told anyone. Not even Mr. Fornoff. My own parents never knew the whole story. You shall be the first to know, and you must keep it in confidence. I'm telling you because I've been wanting to tell someone for fifty years. And for reasons that are clearer in my heart than in my head, I think that someone is you. Are you still sure you want to hear it?"

Sam nodded in the affirmative.

"Okay, but first I want you to look at me and tell me what you see."

Sam looked at the elderly woman with the clean, pressed clothes, the combed hair, the proper speech, and the perfect manners. "I see a piano teacher and a nice lady."

"I'm a bank robber!" Mrs. Fornoff blurted out.

Sam couldn't have been more confused and said nothing in response to this absurd confession.

"What, do I not look like a bank robber?"

Again, Sam didn't respond.

Then Mrs. Fornoff settled in and began a shockingly sordid tale. "I was born in 1860, one year before the Civil War. I was the oldest child. I lived with my parents in a warm little home on Baker Street. We weren't rich, but we were certainly not poor. We always had wood to burn in the stove, and the house constantly smelled of my mother's delicious cooking. By the time I was eight years old, I had three little brothers. By age ten, my mother had another baby, and she told me she needed my help taking care of it, and she taught me to change diapers. I didn't mind so much at first, but over the years she kept on having babies, and I kept on changing diapers. Finally, I grew weary of all the babies and all the diapers. By the time I was fifteen, I must have changed a thousand of them. So I told my mother I wouldn't do it anymore."

"Was your mother mean to you?" Sam interjected.

"She was sweet as pecan pie. She was loving and kind and cheerful, and she filled our home with her radiance. When I told her I wouldn't change any more diapers, she cupped my cheeks tenderly in her hands, like she used to do when I was a little girl, then said very plainly, 'Yes, dear, you will change diapers. Everyone in this house has chores and responsibilities. And you will do your part like everyone else.'

"But there was something wrong with me. I couldn't see what kind of charmed family life I had. So I ran off. I ran off with a boy named Frank. I was fifteen and he was eighteen. He told me we would get married, but of course we never did. Instead, we went to live with his older brother Bill in another town. There were two other men as well, Bib and Hank. I would soon find out that Bill, Bib, and Hank were outlaws. They robbed stagecoaches and banks. Naturally, Frank and I fell in with them. And it became my job to hold the horses outside the bank to ensure a clean getaway—just like in the cowboy pictures. I wore men's clothes and pulled a cowboy hat down over my hair and covered my face with a neckerchief. And I held the horses while they went into the bank." She paused her story and asked Sam, "Can you see me? With the clothes and the hat? And the neckerchief? Holding the horses?"

Sam shook her head back and forth.

"You'd think people who rob banks would have a lot of money, wouldn't you? But that's not how it worked out. We'd rob a bank, then spend all the money. Or the men would lose it all gambling. Then we'd rob another bank and do it all over again. We were constantly on the move, and we stayed in terrible places—dark, cold, dirty places. All the men did was drink and gamble. As you can imagine, they were no gentlemen, and they treated me poorly, even Frank. And there was nothing for me to do all day. I was bored and lonely and miserable.

"Then one day we went into a saloon. I had my hat pulled down extra low so no one could see that I was a young girl. The place was filthy and dingy and stinking of cigar smoke and unwashed cowboys. As I sat in the corner in silent misery, waiting for the men to lose all the money so we could leave, something preposterous happened.

"Bib, who was the least gentlemanly of them all, sat down at the piano and began to play. We were all shocked. None of us could possibly countenance the notion that a brute like Bib could play the piano; he was barely housebroken. But he played this beautiful piece of music, which I later learned was a composition by the great Frederic Chopin. Eventually, the whole room was staring at him, paralyzed with wonder. For a brief moment, that infernal pit was transformed into a stately music hall. Something happened to me that I could not explain then and I cannot explain now. Perhaps it was not unlike the moment when you first heard Natalia play. But I was a different girl than I was when I walked in the door.

"When Bib was finished, everyone in the room was still staring at him. His little musical stunt was so misplaced. So conspicuous. So outrageous. No one clapped or even moved. Bib started laughing like a hyena, then spit chewing tobacco on the floor and resumed his place at the poker table.

"I was stunned. I could not help but ask myself, *Why does someone who can play like that live like this*? And then the even more searching and obvious question occurred to me: *Why am I living like this, in this darkness, devoid of beautiful things?*"

She suspended her story briefly, as if she was reconsidering the question some fifty years later. "When we robbed the next bank, I was outside with the horses as usual when I heard a gunshot. Bib had shot the bank teller. I was horrified and sick to my stomach. I couldn't believe I had allowed myself to be a part of it. I was rattled and tortured with guilt. So that night when the men were drunk and asleep, I sneaked off and ran away, determined to go home. That is, if my mother would take me back. But even if she wouldn't, I'd go somewhere else. I had to get out of there.

"When I got to my home, I walked up to the front door and didn't know if I was a stranger who should knock, or if I still had any right to just walk in. I was so ashamed and embarrassed and felt so foolish and ungrateful. I had been so wrong, and I had done so many wrong things. I had betrayed my parents and surely caused them great suffering, as they were left wondering what had happened to me. I didn't imagine they could ever forgive me. And it took all of my courage to knock on that door. When it opened, my mother appeared in the doorway holding a broom. Without time for a thought or a word, she dropped the broom and leaped at my neck. She wrapped her arms around me and burst into tears. She held me there in front of the door for the longest time, saying nothing. I can still feel her quivering body as she sobbed and sobbed. In an instant, the guilt crushing my soul melted away in her embrace. And my gracious mother gave me the single greatest gift of my entire life."

Mrs. Fornoff pulled a clean white hanky from her pocket and dabbed the corner of each eye. "I told her I would change diapers and do whatever she asked of me. Then I said, 'I know I have no right, but can I ask you for one thing?' She said, 'Of course, dear, what is it?' I said, 'Can you get me a piano?' She said, 'Sweetheart, I'll get you a whole orchestra.' So I changed diapers and studied the piano. It took me ten years to become an accomplished pianist. But I owe it all to my saintly mother. Eventually, I married Mr. Fornoff, who as you know was also a musician, and we became deliriously happy making music together. Ultimately, despite my adolescent aversion to diapers, I grew up and wanted children of my own. But after several years, we had yet to be blessed with a child. We kept waiting and waiting and hoping and praying, but those children never came."

She paused again, having offered up the fading penultimate lines of her little drama, and looked deep into Sam's eyes, preparing her for the finale. "What a tangled irony. The teenage girl who hated changing diapers grew into a woman who wanted to do nothing more than that. So I dedicated my life to bringing beauty into the world through my playing and through teaching music to the children of other people—like you, young Samantha."

Sam was honored to be her confidante but felt immediately conflicted. She had grown fond of Mrs. Fornoff despite her rather formal demeanor and use of big words. She felt a connection with her after hearing her story. And her charming habit of referring to her as "dear" was irresistible. Sam yearned to let her in, to confide in her. But for Sam and Jo, people like Mrs. Fornoff, the very people who showed affection and concern, were the most dangerous of all.

On the other side of the store, Jo opened the bulky case and removed her cello. Tuning was part of each lesson. It is critical that all string instrument players master the skill, and Mr. Fornoff always let Jo struggle with it before assisting her. She bowed each of the four strings one at a time, listening intently, tightening and loosening, and listening some more. When she had done her best, the venerable ear of Mr. Fornoff guided the final stages, and then she was ready to play.

Jo was always thrilled to play her new pieces for Mr. Fornoff. His response to her playing followed a strict dichotomy. He either said "bravo" or "try again." He always said "try again" at first, followed by corrective suggestions. She lived or died by his approval. When she finally achieved mastery of a piece, with that single word—*bravo*—he made her feel like the guest soloist playing a Bach concerto with the Metropolitan Philharmonic.

But this day, Jo was determined to get the *bravo* on the first pass. She took her place on the seat behind her cello and prepared to play.

"Proceed," came the familiar invitation from Mr. Fornoff.

Jo's anticipation was expressed as a covert smile. Then she began. A simple beginner's piece. Regardless, she played it as perfectly as a beginner could play it. Mr. Fornoff listened studiously. When she finished playing, he remained expressionless and did not move. Jo awaited the verdict with bated breath. His response was usually immediate, but this time there was a long delay. It was killing her.

Finally, instead of delivering his decision, and with no other words, he took the instrument from Jo and placed it back in the case. Jo didn't know what was happening. Perhaps she had done so poorly that he had given up on her and was dismissing her. She was starting to tread water when he stepped over to the Montagnana, cradled the neck in his left hand, and motioned her over with his right, still not speaking.

Jo was stunned. Since the first day when Mr. Fornoff let her play the D note, he had not offered to let her play his treasured cello. She had guessed correctly that in all his years of teaching, he had never let any student play it. His less-accomplished students were undeserving, and his advanced students all had their own high-quality instruments—albeit none as high quality as his. Nevertheless, for reasons Jo had no hope of understanding, and with a look of inevitability on his face, he turned over his vaunted cello.

Jo sat behind the sacred instrument, in the spotlight of the cellist's amphitheater, and began to play. Her meager status as a rank novice notwithstanding, she could immediately hear the difference in tone and feel the character in her fingertips. It reacted like a racehorse to her subtle commands. She had never felt anything of such substance and wondered how something so old could be so lively. As she played, she caught a glimpse of Mr. Fornoff's face. His eyes were closed, and he seemed to be in a trance. As the music of the last note trailed off, Jo was consumed with exhilaration. She wasn't sure what Mr. Fornoff had thought of it, but it was a life-changing moment for her. She looked up at him and waited.

"Bravo!"

And there it was. Validation. The kind of adult validation that can only come from a master. Jo flushed all over until she thought she might have hives on the back of her neck. She tried to conceal her joy. After all, outwardly it was a minor musical victory. But she knew she would never be the same.

"Jo," Mr. Fornoff began in the style of a grand announcement, "from now on you will play the Montagnana at your lessons."

"Yes, sir," she said obediently, accepting his highest praise.

As Sam and Jo left the music store, Mr. and Mrs. Fornoff stood at the front door and watched them walk down the street, Jo lugging her cello. "Who are those remarkable girls?" Mr. Fornoff said with wonder.

"I don't know," she replied wryly. "I only know you have more pie to eat."

Chapter 11

Mr. Markel

The summer was half over. Jo's school of literacy had a star pupil. Sam was making unexpected strides in her studies. She had blown through all of the first-grade materials and was deep into the second grade. The girls spent many afternoons in the library finding new books of all descriptions. Jo made Sam write pages and pages of letters and words, then insisted she compose her own lines. She was tough.

As had been their practice since early in the summer, they met Howard on Thursdays for shooting practice. Although neither of them was at much risk of winning a marksmanship contest, they had acquired rudimentary proficiency with the .38, as well as the .22 and the 20 gauge. Aside from the boys at the ball field—none of whom made friendly overtures outside of the serious business of baseball—Howard was their only child friend. They had not had a chance to meet and befriend other girls, and they were wary to do so since they could not bring friends to the house.

The girls continued their immersion in music and baseball. Also, on every occasion, they took to finding sundry knickknacks and decorations for the house. Some afternoons they loafed around the drug store reading comic books, licking ice cream cones, and swilling root beer. As always, they painted with Mrs. Jones.

It was after one of her stimulating art sessions and her delicious lunches that the girls were walking home when a black Model T Ford followed behind them. The car had been parked across the street for some time before they left the house. They chatted merrily as they walked, their batteries at full charge after spending a couple of hours in the invigorating grace of Mrs. Jones. The car stayed discreetly distant. As they approached the corner and turned left across the intersection, the car slowly pulled off to the curb on the right and waited until they were most of the way down the block before proceeding. This went on block after block until the girls reached their destination, their second summer home: the public library. The Model T pulled into a parking lot across the street and down the way and came to rest in a position with the windshield facing the broad cement steps leading to the front door. The engine went silent, and the driver remained inside.

The librarian, Mrs. Baxter, was on a first-name basis with the girls and no longer waited for them to request help. As soon as they passed by the personal fortress behind which she was stationed, and from which she sprang to quell rumblings, she arose and followed them into the stacks. Her knowledge of children's books was as vast as it was indispensable.

"Where can I take you today, ladies?" she said with the enthusiasm of a tour guide. "Did you like *My Mother's House*?" she asked Sam. And what about *Goose Livers*? Were they too advanced for you?"

"Not at all," Jo barged in. "She blazed through them like a champ."

"She is a champ," Mrs. Baxter said and gave Sam a wink. "She's made unbelievable progress this summer." Then she turned to Jo with a solid look. "But make no mistake about it, you are also a champ.

Teaching your friend to read. I can't tell you how much I admire that. And two such erudite children I have never seen."

Jo had a system. First, she would find, usually with Mrs. Baxter's help, a suitable storybook for Sam. Then she would make Sam read it to herself and try to sound out all the words. After checking out the book, and once at home, Sam would read it out loud, and Jo would coach her as needed.

For herself, Jo would find a challenging book and then take a dictionary to her table and keep it at the ready. She loved her mysteries, of course, but she was also fascinated with famous people. She had read the life stories of a dozen of the Founding Fathers as well as Abraham Lincoln and Thomas Edison. She looked for biographies of women and had read about Abigail Adams, Martha Washington, Clara Barton, and Florence Nightingale. Mrs. Baxter had an uncanny knack for selecting books at her reading level and within her scope of interest. Jo wondered if she had possibly read every book in the library. That day, she recommended Madame Curie.

Before leaving, Jo found a dictionary and flipped the pages until she landed on *erudite*: "Er-u-dite: having or showing great knowledge or learning." She smiled proudly.

Two hours later, as they skipped down the cement steps with their new books in hand, the black Model T was still there, the afternoon sun flashing off the windshield. As they turned down the street and headed for home, the car casually rolled from the parking lot and followed. When they reached the house and went inside, the car stopped short of entering the dead-end street, like an animal instinctively wary of entering a baited cage. It stayed there until dark.

By eight o'clock the next morning, the car was back in place. At eight fifteen, Sam and Jo were on their way to clean the music store. They walked past the parked car, unaware it had been stalking them for a day. The driver had ducked down inside the car, out of sight. Once the girls had gone by, the driver popped up and watched them through the rearview mirror until they disappeared. Then he got out of the car and strolled toward the house.

He was in his thirties, well-dressed in a gray suit with matching fedora and shined shoes. He studied the neighborhood as he walked, but a casual observer would not have noticed because his searching glances were obscured by his dark glasses. As he approached the front door, he peered briefly into the window. Then he knocked and waited. No answer. He knocked again and waited some more. When nobody came, he tried the door, but it was locked. He looked about to see if the neighbors were watching, then he ambled around the house, pausing to look into each window. The back door to the kitchen was unlocked, and he went in. Fifteen minutes later he emerged from the house. He walked back to his car and drove off.

Sam and Jo busily set upon the store with brooms, dusters, and wet cloths. Soon, the place was immaculate, and Sam headed to her miniscule concert hall to try once again to please Mr. Beethoven on the piano. Jo hung around the cello amphitheater until Mr. Fornoff noticed her. The deal with the Fornoffs was to clean the store twice a week, Wednesday and Saturday, in return for a lesson on Saturday. On Wednesdays, Jo usually lingered while Sam practiced the piano so they could walk home together. But since Jo had received the esteemed honor of playing the Montagnana for her lessons, she decided to try something new.

Jo caught Mr. Fornoff as he passed by. "Good morning, Mr. Fornoff."

"Good morning, Jo."

"Nice day, isn't it?"

"Why, yes, it is. Delightful."

"I'm just waiting here while Sam practices her piano."

"The store sure looks fabulous. You girls do a great job with the cleaning."

"Oh, thank you, Mr. Fornoff. We're happy to do it." Then she smiled a lingering smile at him. "Yeah, I'm just waiting here . . . for Sam."

"Jo," Mr. Fornoff said leadingly, "I notice you are holding your cello books in your arms."

"Oh yeah, I guess I am." She smiled more brightly this time.

"Any particular reason why you brought your books with you? You don't have a lesson today."

"Um, I guess I'm not really sure," Jo said. "Maybe you could think of a reason?"

Although famously straight-laced and not known for his sense of humor, Mr. Fornoff was not without personality. Of course, he had a gooey if not inexplicable soft spot for her. "Jo," he said, feigning genesis of the idea, "since you are already here and have some time to kill while you wait for Sam, and since, serendipitously, you have your books with you, would you like to practice on the Montagnana?"

"I thought you'd never ask!" She giggled as she bolted for the music stand and placed her book, already opened to the page she had been holding with her thumb.

Mr. Fornoff smiled curtly and offered up a blunted throw of his hands into the air as he went about his business.

That afternoon, the man in the Model T parked it in front of a nondescript building on Eighth Avenue. The neighborhood straddled the transition between the commercial and the industrial sectors, but it was nice enough. The address on the brick building was prominently marked, but the entrance was generic, without other signage. He hustled from the car to the front door and barged through, taking the stairs two at a time to the second floor. Halfway down the hall, he swung open a door with his company name engraved on a small plaque: The Markel Agency. He nodded at the pleasant, middle-aged woman at the desk who was reading a ladies' magazine and drinking iced tea. The office was sparsely decorated, though orderly and comfortable. There were no identifiable personal items, such as family pictures, certificates, or credentials. A somewhat brawny desk telephone sat undisturbed.

"That creepy hotel manager called again," she said to the back of his head as he passed through a second doorway into his private office.

"Mr. Monson?"

"Yeah, him."

"Please don't refer to my clients as creepy," he said with mild despair, as the chances she would do it again were one hundred percent.

"I call 'em the way I see 'em."

"Mrs. Whitaker, I realize it was a long, *long* time ago, but didn't your mother ever teach you that if you can't say something nice—"

"Yes, she did, and *creepy* is the nicest thing I can say about that man."

Realizing his attempt at refining her tongue was futile, he shut his door and hurriedly scratched notes at his desk. She went back to her magazine.

Not long afterward, a tall brunette with brown eyes and a disarming smile came through the door and presented at the desk of Mrs. Whitaker. "Good afternoon. I'm Caroline Jones. I have an appointment to see Mr. Markel. Is he in?"

"Of course, Mrs. Jones. How delightful to meet you," Mrs. Whitaker said with a matching smile as she graciously rose to greet her. "You can go right in." She gestured toward the door.

"Are you sure he's not busy?"

"Honey, I'm the one who decides if he's busy," she said, taking her into confidence with a telling smirk.

At their initial meeting, Todd Markel, private investigator, had gone to see Mrs. Jones at her home. As she entered his office for the first time, she couldn't have known what to expect. On the walls hung prints by some of the great masters, along with other works of art she did not recognize. Classical music played from the phonograph. Mr. Markel sat at his tidy desk, studiously rifling his notes. The tree-style coat rack was adorned with his suit coat and fedora. His holstered iron dangled from the front hook by the shoulder strap.

He arose like a gentleman, smiled warmly, and turned off his music. "Please sit."

Mrs. Jones smiled back at him, but it never went away. It turned into a more-or-less uncontrolled and sloppy grin. "I'm so sorry, Mr. Markel," she said with a squelched chuckle. This whole thing is so foreign to me. And the purpose of your engagement must seem so piddling. I feel like a character in a cheap detective novel. Honestly! The unmarked building. The creaky stairs up to the second-floor office. The surly secretary."

She looked directly at him with wide eyes. "The quirky private eye, sleuthing the seedy underbelly of the city, then retreating to his unexpectedly cultured sanctum. If you just had a broken nose and a gravelly voice, like you'd been shot in the throat with a small caliber bullet, you'd be the whole cliché."

Todd Markel, only a few years older than Mrs. Jones, and without the low-riding fedora, the dark glasses, and the skulking, was not an unhandsome man. He had intelligent, searching eyes and spoke with aplomb. Solid in himself by nature and thick-skinned by profession, he could absorb a fun-loving punch. He smiled back at her and took the opportunity to spar a couple of rounds with the vivacious Caroline Jones, as virtually any man would.

"Todd 'Cliché' Markel at your service, ma'am," he said as he thumbed his nose off to the side and held it there while he lowered his register and tightened his throat. "It's always the same with you mugs!" he said facetiously in a raspy voice. "I solve the crimes, and you cops get all the credit."

Mrs. Jones chuckled again. His self-effacing humor was just what the situation needed. She sat back in her chair and set her bag on the floor. As the levity faded, she turned to the reason for her visit. "What did you find out?"

"Well, I found a couple of pretty nefarious characters, all right," he teased. "When they left your house, they went to the public library for two hours. They came out lugging a pile of books and went to a dead-end street on the edge of town: 210 Walnut. In the morning they left, and I went inside. And no, I didn't have to pick the lock with my special PI tools; the back door was unlocked. The house is small, old, and rundown, but certainly not the worst I've seen. Wash was hanging on the clothesline in back. The lights worked, water ran into the sink, and there was ice in the icebox."

"Was there any food?"

"Eggs, milk, cheese, bread, corn flakes, oatmeal, brown sugar, and a lot of empty root beer bottles," he said, reading from his notes. "The kitchen table was covered with papers filled with hand-written letters. And I don't mean correspondence. I mean pages of As and Bs. Lowercase letters, capital letters, print, and cursive. Like we used to do in grade school. There was a cello in the living room with music on the stand. The two bedrooms upstairs looked freshly painted. Both yellow. The walls were papered with, let's say, *budding* artwork. Their beds were smothered in stuffed animals, like the beds of all little girls. There were books all over the place, ranging from *Madame Curie* to *The Call of the Wild* and all the way down to second-grade readers. The closets were full of pretty nice clothes. All little-girl stuff. The only thing out of place was in the top drawer of the night table in one of the bedrooms. I found a Smith and Wesson Model 10 .38 Special. Just like that one." He pointed to his gun hanging on the coat rack. "Except it was tied up in a pillowcase, along with an opened box of bullets."

He paused and looked at Mrs. Jones, her brow furrowed. "It looked like a playhouse. I didn't see one thing indicative of an adult resident, man or woman—aside from the gun, of course. I think those two little girls are on their own. I'm not sure how that came to be, but there you have it."

"I was afraid of something like this. I knew Sam was an orphan and that she lived with Jo, but I hoped Jo had at least some kind of family looking after her. Although, based on some of the things she has said to me, my expectations were shaky. I tried to get it out of them, but it was like feeding feral dogs. They won't get close enough to take food from your hand; you have to throw it to them. No matter how desperate, the risk of getting too close is greater than the benefit of the food. If you insist they take it from your hand, eventually they run off. And I didn't want those girls to run off."

She lowered her somber gaze as a single tear glistened from the corner of her eye. "But if they are on their own, why would they be so secretive about it? Why wouldn't they tell me? I feel like I have a bond with them, and I get the distinct impression they have no other mature person in their lives more invested than I am. One day those two broke down and cried in my arms until they literally ran out of tears. When they paint, they urgently want to please me. I give them hugs, and they hug me back. They hug me hard, and I know they don't want to let go." She lost the fight with that tear, and it escaped down her cheek. "Why wouldn't they tell me?"

"I can't be certain. We both know you're not paying me enough for that. But let me take at least one wild stab at it. First of all, even though these are just little girls, they are incontrovertibly sophisticated. Somehow, they seem to have acquired singular control of an entire household. The place is neat and orderly beyond their years. They make their beds. They cook at least some food. They wash their own clothes. They lock the front door. It wouldn't surprise me if they know how to shoot that damned thirty-eight! One of them is so mature that she is teaching the other one to read. And the one learning to read is either so simple that she does it out of obedience, or she's so personally motivated that she is willing to take instruction from another eleven-year-old. Now which do you think it is?" He cocked his head to the side and showed her his palms. "One of them, if not both, plays the cello. How many children do you know who practice the cello, or any musical instrument, without badgering from their parents?"

"You're telling me they are smart and sophisticated girls, so why wouldn't they do the wise thing and confide in someone they trust who obviously has more resources, like me?"

"Well, Mrs. Jones, here's where I have the advantage. I have the orphan advantage. My brother and I lost our parents when I was ten years old. We were separated in foster care. He went to live with what can only be described as an award-winning family, and I went to live with the family from hell. Government studies suggest that about eighty-five percent of placed kids thrive in foster care. But I landed hopelessly in the fifteen percent who don't. And I can tell you this for sure: If Sam is an orphan, and she's not in an orphanage or foster care, it's because she also landed in the fifteen percent."

"It's just so tragic that this happens to kids," she said with concern bordering on anger. "It's tragic that it happened to you."

"Don't you worry about me," he assured. Then he leaned forward on the edge of his chair and placed his hands on the desk. "Now let's talk about you. I've been in your home, and I've met you on two occasions. Here's what I think. You stop me if I get it wrong." Then he took a windup like a pitcher and started in. "You were raised in a fine, upstanding, and loving family. Your mother, especially, was a constant example of compassion and goodwill. Your home is practically a shrine to her legacy. It's orderly, clean, and bright. It smells like family, and the warmth is enveloping. Even intoxicating is not too strong a word. Pictures of your babies are displayed like trophies. You adore your children and have no earthly understanding of parents who feel even remotely otherwise. You serve in the PTA, and you give free art lessons to orphans."

Then he sat back in his chair and put his hands in his lap. "How am I doing so far?"

Mrs. Jones was flat-footed. "Go on."

"So," he continued, "when the virtuous—no offense intended—Mrs. Jones finds out that two eleven-year-old girls are living on their own entirely without adult supervision, what is she going to do about that?" He paused and watched her consider. "What is her duty as a concerned citizen? What is her moral obligation? What *are* you going to do with this information, Mrs. Jones?"

He didn't let her answer, of course. "The bigger question is what do the two sophisticated little girls *think* you'd do?" Then he paused, like he expected an answer this time. But still she was silent.

"It's pretty simple, really," he resumed, "because there are only two answers. Number one, you take them into your home and care for them like your own and file for adoption, and they enjoy all the attendant blessings thereof and live happily ever after. Or number two, you inform social services and they go into foster care. He waved his finger at her cautiously. "But not together."

Mrs. Jones pulled a hanky from her bag and pressed it to her nose. "Dear God, what a hideous dilemma. How excruciating it must be for them to come to my home and make happy faces and paint cheerful bowls of fruit and baby animals and be charming and delightful young spirits. And hug me with both arms and thank me politely for lunch, then not say a damn thing about how they live. Not tell me that they are going home to an empty house. Not tell me that they have no one to kill spiders and check on scary noises in the night. Not tell me there is no one to pluck the bugs from their eyes. Those brave little girls."

Mr. Markel went on. "Now you may be honestly considering option number one. Perhaps that's why you went to the trouble of hiring me. But I can guarantee they're not considering it for the same reason that your feral dog won't take food from your hand. The perceived risk is too great. That's how children in their position get their hearts crushed. Besides, the evidence is against it. They've withheld the truth from you."

Mrs. Jones stared blankly at the wall behind Mr. Markel and wiped the tears from her cheek. "So are they just squatting in this abandoned old house?"

"I don't think so. The house is deeded to one Scarlet Jamison. The tax notice is sent to her at an address in Silverton, and the account is up to date. The power is also in her name, but the bill is paid directly from the bank each month. This woman must have some connection to Jo."

Mrs. Jones quickly composed herself. "Are you suggesting this woman, the owner of the house, allows two little girls to live there by themselves?"

"Of course not. I'm suggesting she doesn't know they live there by themselves. I can investigate further, if you wish."

"Please do, but be discreet. I don't want to stir things up for them."

"Discreet?" he repeated. "Me, be discreet?" Then he thumbed his nose off to the side as before and made with the gravelly voice. "Hey, lady, who do you think you're talking to?"

Chapter 12

Man in the Gray Chrysler

A week later, Sam and Jo were on their way home after art school and a visit to the library. The afternoon was hot and hazy with a hypnotic breeze that steered their thoughts inward. They walked with the leisure of summer kids and chatted about their new library selections. Jo was complacent and relaxed, secure in the familiarity of routine. She had walked the stretch of road in front of her house with Sam dozens of times and had come to enjoy the feeling of arriving home instead of dreading it as she had done with Steven. It didn't hurt that she was carrying a paper bag full of Mrs. Jones's delicious, flaky apple tortes. As they approached the house, they followed the well-worn path around the back to the kitchen door, as they kept the front door locked.

Once inside, Jo pumped cold water, and they took turns drinking from the spout as it poured into the sink, letting plenty of it splash onto their sweaty faces. Sam sat at the table and began to read from her new book, and Jo stepped toward the living room to play her cello. But as she reached the threshold between the two rooms, where she could see the back of the couch, she stopped cold.

On the near end of the couch next to the cello, she saw the back of a man's head. He didn't immediately turn around. Jo recoiled half a step backward. She didn't recognize the figure and didn't know what to do. She looked over at Sam for advice, but she was already engrossed in her reading. She could feel her heart stepping up toward her throat and was about to yell at Sam to run out the back door when a voice from the front of the strange head said cheerfully, "Come on in, girls. Let's talk some."

Sam instantly shot a startled glance at Jo. But Jo knew the voice.

"What are you doing here, Mr. Taylor? Why are you in my house?" Jo demanded sternly.

"Relax, little Jo," he said calmly, his deep, smooth voice at odds with his chinless face. "I just came back to talk to Steven."

Sam rushed in and shouldered up next to Jo in a show of solidarity. Both girls assumed defensive postures.

"Steven's not here," Jo said sharply. "I'm afraid you missed him again."

"Well, that's the thing," he said, sounding perplexed. "I seem to miss him every time."

"I'll tell him you stopped by," Jo said. "If he wants to talk to you, he'll come see you. But I doubt it."

"Now that's where you're wrong." He spoke with an unsettling confidence, looking straight at Jo. He wasn't smiling, and he wasn't frowning. He didn't look sinister or accusative. He just looked like he knew he was right, which he was. "That's where you're wrong, because Steven doesn't live here. Does he, Jo? You're not going to tell him anything, and he's not going to come see me. Why? Because he isn't here anymore."

"How do you know that?" she insisted.

"Because when I let myself in—and by the way, you two need to keep that back door locked; it isn't safe—I snooped around a little.

I found neither hide nor hair of Steven." Then he leaned forward and casually reached over to Jo's cello and thubbed the first string. "Do you play this thing, little Jo?"

"Yes, I do," she said smartly. "What's it to you?"

"No need for rancor, little Jo. We're just talking here." Then he leaned back into the couch cushion and continued. "No, sir. I couldn't find a trace of ole Steven. And then I got to thinking, *Well, if Steven's not here, who's taking care of little Jo?* I know your mother is in prison, and your grandmother moved off to Silverton years ago. I can't imagine your little friend here has any grownup people. So what's the deal? The only thing I can figure is that you two are all alone here." He looked at Jo again, like he wanted her to either confirm or deny. She gave him nothing to read on her face and held her answer.

"Yes, sir. I think the only people who live in this house are little girls." Then he tried Sam, an obvious ploy to see if her face would give anything away. But he was way out of luck there. Even a long, awkward pause didn't faze the hardened girl.

He continued as if they had caved. "So Steven is not here for whatever reason. Maybe he died of liver failure or got killed in a fight. Maybe he got drunk and fell off a bridge and drowned or something."

Jo had a flush of panic at the image of heaving Steven's body into the water, the heavy chains working their magic, pulling him down within seconds. She recovered from her momentary disconnect and held a poker face. There was no way he could know. He was just listing any possibility that could befall a drunk.

"Anyway, I should probably get the police and maybe social services to look into this situation."

The stone-faced, silent duo gave him nothing.

"But then we both know Steven never took care of you at all. If anything, you took care of him."

"Don't do that," Jo pleaded. "Don't bring the police or social services here."

Mr. Taylor broke into a smile. “I was hoping you’d say that.”

“What do you want from us, Mr. Taylor?” Sam blurted.

“Now there’s a girl who gets right to the point,” he said enthusiastically. “I like that, all business. I like that because I’m a businessman myself. But I have a problem with my business, and that’s where you two come in. You see, I’m in the moonshine business. And as you undoubtedly know, it’s technically illegal. Now, the two of you probably don’t fuss yourselves much with such concerns, but prohibition is the most consistently ignored and inconsistently enforced law in history. Up until recently, I have been the unmolested beneficiary of police indifference to that law. But now we have a new police chief, a man of exasperating piety on a tiresome crusade to save the imbibing masses from themselves. Do you understand what I mean?”

“You mean you can’t sell your hooch because of the police,” Jo stated succinctly.

“Smart girl, little Jo! You impress me at every step. I can see why you don’t need anyone to take care of you.”

“So what’s that got to do with us?” Sam cut in again.

“Well, I’ll tell you. As you also know, I sell my moonshine out of my grocery store. But now I can’t do that because the police are always watching. So I want to hire you two to deliver it for me.”

“What?” Jo said, outraged. “You want us to be bootleggers?”

“I want you to be my little grocery delivery girls,” he corrected, tongue-in-cheek. “You’ll each have your own bicycle with a big basket on front. The top of the basket will be filled with bread and sundry, lightweight items, and the bottom will be loaded with quarts of my finest corn liquor. The police will watch you come and go with complete disinterest as we conduct business as usual in broad daylight. After all, who would suspect two darling little girls of, as you put it yourself, bootlegging?”

“We can’t do that,” Jo said tersely. “If the police catch us, they’ll try to call our parents, then they’ll find out everything about us.”

"Here's how you have to look at it, little Jo—and I'm sure you can understand this—if you work for me, it's true the police might possibly find out all your secrets. But if you don't work for me, they most certainly will."

Jo looked at Sam in defeat, knowing they had no choice, and realizing once again, they lived in a world owned by adults. She felt powerless against that adult world and was struck by the sheer chance that Mr. Taylor would stumble onto their secret. Or at least part of their secret. The part about them living alone in the house, not the part about what happened to Steven.

"Don't look so glum, girls. I'm offering you paid positions. I'll give you twenty-five cents for every quart you deliver. Most days that will add up to two dollars and fifty cents for each of you. That's fifty bottles of root beer every day. Plus, you each get a bicycle out of the deal."

Two weeks later, Sam and Jo were deeply embroiled in the illicit liquor trade. Every day they rode their bikes to Mr. Taylor's grocery store and loaded the bottom of the baskets with quart bottles of moonshine wrapped individually in brown paper bags. Then they piled on loaves of bread and lightweight items such as toilet paper for cover. Mr. Taylor would give them a delivery list with addresses. At first, he helped them find the approximate location on a map of the city and plot out the best course. But it didn't take long for the girls to graduate to the navigator role. As they pedaled around town, teacher Jo insisted that Sam read all of the road signs out loud and learn the names of all the streets. It was a way of practicing reading while they worked. Before long, their knowledge of the city rivaled that of a veteran taxi cab driver.

Mr. Taylor gave them explicit instruction. He told them not to stop and talk to anyone except the customers, to never leave their bikes unattended, to always stick together, and never go inside a house or apartment.

Resenting Mr. Taylor for the way he strong-armed them into service became increasingly difficult for Jo as he paid them greater and greater sums of money. Not only did they collect the twenty-five-cent bounty from him on each bottle delivered—as he had promised—but they soon discovered unexpected benefits of the service industry when thirsty customers gave them tips. Still, Jo was loath to break the law and failed to see the humor when Sam teased her with the nickname Ole Bootlegger Jo. Sam, on the other hand, was more of an opportunist than a moralist. She appeared to enjoy romping around town on her new bike, delivering hooch, and working customers for tips.

Her approach was uniquely Sam. She would knock on the customer's door, then hold the bagged moonshine in one hand and her white hanky at the ready in the other. When the door opened, she conspicuously wiped the summer sweat from her face while taking deep breaths and exhaling theatrically, dragging out the show for full effect. She would then feign composure, hand over the brown paper bag, assume her most sincere expression, and say, "I'm Sam from Taylor's Grocery Store. I brought the *mayonnaise* you ordered!" The customers gobbled it up. Then she'd collect the juicy tip, graciously refuse the lemonade, and be on her way.

Mr. Taylor's distribution plan appeared to be inspired in design and flawless in execution. On a daily basis, Sam and Jo, on their spiffy, contraband-laden bikes, zoomed past policemen walking beats. They smiled and waved innocently at them. Properly motivated, they made timely, accurate, and discrete deliveries, which led to pleased customers and return business. It was a win-win-win. The little grocery girls soon became part of the neighborhood identity. By the end of July, between their piecework payments from Mr. Taylor and their tips, their combined take was almost sixty dollars—an amount much greater than the monthly annuity allowance from the bank. This was at a time when a Model T Ford could be purchased for three hundred dollars. Sam treated it like an unqualified windfall, but to Jo, it seemed a little too good to be true. And Jo was right.

Loading bicycle baskets with moonshine wasn't the only exploit going on in the back room of the grocery store. Since the police crackdown on local liquor sales, Taylor had branched out into other cities. He had begun to sell wholesale. But the bigger the business, the larger the volumes, and the greater the transport distances, the more risk was involved. The men willing to take those risks were of a certain breed. They were men looking for a shortcut and had little regard for anyone who might have to make up the balance. They were usually desperate men with a penchant for violence. And bootlegging was rarely their only shady venture. They traveled in packs—like wolves in suits—and answered to the alpha male.

One of these men drove a big, gray Chrysler. Sam and Jo saw him behind the store one day. Mr. Taylor was loading crates of moonshine into the open trunk. The driver stood watching but didn't help. His face was blank, and he didn't acknowledge the girls as they rode past on their bikes. He was tall and fat, with shoulders like a beam. His dark-colored business suit struggled to contain his mass. He wore his fedora oddly high on his forehead while squinting in the afternoon sun.

He was there often after that. Each time he ignored the girls, like a cat. A fat, indolent, indifferent cat. One day, after the girls rode their loaded bikes past his car, he groused at Taylor, "I don't like those kids hanging around here."

"What's it to you?" Taylor responded.

"I don't like people in my business."

"What business?"

"This business!"

"Those are my retail delivery girls. They have nothing to do with you."

"Yeah, and I want to keep it that way."

"Like I said, they have nothing to do with you."

"Yeah, well, they got eyes, don't they? And little mouths. Maybe big mouths."

"What are you worried about?"

"Let's just say I cut a distinctive figure. The kind of figure easily tagged in a lineup, and I don't want those kids talking to their mommies."

"Don't you worry about them. I can guarantee they won't talk to anyone. What do you think is in the baskets? More bread and toilet paper? They're my best little hooch hustlers. And I pay them enough to keep the deliveries rolling and their little mouths shut."

As Sam and Jo hit the street, they stood on the pedals to get some momentum.

"Jo, what's that big word on the back of that gray car?" Sam asked.

"Chrysler," she answered. "It's a Chrysler."

"What's a Chrysler?"

"Like a Chevrolet or a Ford, only it's a Chrysler."

"It sure is big."

They leveled off at a cruising speed and sat back down on their seats, the wind flagging Jo's long hair behind her.

"It has to be big. Did you see the size of that driver?"

"I saw him all right, and he gives me the creeps."

"I know what you mean. I think it's the way he ignores us."

"No kidding. He stands there like a stiff corpse and watches Taylor load the trunk."

"Next time we ride by the car, we should run over his foot and see if he's alive." Jo giggled as the girls veered right in tandem and headed up Washington Street.

A few days later, the girls were making a delivery on Cedar Street. Jo had just left the customer's porch. As she returned to Sam, guarding the bikes, she was staring down the street and across the other side. "Isn't that the Chrysler from Taylor's store?"

Jo studied the car briefly. "It's got to be. Look at the pumpkin head on that driver. It has to be that same dufus."

The car lumbered slowly down a pocked drive and disappeared around the back of a weathered, two-story brick building. A few loose shingles dangled from the roof. A first-story window was cracked, and the front entrance looked abandoned and was adorned with a disproportionately small neon sign that read, The Charlston. The modern sign clashed distastefully with the age and style of the building, like a shabby old man with a rose in his tattered lapel.

"Creepy guy, creepy place!" Jo said.

"You think that's where he takes the moonshine?" Sam asked.

"Maybe he lives there," Jo offered.

They were both right, but there was much more to find out.

Another week passed. The summer heat had peaked, meteorologically speaking, but that was of little comfort to the two delivery girls slogging through a muggy August on their bikes. The girls didn't mind it too much. After all, they could afford mitigating measures such as all the cold root beer they could drink and all the ice cream they could eat. Along with their delivery jobs, they continued to clean the music store and keep up with all their other summer activities—except for some of the drugstore loafing and street wandering, which was sacrificed to the cause of commerce. Jo made sure they still had time to read as Sam charged hell-bent through the second grade. Concerned about the security of their growing pile of cash, they each opened a savings account at the bank. It was all going quite swimmingly.

One warm evening after Jimmy and Scotty had gone to bed, Caroline Jones pulled two chilled bottles of beer from the icebox and opened them above the sink. She held them both in her left hand by the necks.

As she approached Mr. Jones in the living room, she grabbed him by the hand and separated him from his newspaper. "Come with me," she ordered softly. She led him through the front door and sat him in the porch swing. Handing him one of the cold beers, she took her place beside him and pushed gently at the floor with her foot, setting the swing in motion.

"Where did these come from?" he asked, looking surprised.

"Canada, I should suppose."

"Where did you get them?"

"That's a federal secret," she responded coyly.

A low cricket symphony played covertly in the background. A bright half-moon peered intermittently through a crack in the leaves of the Jones's tallest tree with the rhythm of a stuttering breeze. The fragrance of hyacinth, honeysuckle, and lavender wafted from Caroline's flower jungle. As Mr. Jones sipped his beer, she curled her hand around the inside of his bare arm, just above the elbow, and strummed her fingertips ever so lightly across his skin. Then she leaned in from the side, submissively nudging her head up against his neck, her soft, shimmering hair draping his shoulder. She kept the lulling motion of the swing going for dozens of cycles as they sat together in the moonlight without speaking. Then she made with the big brown eyes.

"My dear Caroline," he intoned in a manner presupposing a tender sentiment, "this all feels suspiciously of ambush."

"What a ghastly thing to say!" she shrieked facetiously as she pulled away and smiled wickedly. "Whatever do you mean?"

"You know exactly what I mean. You're the most beguiling creature since the Garden of Eden, and no one knows that better than you. Please give me some credit for knowing when I'm being worked. I may be powerless to resist it, we both know that, but at least I know it when I see it. So get on with it. Spit it out. What do you want? What coerced permission followed by my reluctant support do you seek from me this time? Or should I say, what charitable enterprise shall be the next object of your ravenous pursuit?"

"You make it all sound so cunning and sinful."

"Oh, it's cunning all right, sinfully cunning!"

"Fine," she admitted. "I want to talk to you about Sam and Jo."

"What about them?"

"I have learned some interesting things about them."

"Such as?"

"Such as, they are living alone, just the two of them. They have no adult to take care of them."

"Where do they live? On the streets?"

"No, it appears they live in a house but completely unsupervised."

"How can that be?"

"That's not quite clear, but the point is they have no parents."

"Did they tell you this?"

"Not exactly."

"Then how do you know?"

She didn't immediately respond to that question.

"How do you know, Caroline? Did you follow them home or something?"

"Of course not," she quickly replied. "I hired a private investigator."

"What?" he said incredulously. "You hired a private eye to tail two eleven-year-old girls?"

"I had to. Every time I tried to get information out of them, they clammed up like fugitives on the lam. I didn't want to scare them off."

"How much did that cost?"

"Not as much as you'd think. As you can imagine, it wasn't a big job. Turns out, Sam is an orphan like I thought. Jo has a mother, but she is in prison. Her father is unknown. The house is owned by her grandmother in Silverton."

"So why don't you write the grandmother?"

"Because Jo is a smart girl, and she could have easily done that herself. There must be some good reason why she's not communicating with her grandmother."

"So what are you getting at? Are you wanting to adopt these two girls?"

"I want to take care of them," she said solemnly.

"Caroline, you can't take in every stray that wanders through your life."

"These girls are beautiful and courageous. They're talented, resourceful, and sincere. They come over here every week to paint. And they chat and giggle and bring life to the house like only little girls can. They carry on like all other children—which is what they are, children—but then they go home by themselves with no one to greet them and smile at them and be happy to see them. No one to ask them about their day. No one to notice when they're unhappy and ask them what's wrong. No one to fix them a decent meal, braid their hair, and kiss them good night. No one to nag them about practicing their cello, making their bed, or doing their homework. No one to comfort them after a bad dream. They have none of those things, yet they come over here, made of steel, and act like all is well. When I met them, they were broken little girls. Broken! I shudder to imagine the misery and calamity they've endured.

"I know they love me. Because of the simple, pedestrian acts of kindness I've shown them, they practically worship me. I can see it in their eyes. But when I try to dig into their home life, they lock me out and insist on bearing that burden alone, courageously alone. It's remarkable. Think about it. You love someone, you trust them implicitly, and you want to take them into your confidence and bear your soul to them and share your onerous load, but you're shackled to a secret. You're able to walk to the precipice of embrace, only to stop resolutely short at the last possible step and go no farther."

"What do you mean by *take care of them*?"

"I've always wanted a girl; you know that. I want to invite them to live with us, and we'll take care of them as long as they need us. We'll worry about legal matters later. We'll worry about Jo's mother and her grandmother later. For now, we'll just love them. And they will learn to trust us."

It was just another day in the summer. Not another day like most kids would know, to be sure. Most kids didn't serve as their own parents. Most kids had actual parents for that role. And most kids didn't have dire secrets to protect. Indisputably, most kids were not running moonshine for a delicate-chinned blackmailer. But for Sam and Jo, it was just another day. By late afternoon, they were halfway into their deliveries. It was hot and sticky, and the girls made every effort to ride in the merciful shade of the trees that lined the streets and shrouded the sidewalks. They were flush with the cash collected from repeat customers who tipped generously on this particular route. As they rode their bikes from block to block, Sam read the names on the street signs and called them out, as per their usual. Jo corrected her pronunciation when they passed Cincinnati Street. They talked of the upcoming school year, the August heat, and how they might spend their delivery money. Sam said she was saving for a piano.

Midway through the block, they approached an alley on their right. Not less than half a dozen close calls with cars, pedestrians, and the broad side of at least one service truck had taught them caution in traversing such openings. They simultaneously braked and slowed in anticipation. But this time there was no car, no hapless pedestrian stumbling in front of their careening bicycles, and no service truck. This time two men in suits stepped intentionally in front of them, forcing them to stop. One of them was of average height and weight and looked to be in his mid-twenties. He was wearing a brown suit with a matching fedora cocked smartly over his right eye. He raised his hands in both a signal to stop as well as a gesture of self-protection against the oncoming vehicles. His expression was unmenacing, and he even smiled a little as Jo's front tire rolled right up to his feet.

But the other man they quickly recognized as the man in the big, gray Chrysler from Taylor's store. The tall, fat, cat man. As he stepped in front of Sam's bike, his mountainous frame filled the sidewalk. He was expressionless as always.

Sam looked at Jo with concern. "What is this?"

"I don't know!" she replied, equally concerned.

Before either of them could venture a guess, the men took hold of the handlebars of their bikes and steered them into the alley.

"Hey! What are you doing?" Jo yelled. "Let go of my bike!"

"Relax," the cat man said, finally speaking to the girls. "Taylor sent us. He has another job for you. Some 'special' deliveries."

The Chrysler was parked nose-first in the alley, with both front doors already open and the engine running. The far end of the alley was blocked by a tall, rusty fence.

"He never said anything to us," Jo countered.

"I guess it just came up," he replied.

Sam didn't like this at all. She didn't trust the creepy cat man. "Mr. Taylor didn't tell us about any other deliveries today," she confirmed. "But he did tell us not to stop and talk to anyone except the customers. He also told us not to go into any homes or apartments, or get in any cars."

"Yeah," Jo added. "We'll just ride our bikes back to the store and ask him what he wants."

"He seemed to be in a big hurry," the cat man said. "He told us to bring you both back in the car."

Sam looked up at the behemoth of a man, his lumpy figure literally blocking out the sun and casting a broad shadow on the wall of the building, complete with a shaded image of his hat stretched tightly over his expansive head.

His affect was flat, his eyes vacant, and his speech devoid of human warmth.

"We're not getting in that car," Jo stated unequivocally.

But she was about to lose control of the situation.

All at once, the cat man grabbed Sam by the arm with one hand and covered her mouth with the other. He lifted her free of her bike and let it crash to the ground. The other man grabbed Jo and did the same. Both girls were picked up, shuffled to the car, and stuffed into the front seat. The cat man wedged himself behind the steering wheel as the other one climbed in the passenger side and slammed the door shut, trapping the two girls between them.

As the cat man backed the car slowly out of the alley and into the street, Sam, pressed tightly against his right side, could feel hot, disgusting sweat coming through his suit and smell his nauseating body odor and heavy alcohol breath. With the windows up, the car was stifling from the afternoon heat.

"Where are we going?" Jo demanded.

"It's time for you to shut up, little girl!" he barked.

As the car gained speed and the alley became a speck in the distance, the cat man spoke again. "We're going to roll down the windows now, and if either one of you scream, my associate here is going to break your skinny arm."

It was obvious to Sam that they were not going to Taylor's store. It was also apparent that they were unlikely to get any more information from their inarticulate captors. Sam could see more fury than fear on Jo's face. "At least with the windows open we won't suffocate from the smell of filthy man sweat and alcohol breath!"

The cat man ignored her, and the other one actually grinned at her outburst but said nothing. Sam, on the other hand, had more experience with evil characters, and she shot Jo a disapproving glare. She knew the whole thing could descend into violence at any time with or without provocation, and it would serve no purpose to antagonize them. She knew the best thing to do was to keep their cool.

No one spoke as several familiar blocks of the placid city passed by. Sam watched pedestrians and people in cars go merrily on their way. The same way the world had always ignored her plight—oblivious and unconcerned.

The cat man spoke again. "You two are going to switch cars and take a ride with another of my associates. You're going to get out of this car and get into that car. I don't have to tell you what happens if you scream or make a fuss, do I?"

"There they are," the man in the brown suit said. "Pull over."

As the car came to a stop and the doors began to open, Jo turned to Sam. "This might be the time to hit another line drive to Billy Rose."

The cat man pulled Sam from the car on the driver's side by her arm, and the other one pulled Jo out of the passenger side in a like manner—both of them maintaining a firm grip on the girl's arms. The location of the transfer was a quiet, rundown residential neighborhood. The blasting afternoon sun had driven the residents into the shade, so the area on the street was abandoned and unobserved. There were no mailmen, no dog walkers, no kids playing, and no cars passing by.

As the beleaguered girls and their well-affixed tormentors took a few steps toward the transfer car, Jo calmly said, "Hit it, Sam."

Simultaneously, Jo stepped in front of the man in the brown suit and Sam stepped in front of the cat man. Both girls kicked as high and as hard as they could, striking both men squarely in the groin. The man in the brown suit dropped to his knees as his grip on Jo's upper arm slid down to her wrist. She struggled to pull herself free as he covered his groin with his left hand and let out a humph and a moan.

The cat man bent hard at the waist and made a similar deflating groan. His primordial reflex to protect his groin forced him to give up his grip on Sam's arm, if only for a split second, and she was free.

The man in the brown suit, still on his knees and still clinging to Jo's wrist, did exactly what Billy Rose had done in response to the same treatment. He began to barf. Jo struggled to leverage her wrist away, but he held it fast, despite his retching.

In the midst of this fight for her life, she screamed out to Sam, "Run, Sam! Run!"

Sam bolted from the outstretched hand of the reaching and groaning cat man and ran toward a rickety wood fence surrounding a house. The cat man straightened partially and charged off in pursuit. She ran parallel to the fence and into a backyard. As she rounded the corner of the house, she realized the fence enclosed the premises and feared there was no way out. She glanced back and saw the lumbering cat man closing in. The dilapidated fence was too tall to scale, and it looked like she was out of options. That's when she saw the missing slats. In the middle of the far side of the yard, two six-inch slats were broken out of the fence just above ground level. She lasered in on the target and hit the hole at full speed, turning her shoulders vertical and sliding through like a key. The cat man dove on his face, stabbing his arm through the hole up to the shoulder. But that's where it stopped. His fingertips just missing the disappearing heel of Sam's shoe.

In the meantime, the man in the brown suit had finally stopped barfing and raised his head. Still unable to break free, Jo leveled another kick at him. This time directly in the face, snapping his head back, breaking his nose, and releasing torrents of blood. Wobbly and stunned, he held her wrist until he was able to twist it behind her back and incapacitate the kicking.

The cat man, unable to reach Sam through the hole in the fence, too massive to climb over it, and too ponderous to go around it, returned without her. He found the man in the brown suit barely standing, bent over with one hand holding Jo, the other still covering his groin, his brow sweating, his eyes watering, his nose bleeding profusely, his mouth drooling, and his lips spackled with barf.

"What the hell happened to you?" the cat man demanded.

"Just take this little hellcat before I kill her!" he said through bloody slobber and barf chunks.

By then the two associates in the transfer car had gathered to help corral the girls. "The other one got away!" the cat man said frantically. "You guys start combing the neighborhood. We gotta find that kid!"

The kidnapper's plan for a seamless and discreet transfer had been obliterated by the girls. An oil spill would have been a lesser disaster. Not only did they produce a live crime scene in broad daylight in the middle of the street, but they had lost Sam.

Leaving the rickety fence behind her, Sam darted through the block and into the back of the adjacent yard. Her years running from railroad agents and municipal police had trained her for this moment. The principles were the same. Get as far away as possible as fast as possible. Stay off the sidewalks and streets. Hide and observe. Find an ally if possible.

It took Sam three hours to make her way home. She stopped for half an hour to survey the house from a distance to be sure nobody was coming or going. Finally, she went inside and took a long drag from the water spout. She was sweaty and exhausted. Tense, anguished, and frightened. Without Jo, the house felt like a tomb.

She sat at the kitchen table to rest and try to get her bearings, to come to terms with the harsh reality of the day's devastating events. She was alone again, and she had to recalibrate, reconfigure. She had lived her life by the seat of her pants, and she was good at it. She was fast on her feet, both figuratively and literally, and that quality had been her steady life-preserving servant. It had, in fact, risen to the occasion once again on this very day to champion her escape from the clutches of her kidnappers. But now, her safety secured, her immediate crisis passed, she needed a different skill set. She needed a methodical, deliberate, and dispassionate appraisal. She needed a sound conclusion.

As she sat at the table surrounded by her reading books and Jo-prescribed homework papers, she realized Jo had taught her every single thing on every single page—every letter, every word. She recalled something Jo had said to her on the first day of her reading tutorial, *If you want answers, you have to ask questions.*

Yes, that's it, she thought, *If I want answers, I have to ask questions.* Then she spoke the words out loud, "If I want answers, I have to ask questions." Then she said it again, for stability, "If I want answers, I have to ask questions."

Sam began to ask herself every question she could think of relating to her gut-wrenching quandary. "Who are those men? Why did they kidnap us? What do they want from us? Where were they taking us? Why did they want us to get into the second car? Is the man in the gray Chrysler in charge? Did Mr. Taylor really send for us? Is he involved in the kidnapping? Who else could have known where we were? Mr. Taylor knows where we live, but do the kidnappers? Would he tell them? What do I know that they don't know that could help me?"

Glaringly absent from her litany of self-posed questions was, *Should I go to the police?* But that thought never even occurred to Sam. A common-sense assessment of the situation would surely reveal that Jo was in grave danger. Surely Sam was wise enough to know that, and to know she needed help from the police. Even if that ultimately led to a disruption of their living arrangement, Jo had to be saved from those criminals at all costs. Surely Sam knew that. But Sam didn't so much have common sense as she did street sense. The police had never been her friends. They had never helped her in any way. In fact, they had been a source of constant anxiety and vexation. She had spent the last two years adroitly but laboriously dodging them. She was a slave to her history, as all people are to some extent. So there would be no police.

Instead, she did what Jo would have done; she formulated a plan. Meticulously, patiently, and with precocious forethought, she formulated a plan to recover her friend. She started by drinking more water, eating some cornflakes with milk, and using the bathroom. She changed her appearance by donning some dark play clothes and recalling the service of her trusty newsboy cap—under which she compacted her now much longer hair. Then she pulled from the closet one of the handbags—the one with the long shoulder strap—given to them by Mrs. Jones. Inside, she placed some cash.

She went to the drawer of the nightstand by her bed, took the revolver from the pillowcase, loaded all six cylinders, set the safety, tucked it into the handbag, and snapped the clasp. She slung the bag diagonally over her right shoulder, locked the back door, put the key in her pocket, and set out to rescue her friend.

It was nearly dark as she reached Fifth and Main. She hailed a taxi as she had seen other people do at that intersection. The driver asked to see her money in advance. When she showed him the cash, he asked, "Where to, miss?"

"Cedar Street."

Sam knew it would take too long to get to Cedar Street without her bike. It was late, and she had already endured a taxing day. Besides, she couldn't risk being seen on the streets. The cost of the fare would be worth it.

When the taxi turned onto Cedar Street, the driver asked for the address.

"I don't know the exact address," Sam said. "But I'll tell you when I see it."

He kept driving, occasionally glancing at her through the rearview mirror. The street looked vastly different at night. Familiar landmarks snuck up on her and faded obscurely into the dark, leaving her uncertain where she was. *Okay, there's that old tree with the broken branch*, she thought. *And there's that thing that looks like a tombstone in the front yard of that house.* Sam felt like she was getting close, and her cornflakes began to rumble. As the taxi made its way up the mixed commercial and residential street, she recognized the home of one of her deliveries. Now she was certain. The driver glanced back at her again but kept going. She leaned on the front edge of the seat for a better vantage point, eliminating buildings one at a time.

And then she saw it. On the right, half a block ahead, was the rundown hotel where they had seen the man in the big gray Chrysler drive around back. Carefully studying the building through the side window of the taxi as they passed by, she said nothing to the driver. If it was creepy by day, it was positively macabre by night. The garish neon sign depicting "The Charlston" above the otherwise dark front entrance was such a deep red color and so disproportionately tiny against the body of the building that it looked like the wound of an ice pick. It gave Sam a chill. There were no cars or foot traffic in front, and the drive along the side dead-ended into the darkness. No activity of any kind was evident in or around the moribund structure. It just languished there in the night, its face absorbing the radiating heat of the sidewalk, foreboding and forlorn. Nevertheless, Sam surmised that Jo must be inside.

At the next corner, Sam paid the driver and got out of the taxi. She quickly ducked into the soupy shadow of a lilac bush and waited until the taxi was gone and she could see no other headlights. The darkness had long since become her silent companion, if not her intermittent friend. Where others imagined countless lairs of lurking boogiemen, she saw opportunities for stealth. She backtracked haltingly toward her objective, stopping frequently to listen and observe. She saw no one, and she was sure no one could see her. She was comfortable with that. She had practically been weaned on the dark, and she recognized the advantage of being unseen.

But when she reached the drive on the side of the old hotel, something changed. Something felt ominous, evil. In the front, the blood-red neon sign stuck out against a backdrop of emptiness. She felt cold and hollow. She wasn't sure who would win this. The forsaken building issued a screechy warning to stay away, and she wondered if she should heed it.

On the side, by the drive, there was no light at all. She pressed the handbag up against her hip with her left hand and palmed the .38 inside as she stared into the blackness. There was nothing to do but seep gingerly into the murk. Unable to see her foot placement, she ran her hand along the rough exterior wall as she brailed her way through its length.

At the corner, she slowly peeked her left eye around the back. There was no area lamp, but the poorly hung back door permitted wedges of light to escape from inside. She could barely make out the wavering, spectral form of two cars. She was pretty sure one of them was the Chrysler. As she inched her way quietly toward the door, she was suddenly rocked by the unmistakable sound of metal garbage cans toppling like bowling pins, followed by the cymbal-like crashing of the lids hitting the ground. She instinctively crouched, with her back up against the wall, the prickly brick still warm from the evening sun. She couldn't make out the source of the commotion until the otherwise silent night was pierced by the unnerving screams of a cat fight just a few feet away. The howling, hissing, and tumbling sent Sam crouching even lower as she became certain that such a ruckus would raise someone from inside. But no one came, and the chilling, fiendish exchange stopped as suddenly as it had started, and Sam heard the two cats bolt away in opposite directions.

As she resumed her approach to the door, the smell of spilled garbage wafted over her. She kicked into something firm with her right foot and felt the solid object with her hands to augment her poor vision and discovered that it was a bicycle. It was her bicycle. And Jo's was next to it.

"*Jo must be here. Why else would the kidnappers bring our bikes to this place*?" she thought.

The moment of truth had arrived. Her instinct told her Jo was there. If she was to save her, she had to go inside that snake pit. But why should she? The Sam who Jo met on the day of the first baseball game wouldn't have done it. She would have listened to the screechy warning of the menacing old hotel and run for her own safety. She would have done the calculations based on her survival and no one else's. Paradoxically, she might have gone inside out of anger, not really caring if she came out or not. She recalled how desperate her life had become before Jo. How weary she was of fighting the daily fight for a survival of increasingly questionable value. It wasn't part of her plan to stop at this point for self-assessment; these thoughts overcame her like a mouse being pounced on by a cat. Ultimately, she arrived at where she was. She understood that she was going in, and she knew why. She was going in for Jo. Not because she needed Jo. Not because she needed Jo's house and Jo's food and Jo's company. But because Jo deserved to be saved.

Cracking the back door slightly, she peered inside. The long hallway, flanked by closed doors on either side, stretched to the far end where it gave way to a staircase. It was empty, decaying, and dimly lit. As she crept over the creaky threshold, she heard the distant, low rumbling of men's voices and smelled sour, old building and cigar smoke. She silently opened the first door on the left. The room was filled with easily recognized quart jars of moonshine. Behind the first door on the right was more contraband, cases of Jamaican rum, Mexican tequila, and Cuban wine. The second door on the left contained a roulette wheel and a poker table. The second door on the right was a regular hotel room with a saggy bed and some men's things cluttered about. Working her way down the hall, she was getting closer to the voices and could see cigar smoke billowing from the end room. The door was open about a foot. As she peeked in, she saw the back of the unmistakably enormous head of the man in the Chrysler and a partial side view of the man in the brown suit. They were playing poker with two or three other men around a big table topped with green felt. She flitted by the opening and scurried up the stairs. The second-floor hallway looked much the same as the first, except more advanced in its disrepair with a single, anemic light bulb in a loose fixture on the ceiling, flickering precariously between life and death.

Again, she worked her way from room to room. When she reached the middle room on the left, she glanced back toward the stairs. Nobody was coming. As she faced the fateful door of the middle room on the left, she could not have known what a shock lay on the other side. She could not have known that what she was about to learn would impact her life forever. And nothing could have prepared her or cushioned the blow. She had endured so many difficult things in her short life, but her difficulties were not over. Her resolve would be challenged and her faith shaken. But life requires that doors be opened, whatever the consequences.

She put her hand on the knob, but before she could turn it a voice from the other side yelled, "Don't touch me! Let me go! Get away from me!"

Sam instantly recognized Jo's voice. She had found her. She turned the knob and charged through the door, but she was abruptly set upon by confusion and disbelief. The cramped room was feebly lit by a small lamp with a filthy shade in the corner to her right. Next was the unmade bed with a soiled pillow hanging over the edge. Then a nightstand littered with various articles of makeup and lipstick. To the left was a secondhand armoire with the doors missing. Girls' clothing hung from the rod, mostly dresses. In the bottom were strappy shoes and petite handbags. But there were also some dolls and coloring books. The faded curtains were drawn over the only window.

On the far side of the room, in poor light—like someone standing a little too far from the campfire—was the figure of a man sitting in a stuffed chair, holding Jo on his lap. Sam studied him with disbelieving eyes. It didn't make any sense. It was like the sun running into the moon; these two should never be in the same place. How could it be?

But the longer she stared, the better her eyes adjusted to the light, and the more certain she became.

"Mr. Jones?" Sam whispered.

She flashed back to Mrs. Jones's kitchen. She could see him sitting at the table, handsome and charming, with Mrs. Jones doting over him and practically glowing with pride. It wasn't possible. And why was he holding Jo?

"Yes, it's him!" Jo blurted. "He's one of them!" She struggled to leap from his lap, but he held her fast. "Sam, what are you doing here?"

"I came to get you."

"You shouldn't have done that. Now they've got us both!"

"No," Mr. Jones said as he stood from the chair but kept his left arm wrapped firmly around Jo's chest. "It was foolish of you to come here, although very fortunate for me."

"What does this have to do with you, Mr. Jones? Why are you here?"

"I'm here because I owe these men money. And you're here because I couldn't pay them."

"I don't understand," Sam said.

"These men will pay a lot of money for little girls."

Sam tried to process his answer, but it was too unthinkable, too foreign, too insulting. Her mind instinctively searched for a less-vulgar and humiliating conclusion. Ultimately, the rabid and inevitable truth settled in on her. "So you sold us?"

"I had to. They threatened to hurt Caroline and the boys. I had to give them something."

"So you gave them us? Why us?"

"Because I know who you are. I know where you live. And I know that no one will come looking for you. Those are the kind of girls they want."

"What are you doing in this room with Jo?" Sam demanded.

"I came to the hotel to play poker. It wasn't until I arrived that I learned Jo was here. So I came up to check on her and see if she needed anything."

"He was trying to touch me!" Jo cried angrily. "He's one of those creeps who likes to touch girls."

"Well, it's all quite irrelevant at this point," Mr. Jones said dismissively. "Because tomorrow you're both going to a new city far away. And you won't be coming back."

Sam had heard enough. Despite reeling with mortification at the sobering reality, despite the pain of being betrayed and used again, and despite the screaming injustice, she knew she had to rise up and finish this. "Let her go, Mr. Jones," she demanded with all the conviction she could muster.

"Now, Sam, you know I can't do that."

Still struggling to free herself, Jo jerked her upper body forward while stomping wildly at his feet and clawing and biting at his arm. It was a valiant effort, and it almost worked, but he restrained her with both arms and warned her ominously about the biting. But after Jo's flailing distraction, when his gaze returned to Sam, he was staring into the bore of her .38 caliber revolver.

"Let her go, Mr. Jones," Sam repeated.

"Sam!" he scolded. "Put that thing down before someone gets hurt."

"Someone is going to get hurt unless you let her go."

"You don't know what you're doing. Those things are dangerous."

"I know exactly what I'm doing, Mr. Jones."

"I can't imagine where you got that thing, but surely you don't expect me to believe that you actually know how to shoot it!"

Sam, of course, didn't want to shoot Mr. Jones. But the negotiator in her knew that the best way to avoid shooting him was to convince him she would. "Mr. Jones, I know how to shoot this gun. This is a Smith and Wesson Model 10 .38 Special. It shoots a .38 caliber bullet at one thousand feet per second. It has a six-cylinder drum, and I loaded all of them. It is a double action, so I don't have to cock the hammer back before I shoot. But I find I'm a little more accurate if I do. I practice with it all the time, and I can hit a soup can at thirty feet four out of five times. I'm telling you to let her go."

"Sam, this is nonsense," he chided. "You are not going to shoot me. And I'll tell you three reasons why not. In the first place, you might hit your friend, and you're not going to take that risk. Secondly, there are four men downstairs who also have guns. If that thing goes off, they will come running, and then you'll have to shoot them too. And third, killing a soup can is not the same as killing a person. If you shoot me, I'll probably die. I don't think you have the stomach for that."

Jo watched as Sam held the gun steadily. "Don't do it, Sam," she pleaded. "I don't want you to have to do this for me. They haven't hurt me yet, and I'll figure out another way."

"Jo's right," Mr. Jones said. "Listen to her."

"Jo, I've seen bad men like these on the rails, and they will hurt you. They are planning to hurt you." She looked up at Mr. Jones. "I'm not going to let you hurt her. I don't care what it takes."

She cocked the hammer back and flipped the safety, then gripped the gun with both hands and extended her arms in firing range fashion with a slight bend at the elbows. With Jo standing in front of him, the only part of his body well-exposed was his face. As she lined up the center of his forehead with the top of the front sight and dropped it into the bottom of the rear sight, she said, "Hold your ears, Jo."

Then there was silence. The talking was over.

Mr. Jones had a look of dismissal on his face. After all, she was just a little girl. The whole thing was absurd. She couldn't possibly have the sand to actually shoot. She was bluffing. But as he stared directly into the dark hole formed by the bore of the gun, his expression changed slowly to one of uncertainty.

As Sam aimed the gun at his face, she was not trembling. Her hands were not shaking. She was not sweating. There had been no quivering in her voice. No elevation of pitch. No pressure in her speech. No mumbled or misspoken words. No pleading. No smacking of dry mouth or hard swallowing. She wasn't fidgeting; her feet were not moving. Her eyes were not opened particularly wide. Her jaw was not set nor her teeth clenched. She felt no remorse, no hesitation, and shockingly, no fear.

Jo grabbed her ears with both hands as she bowed her head as far down and to the left as she could under the restraint of his grip and screwed her eyes shut. Sam pressured the trigger with her index finger in micro increments in the manner of a marksman, letting the gun make the final timing decision.

"Wait, Sam!" Mr. Jones shouted. "I'll let her go! Just put the gun down."

Sam withdrew her arms in a show of reprieve, but only slightly. Jo dropped her hands from her ears, and Mr. Jones exhaled. He had unsealed his fate at the last possible instant. But for the built-in resistance in the trigger mechanism, he would already be dead. Jo stood straight and took a short gasp.

Mr. Jones, partially concealed behind Jo, slipped his right hand under the left lapel of his suit coat and wrapped his fingers carefully around his own revolver. In a single motion, he pivoted Jo out of the way with his left hand, drew the pistol with his right, and fired at Sam. *Pop!* The percussion of the blast in such a confined space and so close to Jo sent her ducking and reeling toward the corner, grabbing at her ears. Fire belched from the muzzle, flashing grisly shadows of the nightmarish scene on the dismal walls. The bullet tore through the undersleeve of Sam's shirt, nicked the outside of her right armpit, and lodged in the door behind her.

Sam did what she had been trained to do. In the many sessions with Howard at the shooting range, he had taught them the principles of self-defense. He had taught them the overriding principle of incapacitation of the assailant. Do whatever it takes, and keep doing it until the incapacitation of the assailant is assured. And that's what Sam did.

She fired at the center of mass. Mr. Jones flinched hard but raised the gun for a second shot. Sam fired again, hitting his hand and his gun at the same time. The bullet ricocheted into his chest as she fired a third shot, and his gun dropped to the floor. Mr. Jones crumpled facedown into the cheap rug.

Jo sprang from the corner, pulled her hands from her ears, and cut through the smoke of burnt gunpowder on her way to the door. "We have to get out of here!" she exclaimed as she pulled Sam into the hall.

"This way!" Sam said as she turned to the left and ran toward the back door. By the time the four poker players made it upstairs, weapons drawn, and discovered Mr. Jones, the girls had gone out the back door of the second floor and down the outside stairs.

Stumbling in the darkness at the bottom in front of the cars, Sam said, "Here, Jo, grab your bike!"

As they cleared the corner onto the side drive, Sam looked back to see if they were being followed. The closed first-story door was outlined in escaping light as before. The second-story door was dark until it opened slightly and the backlight from the hall made it visible. Sam fired a shot into the door, and it quickly slammed shut. She fired another shot into the first-story door, then tucked the gun into her handbag. Fueled by fear and adrenaline, the girls pedaled frantically into the night, unpursued.

When they reached the house, Sam unlocked the back door with the key in her pocket and they went in. She pulled the .38 from her handbag—there was one round left—and flipped on the light.

"Wait here, Jo." She ran through the living room, up the stairs, and into the bedrooms, flipping on the lights as she went. When she was satisfied the house was empty and secure, she returned to the kitchen, checking the lock on the front door as she passed by, then relocked the back door. In a reversal of roles, Sam was taking care of Jo. She was thinking of everything and exercising Jo-like thoroughness and caution. Sam was playing the hostess and the keeper.

It was four o'clock in the morning. It would have required a demon from hell to mastermind a more physically, emotionally, and mentally exhausting twelve-hour period of tribulation than the one they had just braved. Certainly, neither of them was in any condition to extrapolate the incalculable ramifications. But by all measures, it appeared to be over, and it was okay to decompress—like the air brakes of a bus. Within minutes, they were overcome with wobbly, mind-sludging fatigue and self-preserving shock. Neither of them could think of anything to say. Neither of them had the energy to cry. They simply helped each other up the stairs and collapsed on Sam's bed—because it was the closest.

After a long sleep, Jo woke to find Sam sobbing quietly on her side of the bed, facing away from her. "Sam," she said tenderly, "I'm so sorry you had to shoot Mr. Jones to save me."

Sam took a few labored snuffs and tried to speak, but had to wait for her throat to catch up. She wiped the tears from her face with her sleeve, swallowed the tightness, and said, "Do you remember my hobo English professor I talked about, the lovely one?"

"Yes, I remember you telling me."

"One day we were sitting around a campfire, and these two bums got in a fight over a chicken. They started hitting each other and rolling around on the ground. Then one of them came up with a rock in his hand and hit the other one in the head. The second one fell hard and didn't get up. I don't know if he ever got up. All over a chicken. The professor turned to me and said something I'll never forget. He said, 'Young Sam, I've read the history of the world, and I've lived a long time myself, and I can tell you this: Survival is a violent business.' I think he was right. I think you and me have proved that he was right. I did what I had to do, just like you did. Just like the man with the rock. And I'm not crying for Mr. Jones; I'm crying for Mrs. Jones. How am I ever going to tell her? What am I going to say to her? How will I ever face her again?"

"You're not going to tell her anything," Jo snapped. "We don't even know what happened. We don't know if he's alive or dead."

"He's dead, Jo! You didn't see him because you were turned away with your hands over your ears, but he took all three bullets to the chest, and I know he's dead."

"Maybe so, but we can't do anything until we know for sure."

"So what are we going to do?"

"The first thing we're going to do is take a bath and wash yesterday off of us. We're going to wash off those creepy men and that creepy old hotel. Then we're going to put on clean clothes and go to the library and get a newspaper."

They pumped and heated the water and filled the washtub. As Sam pulled her shirt off, she felt a searing pain in her right underarm and something wet pouring down her side. In the severity of the moment, she had been shot by Mr. Jones without feeling it. The wound had bled briefly but stopped on its own. The bleeding had resumed when the scab was torn off with her shirt. Luckily, the wound was superficial. After washing it, Jo applied a simple dressing and the bleeding stopped. A careful inspection of the shirt sleeve revealed the bullet hole. It was one of the shirts given to the girls by Mrs. Jones.

At the library, Jo anxiously scoured the morning paper. Each page filled her with apprehension and dread as she feverishly searched for the headline about the shooting, then disappointed her when it wasn't there. In front of the library, they sat on a cement bench beneath the leafy branches of a stately maple tree, posted there like a sentry more than a hundred years ago. On this particular day, Jo noticed the magnificence of the tree. She also saw the delicate architecture of the flowers, the fullness of the shrubs, and the green of the grass. A tiny elderly woman in a car of similar age drove by at no more than twenty miles per hour. A young woman pushed a baby carriage as a large, impatient dog on a leash dragged a small boy down the sidewalk in the bright sunshine. As she took in the beauty and the freedom of the neighborhood, she cringed at the memory of her recent confinement in that dreary, frightening hotel.

Sam stared at the ground. "What are we going to do? What am I going to say to her? How do I tell her I just killed her husband? What words do I use? How do I even say it?"

"Sam, that night on the bridge you said to me, 'We didn't ask for any of this.' Do you remember that?"

"Yes, I remember."

"Well, we didn't ask for any of this either," she said emphatically. "And you didn't do anything to hurt Mrs. Jones. Mr. Jones did that himself."

"I just feel like I should go to her."

"I want to go to her too," Jo said, softening her tone as her voice cracked ever so slightly. "I love her just like you do. And I'm confused just like you are. I don't know what to do either. So we're going to wait, get more information, and figure out how to do the best thing."

And so they waited until the next day. But the newspaper disappointed them again. They tried to carry on with their lives as best they could. They practiced their music and read their books. They went to the drugstore and took solace in the cool pleasures of ice cream. But it felt like going through hollow, meaningless motions. Even the ice cream wasn't as sweet. But they did not go back to Mr. Taylor's store.

On the third day, still nothing. The suspense was more than Sam could bear. Thinking of Mrs. Jones tortured her. Questions rolled through her head on an endless, maddening loop that she was powerless to interrupt. *Have the police found his body? Did Mrs. Jones know his fate, or did she only know he was missing? If she still didn't know, is it cruel of me not to tell her? Surely, it's cruel of me not to tell her, right? Should I just go to her house and confess? But how do I do that? Or should I run away? Should I run away back to the streets and the rails and never think of it again?*

The fourth day was Tuesday, art day. The girls had determined that if the morning paper remained silent on that day, they would go to their art lesson as usual, as if they were none the wiser, no matter how hard that would be.

But on that fourth day, Jo did not have to scramble through the paper because the headline was on the front page: "Mobster Slaying in Downtown Hotel." Jo whispered the article to Sam, "Early Saturday morning, police responded to shots fired at closed downtown hotel, The Charlston, at 423 Cedar Street, where they found the body of local engineer Daniel Jones. The 35-year-old father of two had been shot three times in the chest. It is believed to be a mobster shooting related to a gambling debt. Theodore 'Mountain' Scarpini, 29, and Phillip Anderson, 26, are wanted in connection with the murder. They are also wanted on suspicion of loan-sharking, bootlegging, gambling, prostitution, and child-trafficking." Jo stopped reading out loud and hurriedly read it to herself.

"You were right, Sam. He's dead," Jo said. "And he told us the truth about one thing. He did owe those men money, and the police think they killed him for it. But they don't think he was one of them. They don't think he was part of some gang. They don't think he was a criminal. They think he was just an average Joe with a gambling problem who couldn't pay his debt."

"Mrs. Jones deserves to know the truth," Sam said. "We have to tell her the truth."

And then Jo, with forethought and insight decades in advance of her age, said, "No, we can't do that. We can't do that to her. I know it would make you feel better to tell her. And it would make me feel better too. But we have to think of her. She just lost her husband, and that's terrible. And by now she knows he was killed because he was a gambler, and that's even more terrible. But just think of how bad she would feel if she found out he tried to touch me, that he shot you, and that he sold both of us."

It was time for their art lesson. They trudged slowly to the home of Mrs. Jones. It was the longest walk of Sam's storied life. Standing on the porch, ready to knock on the door, Jo said, "I'm not sure I can do this. I'm not sure I can watch her suffering, knowing what I know. It's too hard; it's too much!"

"I want to run away," Sam admitted.

"I want to run away too," Jo agreed.

But neither of them moved. They loved this woman and that was it. In the midst of her stadium of flowers, her well-attended yard, and her swept porch, they held hands and knocked.

When Mrs. Jones appeared, she looked slightly surprised to see them. Her eyes were swollen and bloodshot, her hair uncombed and her face pale and sunken. "Oh, girls," she exclaimed apologetically, "it's Tuesday."

"We saw the paper, Mrs. Jones," Jo said sadly.

With that announcement, the three were momentarily transfixed, staring at each other with the face of defeat that goes with news that's both hard and final. Then the natural tears came and the girls stepped over the threshold and fell into her arms. As the three of them sobbed together like they had done a couple of months before, Mrs. Jones could not have known that only half the tears were produced on her behalf. The rest were wrung from the conflict squeezing the girls like a vise. If she had only known the torment of their quandary, she could have applied her uniquely soothing brand of grace. But alas, she did not know. The girls would bear that burden themselves—silently, stoically, and indefinitely.

When the crying was over, Mrs. Jones invited them inside and gave them each a clean white hanky from one of several tall stacks placed throughout the house. As Sam wiped her eyes and nose, she felt a drop of blood from her wound run down her side. The scab had been torn off again when she hugged Mrs. Jones. She held her arm tightly against her ribcage to stop the bleeding but kept it to herself. Mrs. Jones served them lemonade. "In the past couple of days I've learned that lemonade is the drink of choice to counter the dry mouth of crying and grief," she said in a frail attempt to disperse the gloom. Then she fell into a stuffed chair opposite them, sipped her lemonade, and became serious again. "I need to tell you some things." She looked at them not like a pathetically bereaved woman whose entire world had just been shattered by the loss of her husband, but rather like they were the victims.

"First of all, I love you both. I know who you are and where you live and who you live with. I want to help you. And my husband wanted to help you. I had asked him if we could take you in and live with us. He was in favor of the idea. He was so sweet about it, and I was excited for you to get to know him better. He was such a good husband to me and a good father to the boys. They practically worshiped him. I'm sure you would have grown to love him too."

As she sang the praises of her dead husband, Sam squirmed with discomfort. The wetness under her arm seemed to be getting worse. She worried it would soak through her clothes and Mrs. Jones would notice. But she said nothing and didn't dare look at Jo.

"I was going to ask you today. But now, not only is he gone, along with my only source of income, but I have come to find out that he was a compulsive gambler. Despite all his virtues, he had this one terrible weakness. Apparently, he had debts all over town. He had taken out a loan on the house, sold all of our investments and property, and drained our bank account. I have nothing left. I'll have to sell the house and the car and all my paintings and move in with my sister with the boys until

I can get back on my feet. I want to help you, but I have nothing to offer." Then her voice failed and she could only whisper, "I'm so sorry!"

There was a long pause, and it was quiet except for the sound of Mrs. Jones sniffling her hanky. Sam looked at her with earnest eyes. Despite her heartfelt wishes to the contrary, she was forced to accept that the lovely and seemingly impeccable Mrs. Jones had a fatal flaw after all; she had married an evil man. An evil man of such insidious nature that he had concealed his true character behind the cloak of loving husband and doting father for twelve years. Nevertheless, she defended her. "That's not true, Mrs. Jones. It's not true that you have nothing to offer us. You just said you love us. No one in my whole life has ever said that to me."

"And we love you too," Jo proclaimed. "I hope we can still be friends."

"We'll always be friends, sweetheart."

"Can we still paint? At your sister's house?"

"Of course."

Chapter 13

Hannah

That night, as the girls prepared for bed, it was raining outside the open window of Sam's room. The cool, dense air was palpable to the fingertips and smelled of earth. It was a steady and benevolent storm, offering up life-giving water without the anger of thunder and lightning or the furious shouts of gusting wind.

In the wake of the most heart-rending and emotionally charged day of her life, Sam sought consolation in Jo's arms. She pulled Jo into bed with her, and they folded up together like a sealed envelope. With her cheek pressed tightly against Jo's, she could withstand the weight of the day's events. Thoughts of the cold rain percussing the roof overhead transformed the warm, dry bed into a fortress of safety and calm. In the darkness and rain, her still body betrayed the roiling inside. The ruminations. Reliving the encounter with Mrs. Jones, replaying the scenes, imagining repercussions, and reviewing the prequel. It was a lot for a young mind and young heart to assemble.

"It was a hard day," Sam whispered as a tear fell from her eye but rolled down Jo's cheek.

Jo opened her mouth to speak, but nothing came out.

Sam could feel the pitiful jerking of Jo's chest and hear her attempts to swallow.

It took Jo a long time to find her voice, and when she did, it came out in a squeak. "I wasn't ready for the kind of pain I saw in her eyes. I didn't know there was that much pain in the whole world. I didn't know anything could hurt like that."

"I know what you mean. It was like being punched in the gut with somebody else's pain. It was so hard."

Their mutual suffering melded into a confluence of tears that trickled across their conjoined cheeks as they softly wept. "So hard," Sam repeated in a whisper.

About a billion raindrops fell before either girl spoke again. But Sam heard every one of them. She was alive like she had never been before. Acutely aware of the flurry of emotions in her head. Her heart was broken for Mrs. Jones. Yet at the same time, her heart had never been so full. It felt like a deep massage to a screaming sore muscle. It hurt so much, but it felt so good. Mrs. Jones had told her that she loved her. And Sam believed her. "Surely, if Mrs. Jones were ever to find out the truth about her husband's death, she would understand and would forgive me."

Sam was grateful for that knowledge. She was feeling true gratitude for the first time in her life. She had appreciated many things before. She had appreciated all the back porch handouts by countless kind women. And she had thanked them all politely. But they were anonymous. And all the polite thank-yous were utilitarian. They were uttered mostly to increase the odds of getting a second handout. They were tools. But now, this was different. This sensation was transformative. It made her into somebody else. It gave her hope like never before. She was even grateful for the rain. One of the few simple pleasures in her life had been related to the rain. When she had spent a rainy night in a shed or a boxcar, she loved it when the rain stopped and the clouds rolled away just before dawn so that she could get up and walk out into the sunshine, the world fresh with raindrops. She hoped that's what would happen when she woke up in the morning. She hoped the sun would be shining and she could walk out into a glistening new day.

And then there was Jo. Her confidante and provider. Her roommate and teacher. Her little dark-haired savior. Surely, no two people had shared so much life in such a short time. Finding just the right words to tell Jo how she felt about her, well, she would need to read a lot more books for that. She squeezed Jo a little harder and listened to the soothing hum of the rain.

"Sam," Jo whispered, "what are you thinking?"

"Here's what I think," Sam whispered back. "When two people are crying together for the same reason, and their tears are landing in the same puddle, they must be friends."

The next morning Sam and Jo sat at the kitchen table. The wheels in Jo's head were turning a little slower than usual. Sam appeared to be deep in thought. There was no sound but the crunching of cornflakes.

"What are we going to do without her?" Sam said.

"We still have her," Jo answered. "We'll still paint on Tuesdays."

"You know what I mean. Even though we'll still see her, it won't be the same. She got the wind knocked out of her, and it will take a long time to get it back."

Jo knew she was right. Despite the brave face she had put on the day before, Mrs. Jones could never be the same person she had been. They would have to figure out a way to carry on in the wake of her shocking tragedy. They had to look to other people to pick up the slack. "Let's make a list," Jo suggested. "A list of all the people we know and what we like about them." Jo always felt better with a list.

"Okay," Sam agreed. "Start with Ed Coltrane."

"What do you like about him?" Jo said as she prepared to write down his qualities.

"I like the way he looks at me. He respects me, and I think he cares about me too. He's sincere and I believe him. And he's strong and good at his job."

Jo recorded as Sam dictated. "How about the Fornoffs?"

"They are kind and fair," Sam said.

"And very good at playing and teaching the cello and piano," Jo added.

"What about Mrs. Baxter?"

"She's kind and helpful. And she is smart about books."

"And she's smart about us," Jo said. "She always knows just what we need."

"Yeah, and somehow she makes me feel smart too."

Jo went on. "What did you like about Madam Kaminska?"

"I like the way she played. She was kind and shared her music and her hands with us."

"I loved her strength," Jo added. "I bet she could beat Ed in an arm wrestle." The gravity of the lumbering morning faded a little as the girls flashed each other a weak smile. The growing list of virtues gave Jo some hope. "Howard?" she continued.

"I like the way he shoots. But mostly, I like the way he *loves* to shoot. Like he'd die without it."

"He's been kind to us too. Not like church kindness. He's not all soft and saintly. He went out of his way for us and didn't judge us. He's humble, even though he doesn't want us to know it."

"Who else have we met this summer?" Jo asked.

"We met Mr. Ferguson."

"I thought you hated him."

"I did at first, but he's not so bad. It turned out he had a heart after all."

"Yeah," Jo agreed. "And he was right about the yellow paint. He knew what he was talking about."

"And he wouldn't let us make a mistake," Sam reminded her.

Jo counted the names and reviewed their comments about each one. "We've been pretty lucky," she concluded. "We've met some great people."

"There's one more," Sam said.

"Who's that?"

"Billy."

"Billy?"

"I kinda like Billy."

"The kid who socked you in the eye? The sour kid who's mean to everyone? What do you like about him?"

"Well," Sam began, "for a kid, he's the best baseball player I've ever seen. You gotta respect that. Even after our fight, he let us play. In doing so, he admitted he was wrong and I was right in front of all those boys. He gave me that respect. How many kids would have done that? You have to give him credit."

"Fair enough," Jo said as she added his name. Then she handed the list to Sam for her approval. "What do these people have in common?"

Sam read it carefully. "They're all good at something, and they shared it with us," she declared. "And except for Billy, they all did it with kindness."

"Maybe that will work for us," Jo said. "Get good at something and share it with others. And show them some kindness. Maybe that's how we keep going without Mrs. Jones."

With a plan in place to compensate for the loss of their chief source of emotional energy, Jo felt a little better about their prospects. Sam brightened as well and reached for her reading books. But before they could proceed with their recovery and get on with their lives, they had to get the monkey off their backs.

"We have to find out if Taylor was in on the kidnapping," Jo said.

"How are we going to find that out?"

"We just have to look at his face."

"I don't get it."

Jo knew the relationship between Mr. Taylor and the kidnapping could be complicated. For the first few days after their escape, she only knew one thing: They had to stay away from Taylor's store. Since then, she had thought through the situation, as she was prone to do.

"Here is what we know. From the newspaper article, we know the big man in the Chrysler who kidnapped us is Scarpini. We know he left town because the police think he killed Mr. Jones and they are looking for him. We know that Mr. Jones sold us to Scarpini. We know that Scarpini was in the moonshine business with Taylor," Jo reasoned. "So the way I figure it, there are three possibilities. One, Taylor didn't know about the kidnapping and still doesn't. Two, he's in on the kidnapping and thinks Scarpini took us with him when he skipped town. Or three, he's in on it, and Scarpini told him we escaped before he left town. I don't think it's the third one because Taylor knows where we live. If he had known we escaped, he would have come to the house by now or sent some other jugheads to get us."

"Sounds like we need to pay a visit to Mr. Taylor," Sam declared.

As they pedaled their bikes around the corner of Main and Center, Taylor's Grocery Store came into view.

"What are we going to say to him?" Sam asked.

"It depends on whether or not he looks surprised to see us," Jo responded.

They entered the store through the front door and asked the clerk for Mr. Taylor. "He's in the back," she replied.

Sam shot Jo a fretful glance, like she didn't want to go back there. But Jo was determined. They stepped across the short hallway that separated the retail area from the back room and there he was, lugging a box of lettuce. His face was sweaty and his hair a little mussed. His apron was stained with the juices of fruits and vegetables.

"Where the hell have you two been!" he shouted. The anger in his face was instant and obvious—just what Jo wanted to see. "I've got thirsty customers out there, and I don't have time to make all those deliveries myself." He shoved the lettuce to the floor and put both hands on his hips as he bore down on Jo. "I thought we had a deal."

"We did have a deal," Jo snapped. "Until we got kidnapped."

"What are you talking about, *kidnapped*?"

"Your big dopey business partner in the gray Chrysler—Scarpini. He kidnapped us right off of our bikes when we were making deliveries!"

"Now Jo, I've never known you to make things up."

This time Jo bore down on Taylor. She glared at him and clenched her jaw. "His name is Scarpini, right? And he hasn't been around for a few days, right? The cops are after him for killing that engineer, right? And the last time we were here he saw us leave on our bikes, right?"

Taylor stared at Jo as her questions increasingly shaped a sickening probability. Then his expression slowly descended from disbelief to horror. The kind of horror that only comes from abject guilt. His tiny chin began to quiver as he wiped the sweat from his brow. He sat on the box of lettuce and looked away.

"Dear God," he mumbled. "Dear, Dear God."

Sam and Jo watched without speaking as Mr. Taylor crumbled.

Finally, he looked up at the girls with pleading eyes. "I'm so sorry, Jo. And you, too, Sam," he said. "I'm not proud of the things I do sometimes. I'm greedy and I only care about myself. I sell moonshine, and I'm not above a little soft blackmail here and there. But I'm no kidnapper. I'm no child abuser. I'm certainly no murderer. It never occurred to me that I was putting you in danger. But I did, and I'm so sorry for that."

"We can't work for you anymore," Jo said.

"Of course not," he agreed. "I'm just glad you both are okay. I'm so glad they didn't hurt you." He paused for a moment and rubbed his temples with the tips of his fingers. "They didn't hurt you, did they?"

"No," Jo said. "They didn't hurt us."

"But how did you get away? Did the police rescue you? Do they know your story?"

Jo felt sorry for him. Even though he had taken advantage of them, she no longer believed he would have made good on his threat to report them to social services. She believed him when he said he didn't realize he was endangering them. She believed he was sick with guilt. Nevertheless, she couldn't trust him with too much information.

"We rescued ourselves, like we always do. Nobody knows our full story, not even you. And we're keeping the bikes."

On Thursday, they went to the range as usual. Sam carried the .38 inside the pillowcase where it had been safely stored since the night she shot Mr. Jones. She didn't say much along the way. Jo was worried about her. They arrived early and Howard wasn't there. The familiar clearing that had served as their shooting range was abandoned as usual save for a few scolding squirrels defending their territory and some songbirds high in the trees. The summer was over, and the leaves would soon choose their fall wardrobes. The maples would dress in orange and red, and the willows a brilliant yellow. They sat on a grassy spot in the shade and watched the river ripple by. Jo wondered what Sam was thinking but didn't dare ask. She would wait. Sam would talk when she was ready.

At length, Sam pulled the pillowcase onto her lap and tugged gently at the knot. She slowly reached inside and withdrew the gun while Jo studied her eyes. Sam held it in the palm of her hand, then opened her fingers so she could see the whole thing. She stared intently.

"It's not the same gun, is it, Sam?"

Sam didn't answer. Jo waited.

"It's not the gun I wanted it to be," Sam said. "It used to be a target practice gun. I wish it still was."

"Can you shoot it?"

"I'm going to shoot it," Sam said resolutely.

Jo looked at the gun and saw Mr. Jones's face. She couldn't imagine what Sam was seeing. "You're tougher than me," she said. "I don't think I could do it if I were you."

"It's not the same gun, but it's still a good gun. It's the kind of gun that did what it had to do."

Jo was desperate to comfort Sam. She was also angry at the universe. "Maybe so. But you shouldn't have to shoot someone when you're eleven."

"I don't feel guilt," Sam explained. "But what happened with this gun was big. And I feel that."

Jo was only mildly satisfied, but Sam wasn't finished. "Do you remember when my English professor told me, 'Survival is a violent business?'"

"Yes, I remember."

"Well, there was more to that story. He also said, 'When it comes to that violence, young Sam, you must choose whether you shall be a fighter or a warrior.' Then he told me the difference between the two. 'A fighter's purpose is to fight. But a warrior fights for a purpose.' This summer I've come to understand what he meant. That big kid at the baseball field, he's a fighter. Ed Coltrane, he's a warrior. You fought to save me from Steven. You're a warrior. I fought to save you from Mr. Jones, so that makes me a warrior too. We're warriors, Jo. And warriors don't have to say they're sorry when they win."

As the girls finished up the waning days of summer in anticipation of the new school year, Sam couldn't stop thinking about Ed. She had remained hidden when he was in the music store for fear he would ask too many questions. But something inside was driving her toward him. She felt like she owed him a proper thank-you for saving her life. And she wanted to see his family. She wanted to see the girl with the violin. The one whose happiness Ed had pledged to Mrs. Fornoff, *whatever it takes.*

One morning after piano practice, Sam went to the fire station. It was shift change, and she saw Ed walking down the sidewalk. She followed him from a distance until he turned into a small house on Cable Street. It was a corner lot flanked on two sides by thick dogwoods. On the porch were two large clay pots choked and overflowing with flowers and greenery. Tall trees separated the yard from the sidewalk. Hanging from one of the trees was an old tire swing. Sam wandered over to the swing and leaned up against the trunk of the tree. She wasn't sure about knocking on the door.

After staring at the house for a while, getting her nerve up, a voice came from the tree above her. "Want to swing?"

Startled by the question, Sam looked up into the branches of the tree where she saw a girl in overalls hanging upside down.

"Sure," Sam said. As she climbed into the swing, the girl jumped from the tree and landed in front of her. She was about the same height as Sam with a wiry frame, short blonde hair, and blue eyes. She had a smudge across her forehead and held a bird's nest in one hand. Beneath the overalls she wore a pink cotton shirt with tiny flowers on the collar. Ed had told her the truth about his daughter, and there she was. The girl looked a little surprised as she gave Sam the once over.

"You don't play the violin, do you?" Sam asked.

The girl looked even more surprised at the random question. "I just started. How did you know that?"

"I know your dad."

"What's your name?"

"Sam. What's yours?"

"I'm Hannah."

As the two girls gazed at each other, a small, stocky boy chasing and screaming at a golden retriever emerged from the backyard. The dog ran up to Hannah and offered her the stick in his mouth. She took the slobbery stick and handed it to her brother. He taunted the dog with it, then chucked it at the house without looking. The stick bounced off the clay pot on the porch and ricocheted into the front-room window. The glass didn't break, but it made a big racket. The kind of racket that draws concerned parents into the yard.

After the ruckus caused by the little boy had subsided, Sam turned back to Hannah. "So, do you live here with your mom and your dad and your little brother and your big hairy dog?"

Again, Hannah appeared puzzled and answered the only way she could. "Yeah, I guess I do. Why would you ask me that?"

Sam stared at her longingly. "No reason. I just always wanted a little brother and a big hairy dog."

Before long, the front door opened and Ed appeared.

"What's going on out here?" he yelled.

"Nothing, Dad," the little boy yelled back.

Apparently not satisfied with the assurance of a six-year-old, Ed came out to investigate. The dog fetched the stick from the porch and tried to give it to Ed just as he reached the gathering at the swing. "Who are you talking to, sweetheart?"

Sam climbed down from the swing and looked up at Ed. "Oh, I know who this is," he said. "Are you two friends?"

"We just met," Hannah said.

Ed smiled at Sam and then peered at Hannah. When he turned back to Sam he said, "See, I couldn't have left you up on that ledge."

Even though Sam was wearing a dress and Hannah was in overalls, their resemblance was remarkable. "Do you remember the day after the fire when I came to the station?" Sam asked.

"Do I remember it?" Ed said. "Are you kidding? You became a legend at the firehouse that day. All you said to me was 'nice catch,' then you walked off." He chuckled as he spoke. "The men have been teasing me about it ever since. They're always throwing things at me so they can say 'nice catch.' I even have a new nickname: "Nice Catch Coltrane."

Sam smiled as she thought about how she must have appeared to Ed that day. She thought about how hard it was to say anything at all to him. "Nice catch" was as good as she could do. "I never really thanked you for saving my life."

"Sure you did, kid. That's what you meant when you said 'nice catch.'"

"Well, a lot has happened to me this summer," Sam said humbly. "I've learned a lot of things. I've learned that when someone saves your life, you should probably give him a hug."

"Well, that's the sweetest damned thing I've ever heard," Ed said.

He wrapped her in his massive arms, and she clutched his neck. Once again, she was safe and sound. Once again, she turned her personal security over to him. Inside the perimeter of his embrace, she was bulletproof.

"You know, you squished all the air out of me when we were up on that ladder," Sam said. "I couldn't even breathe."

"This is your chance to get even," Ed replied. "Do your worst."

And Sam did do her worst. She squeezed for all she was worth. She squeezed until her muscles trembled.

It was 1927, the last day of summer. Not the last day as reckoned by the equinox, but rather the last day before the first day of school. The sun had set, and Sam and Jo were taking a final look at the night sky of summer. Once again, they were lying on the cool grass looking up at the stars. There was no streetlight to compete with the sky. The surrounding trees absorbed the glow of the city. They had their own observatory right there in the front yard.

As per usual, the talking didn't begin right away. First there was the marveling, then the wondering, then the introspection, then the questioning, and then the talking. They had a great deal to review. How would they ever complete that inevitable first-day class assignment entitled "How I Spent My Summer"? While other kids read reports to the class about camping in the mountains and visiting their cousins in Toledo, what would Sam and Jo write about? While other kids had learned to swim or plié, Sam had learned to laugh and cry, and Jo had learned to breathe. While other kids had healed their skinned knees, Sam had healed the wound from a bullet.

"Are you excited for school tomorrow?" Jo asked. "Or nervous?"

"What's the difference? They both make you pee."

Jo chuckled briefly. They stared at the stars for a while before she spoke again. "What do you think about our chances?"

"At school?"

"At school, at home, at life."

"I think our chances are good, together," Sam said positively. "I'm counting on it."

Again, there was silent contemplation. Just the crickets and a barn owl.

"Jo," Sam said.

"Yeah?"

"Do you remember when you asked me how I was able to jump from the ledge of that building and I said I would tell you someday?"

"Yeah."

"This is that day."

"Let's hear it."

"Last summer I was in New York City, and I snuck into a Yankees game. I was sitting in left field at the top of the bleachers. Babe Ruth was at bat. He fouled off the first two pitches, and I was afraid he was going to strike out. The third pitch was a ball. But on the fourth pitch he connected with a clean swing. The crack sounded like a rifle going off. The ball came straight at me. I thought maybe I'd catch it. But the closer it got the higher it went. I was on the top row, and that ball was still going up. It cleared the stands by fifty feet. And do you know what I thought as that ball sailed over my head?"

"No, what?"

"I thought, *Nobody can do that.* I saw it with my own eyes, but surely nobody can do that. The same thing happened when I saw Madam Kaminska play the piano. I could hear all the notes, but her hands were moving too fast to see. *Nobody can do that.*

"Anyway, when I was up on that ledge, Ed told me to stand up and face the wall. He said, 'Grab your elbows and tip over backwards. Fall flat like a log.' He asked me if I could do that. I told him of course I could. But that was a lie. I remember thinking, *Nobody can do that.* Then for some reason, I remembered that baseball flying over my head, still climbing. And I realized, people do impossible things."

The next day Sam and Jo put on their best school clothes. They went to the principal's office to register with the secretary. Hundreds of new faces swarmed all about them. Harried teachers and administrators directed the chaos.

"Name, please," the secretary said to Jo.

"JoAnn Jamison."

"Grade?"

"Sixth."

"Have your mother sign these forms and bring them back tomorrow." Then she looked at Sam. "And what is your name?"

"Samantha."

The secretary wrote down her first name, then looked up at Sam expectantly.

"Coltrane," Sam said. "Samantha Coltrane."

About the Author

Corey Johnson, MD, has spent over thirty years practicing medicine in rural Utah, witnessing firsthand the complexities of trauma, courage, and human connection. Drawing from this deep well of experience, he crafts thoughtful, character-driven fiction marked by emotional honesty and narrative authenticity. *Must Be Friends* is his debut novel, reflecting Johnson's keen insights into friendship and resilience, and establishing him as an emerging voice capable of exploring the profound with simplicity and clarity.

www.ingramcontent.com/pod-product-compliance
Lightning Source LLC
LaVergne TN
LVHW091038080826
845145LV00002B/542

* 9 7 8 1 6 4 2 2 8 1 3 4 7 *